"Have you heard of the devil's chord, Annja?"

Interesting conversation change. But Annja could go with it. "Of course. It was a tritone of musical notes that the church banned from being played or used in musical scores in the Middle Ages. It was thought to be evil because it's dissonant."

"*Diabolus in musica,*" Roux recited.

"The devil in music," Annja translated. "I'm not a musician, but I do know the chord is played quite a bit nowadays. The heavy metal bands pounced on the forbidden motif, liking the evil connotation, but a lot of other musicians have used it, too."

"It's not so evil."

"It's certainly not worthy of excommunication or death. So what does a bit of music have to do with a cross that once belonged to Joan of Arc?"

"Nothing. And everything."

Intrigued, Annja propped her elbows on the table, ready for the rest of the story.

D0089660

Titles in this series:

ROGUE ANGEL

Alex Archer

THE DEVIL'S CHORD

A GOLD EAGLE BOOK FROM
WORLDWIDE®

TORONTO • NEW YORK • LONDON
AMSTERDAM • PARIS • SYDNEY • HAMBURG
STOCKHOLM • ATHENS • TOKYO • MILAN
MADRID • WARSAW • BUDAPEST • AUCKLAND

Recycling programs for this product may not exist in your area.

First edition July 2014

ISBN-13: 978-0-373-62169-9

THE DEVIL'S CHORD

Special thanks and acknowledgment to
Michele Hauf for her contribution to this work.

Printed in U.S.A.

THE
LEGEND

...THE ENGLISH COMMANDER TOOK
JOAN'S SWORD AND RAISED IT HIGH.
The broadsword, plain and unadorned,
gleamed in the firelight. He put the tip against
the ground and his foot at the center of the blade.
The broadsword shattered, fragments falling
into the mud. The crowd surged forward,
peasant and soldier, and snatched the shards
from the trampled mud. The commander tossed
the hilt deep into the crowd.
Smoke almost obscured Joan, but she continued
praying till the end, until finally the flames climbed
her body and she sagged against the restraints.

Joan of Arc died that fateful day in France,
but her legend and sword are reborn....

1

Milan, 1488

The night was young and the tavern stank like a hog barn, which was much preferable to the cart of rotting fish parked outside his studio near the park. Leonardo had sought escape from the stench. The tavern's atmosphere of soused cheer always sharpened his senses. There was so much to take in and to record.

Upon choosing a seat, he'd sketched a study of the tavern keeper's face as it had segued through the various stages of reception, duty and amiability. He'd just finished the resentful sneer the keeper cast toward the boastful gent adorned in rich velvet and Venetian lace.

When he'd spied the tall, lean man with a tankard in hand casting about for a place to sit, Leonardo had invited him to join him. Pleased by the invitation, the man sat across from him at the rough-hewn wood table. He had an open purse and enjoyed the taste of the local ale. And he was very willing to share that appetite with Leonardo.

Leonardo da Vinci sat back against the beam in the

center of the tavern—his usual spot—and produced the notebook he always carried with him

"Do you mind?" he asked the man who had introduced himself as Roux. "I like to record things," he explained, pointing at the notebook with his red chalk pencil. "Whatever passes before my eyes. People, places, things. Emotions. Designs. Ideas."

"Don't mind at all." Roux tilted back the ale stein. The man had a French accent, but his sun-browned skin suggested Spanish heritage, perhaps. Leonardo had not visited France—or Spain, for that matter— enough to pick out the various dialects. "But how does one record emotions? Is it possible to draw them?"

"Oh, yes."

Leonardo sketched the beginning lines to the old man's face. His long Roman nose showed a commanding presence and intelligence. His skin tone promised he rode horses more often than luxuriating idly in a carriage. His eyebrows were darker than his silver-white hair, drawing attention from the lines that creased at the corners of his eyes.

"I like to capture the human face as a person experiences many emotions," he explained. "Angst. Worry. Joy. Curiosity. Happiness shows first in the eyes. Drunkenness tends to obliterate the finer details of emotion. And worship. Ah, worship."

"I'll give you drunkenness after a few more steins."

The man signaled to the serving wench, and arms loaded with a pitcher and empty tankards, she nodded that she'd return to their table when she was able.

"I write everything down," Leonardo added as he

swept his hand across the paper. "There is no order," he continued. "But every detail I note engages my thoughts and hopefully inspires me. You see, if I don't put it down on paper, then I can't make room for new ideas. It's so full." He paused to tap his skull. "My mind. And after I've removed one idea, there are always new ones to fill the space."

"You've a restless mind. Always thought an artist would be—I don't know—serene. Lost in the creation of his next work."

"But that's it exactly," Leonardo said. Enthusiasm had him shifting in his seat and he leaned forward to study the wrinkles that dotted the edges of Roux's eyes. "I do get lost. If I didn't have many other notions and interests, I might never take on the next project."

Of course, sometimes it seemed there were simply too many projects jostling for his attention. It was entirely his own fault. He followed his muse. An erratic muse.

He tugged out his purse, which had a few coins in it but more usually held his red chalk and a lampblack pencil. Inside he also kept the key to his special box and a few cards onto which he'd sketched the Lorraine cross he'd recently finished enhancing. Or rather, altering magnificently.

Leonardo set the cards on the table beside the wilted calfskin purse, and when the wench handed him his refilled stein, he thanked her and then ignored the spirits in favor of his subject.

"I've seen a cross like that before," Roux commented. "May I?" He took the sketch with his long, callus-roughened fingers. The cross featured parallel crossbars placed at equal distance on the single center bar. "Referred to as a Lorraine cross?"

"Yes. It's a sketch of a piece I own. A gift from René d'Anjou. He was a friend. Another Frenchman," Leonardo added, since he'd decided Roux's accent was definitely from France.

"I knew the Count d'Anjou. Died a few years ago at his home in Aix-en-Provence. Good King René— isn't that what they called him?"

Leonardo nodded.

"And his mother, Yolande of Aragon. She was kind and strong. A fierce woman. One of Jeanne d'Arc's tutors."

"Is that so?" Looking up from the sketch, the pencil gripped loosely now, Leonardo granted the man his complete attention. René had never talked much about his family. He was possessed of a mind as busy as Leonardo's own and always jumped from one topic to the other with frequency. "Tell me more."

Roux shrugged. "I got to know him when he rode in the siege on Orléans in 1429."

"He and Jeanne were close," Leonardo stated.

There were rumors whispered that René d'Anjou and the Maid of Orléans had been lovers.

"The man traveled to places far and wide in his quest for knowledge," Roux provided. "Did you meet him here in Milan?"

"Yes, we spent some time together. As you've said, his quest for knowledge was immense. That man possessed an amazing mind, and I did enjoy listening to one who could speak with such confidence."

"So this cross—" Roux gestured at the drawing "—it was once René's?"

Leonardo nodded. "Indeed, but before he owned it, it had belonged to Jeanne d'Arc. She'd gifted it to him. D'Anjou implied it was the very cross she clutched to her breast as she prepared to die in the flames."

The old man winced and bowed his head. Indeed, it was a terrible scenario to imagine.

"Once I had the cross," Leonardo said, "I immediately knew I had to fashion it into something more spectacular. As you can see by the notched surface here—" he tapped the card that revealed the back surface of the cross "—it fits a specific lock, of which— That is a secret. Did you know the Maid of Orléans?"

Roux's fingers traced the edge of the card, as if his focus was elsewhere instead of what was in front of him. Leonardo quickly sketched the change in his irises, softening the surrounding whites with a smudge of his finger.

"I did know her, yes," Roux muttered.

Had Leonardo not been sitting so close to the man, he would not have heard the quiet admission.

Possessed of an insatiable need to learn and to experience, Leonardo could not resist the unknown. "What can you tell me about her?"

The old man looked thoughtful for several minutes. He was choosing his words with care. His attention seeming to rise from some distant chasm as he met Leonardo's eyes. "I was one of the soldiers who rode alongside her into battle. I was with her on many occasions. I was there as she was led to the stake."

Leonardo swallowed hard. To have witnessed such a travesty surely was a cruel burden to have to bear and one that would be difficult for a man to erase from his memory. "So you…"

"Yes, I witnessed it all. She was brave to the end. Such a tragic, senseless accusation of heresy."

"She fought for Charles VII. For all of France. Bravely." He leaned on his elbows, curiosity making him bold. "If you were there, by her side, did you believe she was hearing messages from God?"

"I never had reason to question her sincerity," the man answered bluntly.

Leonardo nodded. He longed to explain many things in this world, but some did seem unexplainable.

"If I wanted to do a study, possibly a painting of her, perhaps you could provide me details of the event?"

Roux swiped up his stein. The ale ran down his chin and neck, wetting the silver-trimmed doublet that he'd tied neatly before his throat. "No," he said and abruptly slammed the stein on the wood table.

"I understand it must be a sensitive event to recall—"

"Paint her as an innocent woman who was wronged by those whom she thought to trust."

Sensing the man's ingrained anger for the topic, Leonardo didn't want to push. If he asked of the woman herself, that might restore the right mood. "She was dark of hair, yes?"

Roux slid the sketch of the cross toward Leonardo. "Do you want more ale or am I to up and leave?"

"No, please don't leave. I'll— I'm sorry. Perhaps some other time we can continue this discussion. I do have something else of hers I value. It came from D'Anjou. I traded a sketch for it, a piece. It is one of my prized possessions."

"A piece?" Roux asked.

"Yes. Of Jeanne d'Arc's sword."

Venice—16 months ago

THE GONDOLA GLIDED through gentle waves. Here in the northernmost *sestiere* of the city, the canals glistened as moonlight added the appropriate silver highlights.

Everything should have been perfect for a romantic cruise through the city before they headed to the mainland to catch a flight home to the States. Once at JFK Airport, they would shake hands, perhaps even share a lingering kiss and then go their separate ways.

"I expected more," the woman said, pulling away from the embrace her partner assumed she had wanted. "You lied to me."

"Sweetie." The man caught the gondolier's sad look and subtle headshake. *Been there, done that, buddy.* "I never actually said we'd get married after the heist. I said I'd consider it. And I've done that. I have given it as much thought as I have our escape plans. I don't think it's the right time."

"The right time?"

He always worried about her temper—it could flare at a moment's notice. Now her agitation sent a chilling prickle along the back of his neck. Off-putting and yet so familiar. These days he should have sensed it before it hit him.

"Can we not get into this here?" he tried. "Look around. The city is beautiful. The lights are—"

"I do nothing for you until you apologize."

He sighed and pushed away from her on the padded bench. Another gondola approached, a red-and-white-striped canopy shading the happy couple who couldn't seem to take their eyes off one another. The woman was clutching a bunch of roses. *Hey, look, a romantic couple,* he wanted to point out.

Romance and roses? Hell, he'd forgotten the roses, too. That was the first thing she'd said when they'd boarded the gondola. *No flowers?* The woman had an exquisite bead on what buttons to push to make him feel lacking.

And when the marriage proposal she was expecting had actually been his suggestion for a two-week vacation *apart* while he plotted their next robbery? Her upper lip had disappeared and her mouth tightened. Her silence made him worry more than her usual anger.

Bending forward, he cracked open the cooler cover. They'd brought it along with the steel attaché case. The attaché they'd not let out of their sight for two days. The cooler he'd filled with beer, not wine. And he was pretty sure he'd be reprimanded for that oversight, as well. Did it matter anymore? There was no saving this night.

"I want to get off at that landing up there," she said. "Tell the gondolier. I'll walk to the hotel."

"But we have reservations at that fancy restaurant, sweetie. You insisted."

"Don't *sweetie* me. I'm done with you. No more of this." She shoved the cooler with a foot. "Get another safe cracker. I'm going out on my own."

"Would you keep your voice down?" He suspected the gondolier could speak English, even though he'd shrugged and shook his head when they'd initially asked him. "Sweetie," he said in a harsh whisper, "you know you are a terrible planner. You need me to plot the details of the job and manage the getaway. We're a perfect team."

The gondola slowed near the landing.

"Not this one," the man said over his shoulder to the gondolier.

"Yes, this one," the woman insisted. She stood as they neared the dock. "Ciao, sweetie."

He reached for her leg as she stepped up onto shore, but it slipped through his grasp. She was an expert at folding her body into tight spots, which came in handy during a heist. And she could glide under a security laser with ease. He always marveled at how she could squeeze those generous breasts under a few inches of clearance.

"Do not call me. Ever," she said with a definite finality. She marched into the crowded outdoor café half-filled with patrons.

Perfect escape, he thought. With people around, she wouldn't expect him to cause a scene. Not that he was a scene causer. She didn't want to work with him? Fine. He had the goods from their recent heist. He didn't need her.

Bowing his head over the beer bottle, he slapped his hand onto the hard metal surface of the attaché— but his palm landed on the floor of the gondola. He checked under the padded bench seat where he'd told her to stash the case when they'd boarded.

"We go now?" the gondolier asked.

"Uh, wait. Sweetie!" he called. Even in his panic he was considerate of their rule never to use names in public. "What did you do with the case?"

She was already several yards away, walking the path that hugged the historic canal. But she'd heard him. Turning, she smirked and called out to him, "Dumped it!"

"Wh-what?" He scrambled about the floor of the wide-bottomed boat, thinking he might find a little cubby where the case might be, but there were only life vests stuffed under the seat and the cooler. "It's not here!"

"Because it's in the canal!"

Laughing that bold, spectacular laugh he'd always loved to listen to because it usually followed some great sex, she strolled off and disappeared into the night.

"The canal?"

He peered over the edge of the boat and frowned at the rippling water. She'd dumped the case over the side of the gondola? When had she— It must have been when he'd been digging around in the cooler for a beer, trying to avoid her disappointed gaze.

"We have to go back that way," he directed the gondolier. "I know you understand me. North." He thumbed the direction over his shoulder.

But despite the gondolier's nodding agreement and his patient navigation over their previous route, the thief spotted nothing floating in the canal. The attaché had been relatively heavy, around six to eight pounds. Hell, it must have sunk the instant it had hit the water.

Taking note of the buildings in the immediate area and where they were in the canal, he directed the gondolier to his hotel.

He left Venice that night because he didn't want to miss his flight, and by extension his one shot to maybe repair the damage he'd done to his partnership. He was still hopeful even after he'd found his airplane ticket lying on their bed. She'd bought the tickets because she had always managed their finances. Foolish move on his part.

Equally foolish was his thinking that he might have had eight or nine hours on a flight to convince her not to dump him. She hadn't been in the seat next to him on the plane home. Must have stayed behind?

His bad luck continued when he arrived at the apartment they'd shared in Manhattan, and found his bank account emptied and all the keys and combinations to their secret hiding spots gone or empty.

A knock on the door had been followed by the flash

of an NYPD badge. Accompanying the cop had been a man from Interpol.

A woman scorned knew how to inflict revenge on a man's soul. Maybe he should have proposed after all.

2

Annja Creed checked the cell phone's screen. She had
the phone set to vibrate only because she was conduct-
ing an interview. A name appeared above the long-
distance number. What did that man want with her
now? He'd have to wait. She put the phone aside on
the laminated table.

The woman sitting across from Annja in the bistro
twisted the end of her napkin nervously. She was called
Sirena. That was it—no last name. Doug Morrell,
Annja's producer, had made contact with her online.
A segment for another episode of *Chasing History's
Monsters.*

Beside Annja in the booth sat Ian Tate, her cameraman. He worked freelance and was based in Scotland,
but was fond of traveling the world. He was short of
stature yet filled with the adventurous spirit required
for the job, and she had gotten along with him as soon
as they'd shaken hands and he'd teased her about this
assignment.

They'd met up yesterday afternoon to film shots
of the scenic shoreline here at Isola delle Femmine, a

town in Palermo, Italy. The translation of the town's name was the Island of Women. Annja hadn't done any research on that before arriving, but she seemed to recall there had once been a women's prison on a nearby unoccupied island.

Sirena's hair spilled to her elbows in pale brownish-green waves. Annja wondered if it was a dye job gone wrong or if the woman had purposely chosen the muddy tones. She hoped Serena hadn't paid for it. It wasn't well done, and she needed a retouch.

"So you said you've been living with a man for three years and he won't release you?" Annja posited.

The mythology on selkies fascinated Annja, but she didn't believe in them for a moment. The idea of a seal-like creature coming to shore and shedding its skin to transform into a beautiful woman… Well.

On the other hand, this was exactly the sort of story *Chasing History's Monsters* sought. Something her fans would eat up.

"Yes. Matteo has hidden my pelt so I cannot go home," Sirena said. She toyed with the ends of her seaweed-colored hair. Bright, glossy gray eyes always seemed to be filled with tears, but not a one ever ran down her cheek. "I love him, but…" She glanced out the bistro's window. Across the street the shore sat close. Seagulls swept down from the blue sky and tourists headed for the beach.

"But your home is in the sea," Annja finished for her. She glanced to Ian. He gave her a thumbs-up. The guy was good at hiding his smirk. So long as he got this conversation on film, that was all that mattered.

"Do you ever go in the water now? Swim in the sea? What would happen if you did?"

"I'd sink," Sirena said. The waif sighed heavily. "When in this human form I am bulky and unskilled in the water. But I do like to soak in the bathtub for hours. Matteo laughs at me because I insist on remaining even after the water has grown cold." She shivered and pushed aside her empty coffee cup.

Annja was not a good judge of another couple's relationship. But something about Sirena seemed wrong. And it wasn't at all related to the bleak possibility she may have once lived in the water.

She reached across the table and placed a hand over Sirena's, knowing Doug would whoop when he saw the footage. Whenever she could capture an emotional moment, her producer always rubbed his fingers together in the universal money sign. Ratings gold, he'd say.

But she wasn't forcing this feeling. She was genuinely concerned for Sirena.

"Are you and Matteo okay, Sirena? Is he…harming you?"

The woman's head snapped up, and her gaze met Annja's briefly. She pulled her hand from Annja's and reached for the macramé purse at her hip and slid out of the booth so quickly, Annja slammed into Ian in an attempt to follow her.

The cameraman shuffled out of the booth, allowing Annja to pursue the escaping interviewee.

"I'm sorry, the interview is over," Sirena said firmly. "I thought you wanted to know about my kind, not delve into my personal life. I have to leave now.

Please don't follow me. You are not welcome at my home."

"Sirena, I'll tell him to turn off the camera."

Annja nodded to Ian, and he lowered the camera. She rushed after the anxious woman, who hustled outside.

On the sidewalk, Annja grabbed Sirena by the arm, standing so close she got a whiff of salt, as if Sirena had been swimming in the ocean and hadn't rinsed off. "Wait. You can talk to me, Sirena. Woman to woman."

Sirena tugged away from Annja's grasp. "You could never understand the sacrifice I made for love."

With that, she scampered across the street, and for the first time, Annja noticed that beneath the long skirt dusting her ankles, Serena was barefoot. A bohemian refugee plunked in the middle of a seaside village? Probably not a drastic leap to concoct and believe in her story of waves and woe.

"You think she's going to be okay?" Ian asked from behind Annja.

"I'm not sure."

Sirena stopped at a beat-up red pickup truck. A man slid out from behind the wheel and kissed her. When she spoke to him, his eyes darted across the street and targeted Annja.

"I guess that's the boyfriend." Annja offered a wave, then, sensing she wasn't getting a warm stare in return, she nodded to Ian. "Let's head back to the hotel and look over the footage. See if we have enough for a segment or if we need to entice Sirena to talk some more."

After an afternoon of going through the footage, Annja determined they did have some great shots. She could cobble together a short segment for the show. Though Doug would still want to see fins slapping the water's surface or some other bit of silliness. He could add that himself.

During supper Ian suggested they do a follow-up with Sirena, perhaps in a week or two. By then she would have had some time to think about what Annja had said to her today. It sounded like a good idea. Annja was not beyond extending her stay in Italy for a few weeks. If Doug would cover her expenses, she'd dig around for another story idea. She'd start with Rosalia, the patron of Palermo, who had lived during the twelfth century and saved the city from the plague. Her bones were interred here.

After supper, and still waiting for the okay from Doug to stick around in Italy, Annja and Ian headed back to the shore to capture some night shots. Moonlight glimmered across the water's surface. She stood back, toeing a thatch of ragged grass while Ian strode the rocky shore.

The clatter of stones and footsteps alerted her just as someone grabbed Ian's camera and shoved him hard enough to make her colleague fall backward and land on the ground.

Recognizing the man who'd pushed Ian, Annja rushed him and prevented him from swinging a fist toward the fallen cameraman.

"Shove off!" Matteo hissed at Annja as he wrestled

away from her. "You two get out of town and stop harassing Sirena."

"We're filming a story," Annja defended. "And we were invited by Sirena. Is there something you want to tell us?"

"I just did. Keep away from Sirena. You are not putting footage of her on TV."

"Why? Because she believes she is a selkie?"

The dark-haired bruiser with a few days' beard growth stared at her. He seemed overly worked up considering the circumstances. Why was he so uptight about them and what Sirena could tell them? Annja noted the reek of alcohol, which was likely only fortifying his mean streak.

Sirena had been afraid of him.

Matteo lunged for her. Annja bent at the waist, twisting, and kicked low, catching him below the knee. He yelped and toppled forward, but managed to grip her by the hair as he went down. She rolled over his body, landed on the loose shore stones and came up to her feet in a squat.

"Do you hurt her, Matteo?" she asked.

He sneered and pushed off the ground, coming to a stand.

Annja jumped up before him. She could feel the sword hum from within the otherwise, there if she needed it. But she didn't want to introduce a weapon to this scuffle. She didn't suspect Matteo was armed with anything more than fear of exposure.

"She tells lies," he hissed.

"So you're not keeping her with you against her will?"

"She…she said that? You're lying to me!" He swung at Annja, but she dodged him easily. The man wasn't so drunk. He maintained his footing and, bouncing back and forth, showed her his fists. "Stay away from her!"

Out the corner of her eye, Annja saw Ian fumble to his feet. He didn't go for his camera. Thankfully, he had the good sense that this would not make for good television.

Matteo dived for her and gripped her about the waist, pushing them both to the hard ground. "You give me what's on that camera." He punched, landing a bruising set of knuckles against her throat.

Annja kicked, connecting her boot toe with his gut, but not hard enough to injure. Instead, she flipped him onto his back and crawled on top of him, straddling his hips. A right fist to his jaw spattered blood across the rocks. She'd never backed away from a fight, and admittedly, it adrenalized her. Frankly, it was easy when she fought against a man like this.

"You let her go," she insisted, landing another punch that served to loosen his tense jaw muscles.

His shoulders dropped and Matteo stopped fighting, though he hadn't been knocked out.

"Let her do as she wishes. If Sirena wants to leave you, let her go."

"But…" He fisted the ground at his sides. Growling in frustration, he sputtered, "I don't know where it is!"

"Where what is?"

Behind her Ian scrambled with his equipment.

"The pelt!" Matteo cried.

Annja frowned and delivered another swift strike up under the man's jaw. That tilted his head to the side sharply, stealing his consciousness. Blood drooled from his mouth. "He's out."

She rose and wiped her hands down her pant legs.

"He believes it, too," Ian said, the camera pointed toward the ground, the green run light showing he'd filmed Matteo's confession. "Now what?"

The cell phone in Annja's pocket vibrated. She swiped a loose strand of hair from her face and over her ear and strode toward the parking lot, gesturing for Ian to follow. Matteo would be fine.

Annja answered the call in a harsh tone. "Seriously? This had better be good."

"Sounds like someone needs a nap."

The French accent had become a familiar voice in her life. Yet it had been a while since she'd talked to the old coot. Usually it was she who contacted him.

"Roux." She blew out a breath, calming her thundering heartbeat. "Sorry. It's been a long day. And I think I've spent most of it with a selkie."

"Selkies, eh? A bit fantastical, even for your wild adventures. I thought you preferred kneeling hunched over a pile of dirt?"

"I do, but I do work for a television program that tracks monsters. Selkies are not so fantastical when you think about it. You do know it's—" she cast her gaze toward the sky, then turned the phone to check the time display "—close to midnight?"

"Not where I am. The sun is shining and I'm, well... What can I say?"

No details. Never any details unless the man considered them salacious or wanted to tease her, which was often. But Annja wasn't interested. She didn't want to do the math to calculate what time zone he could be in to be calling her during the day.

"Like you said, I need to get some rest, so make this quick."

"I've a simple question. One I thought would intrigue you."

She closed her eyes and blew in and released a deep breath. A half-hour shower was the only thing she could think about. Her neck ached. She'd have a bruise there by the time she hit said shower. "What's that?"

"Very well. Do you know what Leonardo da Vinci and Joan of Arc had in common?"

Any mention of Joan of Arc straightened Annja's spine. She opened her eyes wide and, seeing Ian's intent interest, turned her back to him. Some things she only talked about with certain people. And those few people—actually, only two—also had a keen interest in the sainted martyr.

"Bonus points if you can name their common benefactor," Roux added cheerily.

Well, that narrowed it down to one person. Annja liked a good quiz. But she needn't the clue.

She'd read a lot on the young woman who had boldly led the French army to war in the fifteenth century, only to be labeled a heretic and burned at the stake by the English forces. Joan interested her because Annja had an inexplicable connection to her. One that she could never completely explain and so had accepted on blind faith. And there was the fact that whenever she was in trouble and needed protection, she could call Joan of Arc's sword to hand from the otherwhere.

Cool. Weird. Fortuitous when she was in a bind. And she tended to find herself in a bind more often than the average archaeologist. Just call her a jet-setting dirt digger and sometime crime fighter and defender of the innocent.

It worked for her.

"Let's see…" Annja kicked at the smooth stones that had been turned over and over by high tides and infinite time. "Joan was burned in 1431. Leonardo da Vinci wasn't born until 1452. So someone who had known Joan and was very young at that time, who then later traveled to Italy, possibly— Aha!

"Good King René," she answered. "I believe René d'Anjou's mother, Yolande, tutored Jeanne at a young age. And René and da Vinci were quite possibly known to each other as well, both being men of the Renaissance."

"Exactly. The Duke d'Anjou, besides being a philanthropist, was literally one of the first men of his age and time who sought to share knowledge instead of suppress it. He wasn't as close to Jeanne as was his mother, but still, there was a loose connection, we think."

That he paused now piqued Annja's interest even more. If ever there existed someone who knew historic details—firsthand—it was Roux. He had lived through the past five hundred years. It meant that Roux had witnessed Joan's sword being broken beside those very flames that had ended her life. Flames were a recurring nightmare of Annja's. She hadn't had any bad dreams lately and wished that would continue forever.

"That's not the reason for my call," Roux said, sidestepping what exciting secrets Annja had hoped he would reveal to her. "You guessed right. René d'Anjou was likely associated with both our Joan and Leonardo. Are you familiar with a theft that took place six months ago at the main antiquities museum in Poland?"

Annja glanced over her shoulder. Ian strolled along the waterline, kicking stones here and there, the camera held slack at his side.

"Are we on a new topic now?" she asked. "Renaissance painters, burned saints and add to that the fact my day has been occupied by a possible selkie sighting. My brain is fried, Roux. If you've got a point, please get to it."

"The stolen items from the museum were believed to have been abandoned in a Venetian canal due to a quarrel between the thieves. Both were arrested, one in Milan, the other in the States. Neither has revealed where the items were dropped into which canal. And with little evidence, they were set free."

"So there are valuable ancient artifacts sitting somewhere at the bottom of a Venetian canal? What's new?"

"It's not what is new, Annja, but what was old and

possibly dumped in the drink. A Lorraine cross believed to have once belonged to Leonardo da Vinci."

There were so many styles of crosses. The Lorraine cross was a particular favorite of hers. "Right. A heraldic cross with two horizontal crossbars of the same length. Got it."

"The Lorraine type of cross was carried into the Crusades by the Knights Templars, and later, the image was adopted by the Duke d'Anjou, but only after receiving such a cross as a gift, reputedly from Joan of Arc."

"So what you're saying is…" She strode over to Matteo's inert body and leaned over him. Still out yet, oddly, smiling in his unconscious slumber. "I'm not following you, Roux."

"It is speculated that the cross that belonged to Leonardo da Vinci was gifted to him by René d'Anjou."

"Are you supposing that the cross stolen from the museum was originally a cross that belonged to Joan of Arc?"

"That I am."

"Huh." Annja stood, hand to her hip, and paced the clattering stones. Ian now sat on the grassy hillside that inclined toward the parking lot, camera on his lap. A giddy excitement stirred her from exhausted to merely semi-tired. "So, are you thinking what I'm thinking?"

"Absolutely, Annja. What do you say to a diving excursion in Venice?"

He was inviting her to do something together? Suspicion immediately set off Annja's warning bells. Roux was always in it for himself, and he'd step over others to get what he wanted.

On the other hand, she'd just been invited to go diving for lost treasure. And she now had a reason to stay in Italy, as she and Ian had just been discussing. And if the stay was funded by Roux, she didn't need to bother Doug Morrell with the expenses.

"Sounds good. When were you planning this adventure?"

"Now. I know you're in Palermo. I'll let the other diver know to expect you at the Fondamenta della Sensa tomorrow, probably afternoon, if you allow for travel time. I have a ticket waiting for you at the Palermo Falcone-Borsellino Airport now. Can you make it?"

How Roux almost always seemed to know where she was, was a question Annja had long ago given up attempting to answer.

"Yes, I can make it, but what about the other diver? You already have someone in place?"

The fact that Roux had expected her to say yes didn't bother Annja. He knew her well enough to realize that any artifact related to Joan of Arc would pique her interest. And she was always up for an adventure, most especially after days of tracking selkies and only coming up with a bad romance plot.

"Generally I like to gather my own team," she said.

"This is my expedition, Annja, and I am the one gathering the team. Have a problem with that?"

"Not if you're footing the bill."

"I am."

"Great. What's the diver's name?"

"All the information has been gathered in a dossier that will be waiting for you along with the plane ticket."

"I'll need two tickets. I've got a cameraman."

"Oh, hmm…"

While Roux considered that one, she gave Ian a thumbs-up and asked, "You want to fly to Venice to film underwater for a few days?"

Ian jumped up eagerly. "I'm in!"

"I'd like him along," Annja said to Roux. "We're scouting segments for the TV show."

"A show which has given me a few knowing smiles and a couple of laughs. Very well, two tickets," Roux said. "I intend to fly out in a few days. I'm tied up at the moment with, er, details. But fear not. I wouldn't miss this discovery."

"That's it? Just a cross?"

Much as she knew artifacts related to Joan were a love of Roux's, Annja found it hard to believe he'd invest in a mission simply to bring up a little memento that should by rights be returned directly to the museum from which it had been stolen.

"Just a cross," Roux replied. "Have a good rest on the flight, Annja. See you in a few days."

He hung up, and it occurred to Annja that he hadn't told her when the flight departed.

"Soon," she guessed.

The airport was a good hour's drive to the south. The flight to Venice shouldn't be more than ninety minutes if direct.

In the parking lot behind Ian, a black limo suddenly arrived. The limo driver got out of the expensive vehicle, introduced himself and informed her he was at her beck and call.

"Leave it to Roux to control me like a puppet," she muttered.

"You were expecting this?" Ian asked.

"Nope. But it's not a surprise. We'll head back to the hotel, pack and then on to the airport."

"But what about the selkies?"

Annja glanced to Matteo. He'd curled onto his side, apparently sleeping off the effects of the alcohol as well as her punch. "We'll swing by after Venice. But I have a feeling if there is a pelt, it'll never be found. Too bad for Sirena."

"Maybe we should call a women's shelter?"

Annja ran her hands through her hair. She was dirty and tired and yet exhilarated about the new assignment that lay before her.

"Yes, good idea, Ian."

And then she smiled widely. Sleep? She'd worry about that on the flight like Roux suggested.

"I should let Doug know about our new plans."

Her producer would probably research every Venetian myth to see if he could come up with a good episode idea for Annja to look into. If she had the time while she was there, she'd be all for it.

The twosome slid into the back of the limo, and the driver offered champagne, which Ian accepted. Annja refused. She was already mentally preparing for the next leg of the trip. It would take five minutes to pack her things because she generally traveled simply, always ready for just such spur-of-the-moment trips.

"On to my next adventure."

3

Roux had purchased her a seat in first class, though Annja wouldn't award him brownie points. Ian's seat was back in economy. The cameraman took the news with his usual good-natured attitude, knowing he'd been a last-minute add-on. Besides, economy was not filled to capacity, so he planned to snag a row of seats in the back and lay down to sleep through the flight.

The dossier was handed to Annja in a sealed envelope when she received her ticket. Once the plane was in flight, she pored over the information, which was sparse.

The man she was to dive with, Scout Roberts, was a former archaeologist who'd been stripped of his tenure at his university after he'd been involved in a sketchy dig in Peru. The operation had resulted in the unsolved deaths of two crew members. He'd insisted poisonous gases had leaked from the cave walls, yet a forensic team hadn't found any trace of poison. He'd disappeared approximately five years ago and apparently hadn't been seen or heard from since. He'd stopped publishing and there wasn't a phone number or address for him. He'd turned himself into a ghost.

But ghosts didn't accept offers to dive for lost treasure. He had to have a reason for accepting the invite from Roux. Unless cash was the motivator?

"Could be," she muttered, knowing Roux's pockets were deep.

Even deeper, though, was Roux's love for Joan and anything associated with her. The cross qualified on that score and was likely enough to spur his interest in the artifact. It would probably only look good under glass or on one of the walls in Roux's château.

The fact that Roux had brought her in on the job also didn't make sense if he intended to keep the artifact.

"Very odd…"

Flipping over the single page in the dossier, Annja was surprised that was all the information he had. Apparently, Roux knew little about Scout Roberts. Where had he found him? On a street corner? While strolling a stretch of the French countryside in search of treasure?

Annja smiled remembering how she had first met Roux. It had been on just such a stretch in the French countryside. In the Cévennes mountain area in search of a loup-garou, she had stumbled upon a hiker, who'd told her he was after something that was lost.

She'd thought Roux a curious old man who possessed the strength of many, an agility that belied his age and a charm that had won her over despite his obvious nefarious dealings. Over an initial get-to-know-each-other meal, she recalled thinking how the twinkle in his eyes could mean trouble for her. And she hadn't been wrong.

When they'd finally found the lost item he'd been looking for, it had been the final piece to Joan of Arc's sword.

Who would have thought that meeting Roux would have led to her owning a sword that once belonged to Joan of Arc, and to a love-hate friendship with a man who had seen and done so much?

At times Roux was harsh and insistent, in it for himself and yet always on mark and aware. He may look old, but the man was agile and swift and could expertly handle any weapon he got his hands on. After she'd claimed the sword, he had mentored her and taught her how to handle the blade correctly and efficiently. At times, he felt very much like a father to her.

But Annja always cautioned herself against letting her guard down completely around the man. At times, Roux allied with Garin Braden. He'd been tied to Roux since Joan's burning back in the fifteenth century. Braden was another man who possessed the same in-it-for-himself attitude as the older man. And he was not beyond lying to her to get what he wanted.

So that left Scout Roberts as a possible ally in this new adventure. A ghost working for a person of questionable integrity.

Annja shook her head as she perused the sketchy details she held.

She'd worked with strangers before. The nature of her work—traveling to foreign countries, traveling to

the middle of nowhere to dig in the dry, dusty dirt—
led to interactions with all sorts. Unwilling to pre-
judge someone she had never met, she looked forward
to meeting Scout and delving into the mystery of how
he'd gotten involved with Roux.

Setting aside the dossier, she settled into the cozy
first-class nest and pulled up the blanket to her forehead. She wanted to be in top form when she arrived
in Venice.

UPON DISEMBARKING AT Marco Polo Airport, Annja felt
refreshed. It was 6:00 a.m. and the day was bright. Ian
was also chipper. He'd had extra bags of peanuts and
a couple of free drinks and was currently balancing
his equipment on one shoulder, his backpack across
both shoulders.

"We'll eat after checking into a hotel. Deal?" Annja
asked.

"Deal."

Annja strode directly to the cabstand and was
greeted by a tall, solemn man in black trousers and
black turtleneck who held a placard with her name
neatly written in block letters.

"Miss Creed. I am Paulo. Your driver here in Venice." He spoke English well. "I've picked up the diving
gear, as was requested by Monsieur Roux. Two sets.
I've had them delivered directly to the boat docked in
the canal." He nodded to Ian. "Welcome to Venice."

The men shook hands.

"You're punctual," Annja said. "I appreciate that.
On to Venice?"

"I've a car waiting. There's a bit of a traffic bind, I'm afraid. Accident as I was coming toward the airport. We may have a wait. And then we'll travel on a water shuttle to the island. I live in the city, so I'll be at your service. I do have a car and a boat."

"Thank you. We'd like to head straight to the hotel. If you could recommend a good place to eat nearby, that would be great."

"I'll bring you there myself."

Three hours later—indeed, the traffic had been backed up for kilometers while a crane worked to clear away lumber from an overturned truck—Annja and Ian dropped their things in their respective rooms at the hotel. Then they accompanied Paulo to a quiet restaurant that seemed lacking in tourists yet had immense personality. The cook sang from the back room, and the waitresses giggled as they delivered plates to the tables. Though they'd both skipped breakfast, Annja cautioned Ian against the full plate of pasta if they planned to dive anytime soon, and he reluctantly ordered the smaller size.

After they'd eaten and Paulo had given them directions, Annja and Ian strolled down the streets in the Cannaregio, where they were to meet Scout Roberts dockside.

"They say the city is sinking nearly a tenth of an inch a year," she remarked as they passed a wet tiled courtyard sandwiched between two buildings.

"Point zero eight, to be precise," Ian replied. She gave him a look that said she was impressed. "Two years ago I spent a summer here filming at San Michele."

Named after the archangel Michael, the Isola di San Michele was located in the Venetian lagoon, northeast of the Cannaregio. It was about half an hour away. One of the first Renaissance churches in Venice, it had been built on the island sometime in the mid-fifteenth century. The same island that had also once served as a prison.

"The team I was traveling with was actually a forensic unit from New York City," Ian explained. "They were digging up bones in the cemetery. One of the women was full of interesting details about Venice. You know the city is tilting, as well."

"Yes, I had heard that. But let's hope it doesn't topple over while we're here. I haven't gone diving in these waters," Annja said.

"I had the displeasure while at San Michele."

"Displeasure?"

"The waters around the island were not bad at all. That's fresh seawater. It's the canals in the city proper. They're not really fit for leisurely dives, especially during the hot summer months."

"Right. Like now."

Since the canals were the Venetians' principal method of travel, cars in the city were rare and the water became unhealthy and murky. She wasn't even going to think about it. On the other hand, the tidal flushes should remove much of the sewage. She'd think positive—only way to go.

Though, now that she'd begun to think about it, she

picked up the salty wet-wood scent in the air. The sun was high today, and she sensed it wouldn't be long before the obnoxious odors would really blossom.

"I understand there's a crew of volunteer divers who have made it their goal to do an underwater version of street sweeping through the Grand Canal," Ian added. "They've collected quite a bit of rubbish."

"Good for them. You've got to hand it to grass-roots efforts. They will improve our world one project at a time."

"Most of the canals are only about three meters deep. I've a headlamp on my camera. I certainly hope there are lamps included with the diving gear. We'll need them. You didn't say exactly what artifact you are diving for. Something about Leonardo da Vinci? I can't imagine we'll find one of the master's paintings lying at the bottom of a canal, surely."

"It's a cross that once belonged to Leonardo. It was stolen from a museum six months ago."

"Fascinating. I'm not much for old stuff myself."

She shifted her backpack, which held a few personal things and her laptop, higher on her shoulder.

"Let me guess," she said. "You like the unknown."

"Actually, I'm all about finding the truth. That's why I've partnered with your television show on occasion. Legends and myths fascinate me. Their origins and how they grow and take on a life of their own, becoming real to some, is intriguing."

"For a guy who doesn't like old stuff, you must run into a lot of history searching for truths."

"I do. Like it or not." Ian chuckled. "It'll be a good

adventure, as you've said. I just wish I could get Sirena out of my head."

Annja offered, "I made sure she got the number for a women's shelter. And she has my number, of course. I told her if she wants to talk, she can call me any time."

"Guys like Matteo don't deserve anyone. And a girl so vulnerable and...beautiful like Sirena should be with someone who can appreciate her for whoever she is."

Annja smiled. Her cameraman seemed smitten.

"I gave Doug a call, as well," she said. "He's psyched about this dive, even though I told him not to get his hopes up. I can only see this being of interest to the show if we run into sea monsters."

"Always a possibility," Ian suggested a little too cheerfully.

She and Ian walked on, taking their time as they followed Paulo's directions to the dive site, as specified in Roux's dossier. The spot they were heading toward was in the Cannaregio, a central neighborhood that was one of the largest of Venice's six boroughs or, as the Italians called them, *sestieres*. Annja noted that Canal Regio was Italian for Royal Canal and that this district had once been the main route into the city before a railway from the mainland had been constructed.

"The Ca' d'Oro," Ian announced with reverence from behind her.

Annja swept her gaze up the Gothic facade of the fifteenth-century palace that had been heavily adorned with gilt. It had been built with a garden and courtyard. And it housed Giorgio Franchetti's private art collection. She'd have to make a point to visit the gallery if she could find some free time while in the city.

She loved Venice. No matter what time of day, the city always seemed to glow as if the sun were constantly setting upon the ancient buildings and water. So few cars made it a joy to wander about, and even the constant barrage of tourists in the major piazzas didn't bother her. So much history surrounded her, she was a bit awestruck.

"Off to find the treasure," she murmured as they turned down a narrow passageway.

Could Scout have become a treasure hunter after he'd been ousted from the University of Columbia? It was what tended to happen to archaeologists who couldn't stay away from the dig and the thrill of the find, yet who needed to subsidize their income to survive. She'd gotten a sense from the sparse details in the dossier that she may be dealing with a treasure hunter. In which case, he may not specialize in diving but rather be a jack-of-all-trades. A necessity when country hopping across the world in search of hidden wealth.

Speaking of hidden wealth, if and when the Lorraine cross was found, would Roux add it to his private collection of amazing artifacts, some of questionable provenance? Annja felt sure he would. They would have to come to terms about the ownership of the item if, and when, it was found.

Having dressed for a cool day, she was pleased to peel off her windbreaker to reveal a T-shirt because the sun promised a warm afternoon. Cargo pants and hiking boots were de rigueur, and generally a hat when digging under the hot sun. She'd gone with a pony-tail today and left the hat behind. If she were heading underwater, a different sort of hat and gear would be required. She hoped the diving equipment was in good condition.

Making a right turn down an alleyway, she and Ian emerged onto a wide sidewalk edging a canal. Spying the boat named *Piuttosto,* their destination, she took a bridge across the Fondamenta della Sensa and went west until she arrived at the appropriate dock. Only one man stood on deck. He waved to her, but didn't act as though he expected her. When she stepped onto the boat, he raised a brow.

Annja offered her hand. "Annja Creed. Scout Roberts is expecting me."

"Oh, right. The babysitter," the man said. "Name's Kard. Not like the game, but with a *K*."

"You work with Roberts often?" she asked.

"Nope. This is the first time. But when a guy offers me a stack of bills, I'm on the team."

Great. So this guy hadn't been vetted, apparently. But if he owned the boat, then he must have experience with diving crews. She'd cross her fingers for that outcome. It occurred to Annja that they didn't even need a boat. They could have dived from the dock or sidewalk. But privacy was a concern, so having the boat would allow them to set themselves apart from anyone on land.

"So how am I a babysitter?" Annja asked, leaning against the steel railing. Ian passed her and set down his camera equipment on a bench and began to unpack it.

Kard shrugged. "Roberts said he was hired by an old dude who intended to send in another diver to keep an eye on him, seeing as how they hadn't worked together before."

Roux had neglected to mention the babysitting aspect of this job. Annja was none too pleased. She preferred to focus on the task rather than on her partner's character. Roux had never worked with Roberts before? Great. Nothing like going into something blind.

A large crest of water splashed the starboard side and up popped a diver. He tossed a hard-shell hand-held lamp onto the boat and then gripped the aluminum stairs and climbed up over the side. After he peeled the tight diver's cap off his head, the man's dark blond hair spiked this way and that. He looked young. Annja's age. Too young to hold tenure and to have been through such nefarious experiences as listed in the dossier.

He took in Annja from head to toe, noted Ian with a frown, winked at Kard, then slapped a wet palm into hers.

"Scout Roberts. Delighted to be at your service, Miss Creed. But not so delighted about that guy. You a cameraman?" he asked Ian.

Ian nodded and stood, but after the cold reception, did not offer a hand to shake.

"He's with me," Annja clarified. "I'll be documenting the dive for possible use as a segment on *Chasing History's Monsters.*"

"No, you won't," Scout confirmed confidently. He slapped a wet palm against his suit, and the spray of water misted Annja's face. "I know that show. They do monsters. We're not monster hunting, Creed."

"No, but we are diving for buried treasure. I've occasionally featured lost treasures on the show."

"Yeah, I don't know about that." The man hooked a hand at his hip, glaring at Ian for a while. "I wasn't even expecting you, Creed, until I got the call from Roux last night. A babysitter I can deal with. But no camera crew is getting in our way. The canal is relatively shallow and narrow and we don't have the space."

"The camera crew consists of one," Annja corrected him, "and you don't get a say in his being here. Roux approved it." Buying the extra plane ticket was as good an approval as any. "You've already completed a dive this morning?"

"Nothing official. Just stuck my head down to get a lay of the land, or canal, if you will." Scout addressed Ian. "If you get in my way—"

Annja stepped between the men. "He's a professional and has filmed while diving in Venice before. And you're out of line. Can we agree to keep things genial, since we must trust one another to have our backs while underwater?"

Scout whistled and turned his back to them. Let him pout about it, she thought. If Mr. Cocky couldn't handle another diver on this team then Annja would take the lead, if necessary. Until then, she would stand back and let him run this show. For the most part.

"Scout?" she prompted him for a reply.

"Yeah, yeah." He swept a dismissive hand behind him. A poor agreement, but she imagined it killed him to show that much assent.

"So this is the correct area?" she asked, hoping to settle both mens' ire by changing the subject.

"According to the few details I've read about the heist, it should be," Scout said.

He unzipped the wet suit to reveal defined pecs and abs that again made him appear much younger than Annja had expected. Sitting on the bench before her, he bent to pull off his fins. She couldn't deny he was a handsome blond, with blue eyes and a sweet dimple that poked into his left cheek with each smile. Judging from his looks and quick wit, she'd bet he had no trouble making friends almost anywhere. But could he be trusted? His response to Ian being there didn't bode well, or maybe she was being too paranoid.

Still, a hotshot? She could deal with that. Might prove more interesting than some of the shy academics she'd spent weeks with on a dig.

"And what are the few details?" she asked. "I'm afraid I'm at a disadvantage. After Roux contacted me, I immediately hopped on a plane to Venice."

"You at the man's beck and call?" Scout cast her a curious glance. "Thought you were more independent. I've heard of you. Recognized you the minute I surfaced. Annja Creed, the host of her own TV show. A world-famous archaeologist. Author—"

"Roux's a friend," Annja interrupted. "Most of the

time. And we both share an interest in Joan of Arc artifacts and history."

"So do I." Scout stood and gestured to Kard, who tossed him a bottle of beer that he'd taken from a minifridge. "More so on the da Vinci stuff, but I like a good saintly knickknack any day."

"Whatever will earn you a few bucks, eh?"

"Creed, please. You calling me a treasure hunter?"

"I'll reserve judgment. But what's in it for you? What is Roux paying you for this job?"

"I don't share salary information, sweetie. Would you?"

Salary? From Roux? That was a joke. She'd be lucky if he didn't stiff her with the hotel bill. She might have to call Doug yet. "Sorry, that was crass."

"If it matters, I approached Roux. I overheard him discussing Joan's history at an auction, and having been studying this theft-gone-wrong for a few months and yet not put together the budget to recover the lost relics, I sought Roux out. Wanted to see if he'd like to invest in something that would net a valuable artifact for him."

"So you're just going on the dive for the thrill?"

"And the fame, of course. Maybe a spot on your show?" he added.

"As you pointed out, we only feature monsters. You fall into that category, Roberts?"

"Me? No way. I'm as harmless as they come." He gave her a wide, warm smile and took a long drink of his beer.

"Again, I'll reserve judgment."

Yeah, the man would be able to work fame like a pro, she guessed. But with his background? If he were seeking fame, that didn't jibe with the dossier that marked him a pariah among his fellow archaeologists.

"Why don't you two suit up?" Scout said. "Then I'll show you the maps."

4

Scout hadn't expected that someone would be scrutinizing his every move while he recovered the case. But he could live with it. Actually, he could use the backup when diving. And the backup was gorgeous. That would make the day go a little faster.

But the cameraman?

Scout shot a look toward Ian Tate, who pulled on a wet suit as he chatted with Kard about the tidal flows in and out of the canal. Scout had found Kard and hired him late last evening. The boat wasn't the greatest, biggest or best, but it was cheap and would ferry them around the canal safely, and Kard seemed reasonably able, even with a few beers down his gullet. While he wasn't footing the bill, Scout did like to keep expenses to a minimum. Fat bills attracted questions.

With luck, this operation should prove an in-and-out foray. Even with the close proximity to the sea, Scout didn't suspect the tides could have moved the lost treasure that far. Or he hoped they had not.

Too bad the tides weren't so rough they could wash a cameraman out to sea.

"You want a beer?" he asked Ian.

The cameraman shook his head. "You crazy, man? We're getting ready to dive."

Scout shrugged. It had been worth a try.

So Roberts was the one who had gone to Roux with the information about the Lorraine cross. Interesting. Roux rarely trusted those not within his circle, so he must have a serious need for this thing. That it had possibly belonged to Joan of Arc and then Leonardo da Vinci made it valuable, but again, Roux had to know if Annja found it she would insist it be returned to the museum that had formerly owned it.

Dialing Roux's number, Annja tugged up the zipper at the back of the wet suit using the long cord. She padded about in the small room belowdecks. Roux didn't answer.

"You ready, Creed?" Scout called down from above.

"Always."

On deck, Scout had laid out a laminated map on the bench beside the steering wheel. Kard sat back, visor cap pulled down to shade his eyes from the afternoon sun and a beer bottle in hand nestled against his stomach. Ian had suited up and looked over Annja's shoulder as Scout explained what he'd learned about the heist.

"So the thieves, who were also lovers," Scout said as he straightened the map, "snagged the stuff from the museum in Poland. They had intended to vacation in Venice, the City of Love." He gave that label a dramatic tone.

Annja stepped forward, drawn into the man's tale.

And yet... "How do you know the thieves were lovers? A man and a woman?"

"It was in the police report. They were arrested, Creed. You should do your homework."

She usually did. The police report should have been included in the dossier. She'd have to look into it as soon as she got a few minutes to fire up the laptop.

"But the man mistook the woman's intentions—he thought she wanted a break from their relationship as much as he—and his partner revolted against him. An argument ensued as they were taking a gondola ride down the Fondamenta della Sensa, very near here."

Scout circled the map where the boat was currently docked.

"As an act of spite, the woman tossed the attaché over the side of the gondola and took off. The man searched for it at the time, but it was hopeless that late at night. The case had been lost. Unbeknownst to both, the gondolier, a part-time fireman who spoke English well, called in the matter to his policeman friends. The couple, while escaping the city separately, were arrested, one at the Milan airport. The other managed to make it all the way to New York City, where a police escort waited for him."

"Don't tell me the gondolier didn't try to find the dropped attaché?" Annja asked. "It should be fairly obvious that what was dropped would stay in the area."

"The tides are pretty strong here. Only one more canal paralleling us, and we're northernmost in the city."

"Yes, but the moon is waning. We should be safe

from high tides while we're here," Annja noted. "Whatever happened to the gondolier?"

Scout shrugged. "Still working the canals? The police reports reveal he had an idea that the couple was arguing about something that had been stolen. He wasn't aware of what had happened with the case, until the man asked him to cruise back down the canal in search of it. So it's been established he did not witness the drop into the canal, either. As well, he had no clue what was in the case. And the police did not divulge that information to him."

Annja gazed out over the water. The scent was not unpleasant, though tendrils of rotting wood and sea flora lingered in the air. This canal was quiet, the sidewalk on one side wide and inviting for tourists; the opposite side featured only a small ledge, perhaps two feet wide but in some spots it narrowed to a foot, the docking worn from years of water running over it.

"Like you said, the canal is not that deep," Annja said. "And despite the tides, if anyone wanted to find something that had been dropped half a year ago, I suspect it wouldn't take long. And you just went down."

"Yes, but only to test the equipment. The waters are dark. This headlamp only beams about two, three feet before me. It'll take some time to scour the area. Come on, Creed, where's your sense of adventure?"

"Oh, I've got it in spades. You have a permit to dive here?"

She scanned the stone-fronted buildings, marking most as private residences. Here and there were canal garages, which she expected would provide an excellent nook for a lost suitcase surfing the tidal rhythms to wedge into. She briefly wondered if a resident had already come upon the case while using their private dock. A few were under construction and, she guessed, unoccupied at the moment.

"I did get permission to dive, Creed. And the authorities know exactly what it is I'm diving for. It's all aboveboard, if that's what you're worried about."

"That's what they all say. And then they disappear."

"Do I detect a bruised ego? Perhaps a tragic romance in your past for such a reaction?"

"Please. I don't know you, Roberts, so I won't be sharing."

"What do I have to do to earn your trust, sweetie?"

"For starters? Stop calling me *sweetie.*"

"But I thought you were here to keep an eye on me."

Grabbing the closest headlamp, she said, "Let's go have a look around."

THE VENETIAN CANAL swirled with sediment, murky at the lightest spots. The headlamps allowed Annja and Scout to see about four feet in front of them at the most, and less than two feet the majority of the time. The canal was a few meters deep, and the bottom was littered with timbers, stones and building materials that had been abandoned through the centuries of construction, remodeling and growth. Iron rebar was the most dangerous obstacle, and Annja brushed her hands over the rusted metal often.

Annja loved to scuba dive and had done so all over the world, from the indigo waters of Phuket in Thailand to the volcanic outcrops in Bali. She preferred the bright coral reefs of the Red Sea in Egypt, but the dark and manta ray–infested waters of Belize had fascinated her equally. There was something about the mystery of what lay immediately before her that kicked up her adrenaline and beckoned her forward to discovery.

Ian's dive light, specially designed for underwater filming, cut a deeper and wider swath through the dimness. He intended to film some initial shots of the canal, then wait for her cue to continue filming. It wasn't necessary to film the entire dive, and she wanted to reduce later editing.

This area of the canal hugged the buildings and Annja noted the crumbled cement chunks and lots of garbage, including tin cans and broken wood oars.

Venice's buildings sat upon oak and pine pilings, most having existed since Renaissance times. Since the wood was embedded in airless, muddy soil, it did not decay or rot. It was the constant wetting, drying and shrinking of wood that caused it to rot and that only occurred in wood above the waterline. Another torment to the abovewater wood was decay from fungi and mold. She imagined upkeep on the pilings alone must tax the city's budget.

Scout's headlamp beamed in her face briefly, and she saw his hand gesture. Annja started to follow. Yet Scout swam quickly, and she was compelled to pause and beam her light down a narrow channel to her right. Looked like a passage under a building. Couldn't be more than a foot wide. No way a diver could risk entering. Flashing the headlamp around, she looked for a glint, as the light would catch on the lost object. Scout had said it was in a silver attaché case, so that should stand out in the murk.

Marking off the channel, she pushed back and started in the direction Scout had pointed.

Annja felt something touch her arm, and she swung her head to the right to acknowledge Ian—but it wasn't him. In fact, she caught a glimpse of the white glow-in-the-dark ribbon sewn down the diver's arm. Scout hadn't such a design on his wet suit. Ian had complained about his suit lacking the racing stripes.

There was another diver down here? What were the odds? Had Kard, manning the boat above, seen someone go down?

Veering to the right, where she had last seen Scout, Annja swam into a fizz of oxygen bubbles. An arm slashed across her headlamp beam. Silt stirred up from the canal floor. As she swam closer, she spotted blood in the water.

A pair of fins hung motionless, then kicked as she neared the person. Gripping Scout's arm, she turned him to face her. His eyes were wide behind the goggles and he slapped his arm. Out spilled more blood in a red cloud. He'd been injured by the other diver?

She tugged him upward, passing Ian. Signaling to him that they intended to surface, the cameraman nodded.

Surfacing, Annja pulled off her mask and tugged out the breathing apparatus. She did the same for Scout. "What the—"

"Didn't recognize the guy," he blurted. "Thought

it was the cameraman at first. He got me with a harpoon." He lifted his arm to reveal the slash through the dive suit. "It's only minor."

"Kard!" she hollered.

The boat master nearly tumbled over the side of the boat as he righted from what must have been some serious REM sleep. The clatter of beer cans near his feet shouldn't have been so easy for Annja to hear from where she treaded water.

"Trouble?" Kard called.

Annja pushed Scout toward the boat. "You're done for the day. He's been injured!" she yelled to Kard, who reached down to grasp Scout's good hand. "Ian, we're done filming."

The cameraman had followed them and now handed his equipment up to Kard. After a second try, he managed to grip the ladder to climb into the back of the boat.

Too curious to leave the water just yet, Annja slipped her mask over her eyes and adjusted the fit. "I'll be right back. I want to see if the person's still around."

"You can't go down there by yourself," Scout shouted after her. "Not without a weapon!"

Reinserting the breathing apparatus into her mouth, Annja dived. Scout's last word was distorted by bubbles as she kicked her flippers and headed in the direction where Scout had been injured. It wasn't wise to return without a weapon, but she did have one that worked in water, on land, in the air and anywhere else she might get in a bind.

Her headlamp swept over the darkness. She assumed if the diver was smart, he or she would have already vacated the area. But if the person was eager and desperate to find the case, then he or she might still be around. Seeking bubbles, she swam slowly through the murk.

Twisting her head side to side, she swam into something solid on her left—that kicked away from her. Jackpot.

Calling the sword from the otherwhere, Annja knew she wouldn't be able to swing it with any effectiveness, but as she drew it before her and grasped the tip of the blade with her gloved hand, she used it as a deflector.

A flipper kicked near her face. She stabbed the sword toward it, slicing through the heavy rubber. Unsure if she had cut through the shooter's foot, she kept the blade before her to deflect a return blow. No return contact was made. He swam away from her, swiftly, to judge the trail of bubbles.

She followed him to a concrete wall, where he swam through an open iron gate. Her headlamp beamed on his hand, pulling the gate shut behind him. A padlock and chain secured the gate, so by the time she reached it, she struggled with the lock only momentarily. There was no way in.

She released the sword into the otherwhere. The man who had shot Scout was obviously familiar with the area. He'd probably readied the gate for the quick escape he might need.

She surfaced, her shoulders bobbing in the cool water as she took in her surroundings. The dive boat was anchored twenty yards north. She treaded water on the opposite side of the canal from where she had begun. She waved, signaling to Kard, who waved back. Grasping a heavy iron ring set into the concrete curb once used for docking boats, Annja pulled herself up and heaved her body onto the narrow ledge, twisting to sit with her back against the wall of the building, her flippered feet dangling in the canal.

Looking up and back, she noted the building behind her, where she sat, was under construction. White plastic tarps had been secured over the windows, the tattered ends fluttering in the breeze. The place was abandoned for the time being; no sign of any workers.

The tunnel the shooter had escaped through was just below, so she should have seen him surface within the building. Annja pushed up and pressed her body against the wall. Through a window she could see an empty room littered with plaster buckets, more tarps and several ladders. The tunnel probably led out the other side of this block and into the next canal. She should pursue on foot, but she'd have to take off her flippers and run barefoot. It wasn't a good idea.

The boat chugged up to the shoreline, and Scout, his wet suit around his hips, waved for her to come aboard.

He'd tied a thin strip of medical gauze around his biceps. Blood stained the tape. Annja guessed it had just been a flesh wound.

"You see anything?" Ian called.

"Followed him but he escaped through a tunnel. Closed an iron gate on me and locked it. I'm positive it's below this building. I need to investigate further."

"Why?" Scout leaned over to offer her his hand as boarding assistance. "You want a smackdown with some angry dude carrying a harpoon?"

She jumped onto the boat.

"Don't you want to find the guy who could have killed you?"

"I'm still alive. I don't think he was going for the kill. He was close enough to make a kill shot if he'd wanted to."

"At the very least, we need to report this to the authorities."

"Creed." Scout placed a hand on her shoulder. "I admit it, I'm a treasure hunter. Trouble follows me wherever I go. This is nothing new."

She quirked an eyebrow at him. Most people wouldn't be so casual about being attacked. Shrugging off her air tank, she bent to remove her flippers. "What do you have against my reporting this to the police?"

"Nothing. Go for it." Scout's indifference only made her more suspicious. "I'm just saying encounters with idiots wielding harpoons are to be expected. I go after a treasure, the bottom-feeders follow in hordes."

"Nice." *Not.* She unzipped the wet suit to reveal her skintight tank top beneath. "Let's call it a day."

"Swell. You go to the authorities and explain to them we almost saw the guy who did it—did you get a good look at his face? Didn't think so. Meanwhile, I'll mark out the map for tomorrow's dive."

She glanced at Ian. He shrugged, evidently as baffled by Scout's disregard as she was.

"You want to get something to eat?" Scout asked.

"I think I'll head back to the hotel after I've been to the police station." Scout's comment about her not getting a look at the attacker's face annoyed her. She didn't need his attitude. And really, she should have paid closer attention to the bad guy's features. "Reconvene in the morning? Same canal, same boat?"

"Fine," Scout said. "Give me your cell number?"

She gave it to him, and he promised to text her his number so she would have it, as well.

Ian packed up his gear, and Annja hung the wet suit in the closet provided belowdecks.

Kard offered Annja and then Ian a beer for the walk to the police station and both refused.

"You think they're a couple cards short of a full deck?" Ian asked as they strolled down the street.

"Possibly."

"Nice crew, Annja. I'll count myself lucky if I come out of this unscathed."

She winced because she took seriously the safety of those around her. She'd have a proper talk with Kard tomorrow. And she'd keep a much closer eye on Scout. The man could be too adventurous for *her* own good.

5

At the police station in San Marco, Tomaso Damiani greeted Annja with a warm smile and welcomed her into his office. The small room held only his desk, two chairs and on the wall a map of the canals. No family photos. No knickknacks.

A new hire? Or was the man so regimented that he couldn't bother with clutter?

She explained she was in the city on a dive for stolen artifacts. Tomaso was aware of that. The city had forwarded the dive permit Scout Roberts had applied for just this morning.

Pleased that the city was in close contact with the police, Annja detailed the encounter with the mysterious diver in the Fondamenta della Sensa.

"You are sure you did not surprise another who was merely diving?" Tomaso asked as he jotted down the information on a yellow notepad. "Perhaps the harpoon went off during the surprise?"

"Then why would he swim off? Wouldn't he want to make sure he hadn't wounded anyone?"

"Yes, of course. That is what we would hope for."

Tomaso ran a hand over his close-cropped dark hair. His narrow face fit with his tall, tight frame. He was young. A wedding ring shone on his sun-tanned hand, but there was no visible tan line beneath. New job, new wife? "Perhaps he was shocked that he had done such a thing. Perhaps not."

"Who dives beneath Venice with a harpoon in hand?" Annja asked. "It's not as if the canals are populated with edible fish. Are they?"

"We have much flora and fauna in the canals, Signorina Creed. But the fish are smaller, such as mullets and bullheads. Still, some are edible. We even get the occasional shark in from the sea. Perhaps your harpoon man was pursuing bigger game?"

"Like humans?"

She hadn't meant it as a joke, but Tomaso chuckled. Then, noticing she didn't share his humor, he abruptly stopped.

"I take your report very seriously, *signorina.* There are drainage pipes and tunnels beneath much of our beautiful city. Some are registered. Others lead into private homes and still others may no longer be used."

"Which is why I didn't try to break through the gate—I didn't know if this was a residence."

Annja realized there really wasn't a lot the police could do. Might it have been an accident? Possibly. And the man could have been frightened or even ashamed, so he'd fled.

"I appreciate you taking the time to listen to my complaint. I know there's likely nothing you can do without a description of the man."

"Unfortunately, that is so. But I am personally eager for you to discover the missing treasure you've described. A cross with a possible connection to Leonardo da Vinci?"

"It was likely a gift to him from René d'Anjou."

"Ah. Our beloved Leonardo. I am so taken with the man. He did so much. And has inspired so many."

Surprised the man was such an enthusiast of Leonardo's and of René's, Annja perked up.

"Details linking Leonardo da Vinci with such a cross and so many other artifacts causes much interest. And sometimes from dangerous people," he went on.

"I find I'm more of a Leonardo purist myself," she said. "Though there are academics and art historians who think there was more to his works. But I'm not inclined to search over his paintings or drawings for symbols and clues he may or may not have left in them. His output was so vast. I can only imagine how many European castles and manors are hiding a forgotten da Vinci in the attic or dungeon."

"Yes, it is an intriguing thing to wonder about. The Renaissance artist was a great genius and I wonder what it might have been like for him if he could have possibly traveled through time."

"Da Vinci a time traveler?" Now Annja chuckled.

"I know," Tomaso agreed, "I have a tendency toward the fantastical—it has to be with the books I read. I like the science-fiction novels." He gave her a warm smile. "Signorina Creed, have you been to Il Genio di Leonardo da Vinci Museo? They've re-created dozens of the inventions Leonardo designed. Quite a fascinating study."

"No, I haven't been able to do any sightseeing since arriving in Venice, but it sounds like a stop I'll have to make while I'm here."

Tomaso stood and shook Annja's hand. "If there is anything you need from me, do let me know." He offered her his business card. "It was a pleasure to meet you, Signorina Creed."

ANNJA BOUGHT A sandwich on her way to the hotel. Glad she'd gone with the panino instead of the soft-crusted tramezinni, she wondered now if she could eat it all. Calling the huge chunk of bread, cheese and meat a sandwich was like calling the Canal Grande a stream. The prosciutto was so thin she could read through it, and stacked thickly within pillows of fresh mozzarella. She ate half before forcing herself to sit at the desk in her hotel room and power up the laptop for a little research.

She started with the antiquities museum located in Kraków, Poland. It featured artifacts she'd label as sentimentally significant. Annja assumed the Lorraine cross must have fit right in with their collection.

The museum had a history similar to a number of others in Europe during the turbulence of the 1800s. Items had been looted and recovered a number of times during this age. And it was all repeated again in the early part of the twentieth century when the Nazis eventually got their hands on the museum's pieces and there they stayed until the place was restored and reopened to the public after the Second World War. Though it housed many important relics and documents, a lot of the most valued pieces had been lost as they changed locations over the decades and centuries.

The recent burglary was a bold and well-planned heist that had taken place just after the museum had closed its doors. The one employee who had locked up for the day had only been in the parking lot for minutes, the online newspaper account reported, before the theft had occurred. Suspicion fell on two suspects, but neither was captured by security cameras.

Annja speculated about the thieves who were arrested in the Milan and NYC airports. Why had they not been detained if they were known to be related to the theft? Or had the gondolier's report merely alerted the police to the pair, and after questioning them, the police hadn't obtained the details required to charge them with the crime?

Most likely. But still odd.

There wasn't anything else online regarding the theft, and she couldn't get access to the police reports. Although, she might be able to get something on the thief who had been questioned in New York from her friend on the NYPD, Detective Bart McGilly.

"Good idea."

She sent Bart an email with the details, and the situation surrounding her dive, and asked if he could find anything on the thief who had been arrested.

Satisfied she had done what she could to follow up on that angle, Annja switched to the history associated with the stolen items. She already knew quite a bit about Leonardo da Vinci and Joan of Arc, so she looked up the third party.

She was familiar with René d'Anjou as an integral force behind the Renaissance, but she was also aware d'Anjou was sometimes glanced over or even excluded from the history books. Could it be because of his rumored associations with the Priory of Sion and Order of the Crescent?

Annja shook her head.

René d'Anjou had held ties to royal houses in France, England and Spain. His sister had married Charles VII of France. His daughter married Henry VI of England. He had control of three duchies, Anjou, Bar and Lorraine, as well as being king of Jerusalem and Aragon, including Corsica, Majorca and Sicily. He had been duke of many places, yet his most common title was Good King René.

His involvement in Joan of Arc's life may have been orchestrated by his mother, Yolande, who had been a supporter of Charles VII of France. There were rumors René had traveled with Joan to Orléans, possibly disguised as the king's messenger. Evidently, he was also along when Joan had escorted the dauphin to Reims for the coronation. Once there, René had been knighted by the Count of Clermont.

René had been with Joan in a few more battles that followed, including the siege on Paris. But soon after that, family deaths turned René's attention away from Joan. He had been detained during a battle against the Duke of Burgundy and subsequently imprisoned.

While imprisoned, Joan had been branded a heretic and…

"So René d'Anjou wasn't able to speak up for Joan of Arc because he had been possibly held captive at the time," Annja muttered, leaning back in her chair.

She grabbed the panino and took another bite. Heaven. She'd left Ian to do his own thing, and he'd gone in search of pizza. Normally, she'd invite him to eat with her, but her mind was still reeling from the harpoon attack. It had been so bizarre and out of place. It didn't make sense to her.

And Scout claimed it was the norm, him being a treasure hunter? He'd acted as if the attack was to be expected. Could he have hired the man to take out Ian, whom he hadn't wanted there in the first place?

"No." He had only found out about Ian just before the dive.

"Something not right with that guy."

She focused again on René d'Anjou. He headed to Naples in 1438 and later returned to France amid further political turmoil and controversy.

D'Anjou had also been a painter and a poet. He set up court at Aix-en-Provence, although she guessed that René must have interacted with Leonardo on his own turf in Italy. D'Anjou had died in 1480. Leonardo had been born in 1452. Annja knew Leonardo had traveled with his father to Florence and had received an apprenticeship when he was fourteen. Possibly, René d'Anjou had met Leonardo between 1470 and 1480, which was around the time Leonardo's father had been employed under d'Anjou.

And if Roux had said he'd met Leonardo at the end of the 1480s, that made sense to her and would fit the timeline of when d'Anjou had supposedly gifted Leonardo with the Lorraine cross.

"Amazing."

Annja experienced the same adrenaline rush she felt when uncovering a valuable historical treasure. The thrill of the find, or knowing that with further research a discovery could be made, was something she never tired of.

And now, before her, was the idea of a significant connection of three incredible historical figures: René d'Anjou, Leonardo da Vinci, and Joan of Arc.

She was deeply involved, too, more so than on a usual archaeological dig, because she was inexplicably tied to Joan herself. And Roux had known all three?

Thinking of him, she dialed Roux's number. She wanted to check when he planned to arrive. Voice mail. She didn't leave a message, didn't want to reveal her irritation. He'd get a real kick out of that.

Finishing off the panino, Annja then scanned through the local television news stations. Nothing of interest. The night had grown long while she'd been hunting for information. She'd save the check on Scout's story for the morning.

Stripping off her clothes and pulling her long chestnut hair out from the tangled ponytail, she padded into the bathroom and made good use of the hot water for the next twenty minutes.

Milan, 1488

"You said..." Roux leaned forward across the table, knowing he could not possibly have heard the artist correctly. The tavern was noisy, and the hissing back-and-forth sweep of a sword blade across a whetstone nearby didn't help matters. "Something about a sword piece?"

"Indeed. From Jeanne d'Arc's sword. The one she wielded in the siege on Paris," Leonardo explained. "Though it's malformed. Melted, I believe. I was to understand they had burned her ashes twice to be sure nothing remained. The English army didn't want to leave anything that could be sifted from the ashes and later passed on. Obviously they missed the sword."

Roux rubbed his chin, thinking back to that moment when the flames had wrecked Joan's life forever. And his. The sword had been held aside, along with the few items of clothing she'd worn while imprisoned. How the sword had made it out into the crowd, and then had been broken before all, was beyond him.

It felt surreal to place himself back at that heinous event. He'd never felt helpless before that moment and never had since. But the sense of anguish returned now, made him uncomfortable.

Leonardo was unaware of his distress. And he wished to keep it that way.

"If you guarded Jeanne— She was burned in 1431, wasn't it?" he asked. "That was sixty-seven years ago. You must have been quite young. You've certainly aged well."

"I've been living well," Roux boasted, smiling.

"Ha!" Leonardo cried and took a hearty swallow of his ale.

Roux tried to act relaxed and purposely pitched his voice low, so that only da Vinci would hear him. "Tell me about this piece from the sword?"

"Ah, you are one with the eager questions?"

Leonardo sketched a few more lines on the drawing he'd tended since Roux had sat down and, seeming happy with the composition, closed his leather-bound book. Placing both palms about the beer stein, Leonardo spoke quietly. "Her sword was broken after they burned her."

"I know that."

"Ah? A confirmation of what I had only, until now, known to be rumor. Excellent."

Yes, yes, so he'd tricked the truth out of him? It wasn't as though it had been a great secret to begin with. Roux wanted to wrench the man up by the back of his tunic and hustle him outside, where they could speak privately, but he dismissed the idea.

"René d'Anjou had the pieces."

"All of them?" Roux had thought they'd eventually been scattered to the far parts of the world, and indeed, his quest to locate them was proving nearly impossible.

"No, only so many as he was able to grab among the crowd, who were hungry for a piece of the Maid of Orléans. Can you imagine that calamity? Dreadful. The human soul has insatiable curiosity for the macabre when compassion is what is needed most."

Losing his patience, Roux gripped the edges of the table. "I was there. I did witness the horror."

"Yes. Right. Forgive my callousness. But you didn't manage a piece of the sword?"

"No," Roux said tightly. "And yet you possess a piece?"

"Yes, yes. When I was so elated by the Lorraine cross, René d'Anjou showed me the few sword pieces he had remaining."

Roux tapped the table with a finger. "I'd like to take a look at the piece you have, if you wouldn't mind?"

"I do mind. It's locked away." Leonardo took the sketch of the cross, waved it in demonstration and then tucked it in his purse. "Prized possessions, the cross and the sword piece. I don't have many. Now, sir, it's time I bought you a drink."

6

Annja met Ian in the hotel lobby, and they arrived at the boat before Scout. Both suited up and were checking the equipment when Scout sauntered aboard with a beaming smile on his face.

He made a show of looking over Annja appreciatively.

She dismissed him and turned to study the marked-up map. "You're late."

"I can't begin the day without my orange juice and coffee. The fresh-squeezed stuff is hard to come by here on the island. Had to order it from the mainland."

"Seriously? Your budget allows for such luxury?"

"Hey," Scout said, tugging off his jacket, "take it up with the old man."

Annja hadn't thought Roux would offer such an expense account. On the other hand, Scout probably wasn't aware that he didn't have carte blanche with his employer, and so was testing the waters.

"I think we should head northwest," Annja suggested as Scout descended belowdecks to change into his dive suit. "The general direction of traffic in this canal may have pushed the case downstream. And depending on what the treasure was in…"

"A silver hard-wall attaché with digital lock!"

"Really? I thought you said it was a nondescript case. How do you know that?"

"Come on, Creed, do a little research. You always just leap into things for your television show?"

Day two, Annja decided, was when Scout had succeeded in getting on her nerves. Generally, she was pretty accepting of people and the attitudes that came with them. "Difficult to casually toss over the side of a gondola during a lover's spat without the other noticing, wouldn't you say?"

Scout emerged, tugging up the zipper on his suit. "Who said the spat was casual? Did you read the incarceration report for the pair? Wait. Right. You didn't."

"I don't have access to it." Which reminded her, she hadn't heard back from Bart McGilly yet. Blame it on the time-zone difference. "But apparently you do. So enlighten me."

"There was a heated argument. And I guess when the guy wasn't paying attention, the woman ditched the case."

He guessed? That wasn't going to help her until she got the chance to look over the reports.

"All right, then," Annja said. "We're looking for a metal attaché case. Let's hope it's waterproof."

"It is. I mean, I'm sure it is. They make those cases to be almost indestructible nowadays."

Having little hope that indeed the attaché would be

intact, Annja conceded and directed Kard to the spot she had chosen down the canal.

"How's the arm?" she asked Scout, remembering yesterday's close call.

"Doesn't hurt a bit. A scratch." He slapped the biceps where he'd been hurt.

"You should have at least had it looked at. What if the harpoon had been rusty?"

"I'm tough, Creed. Let's dock here, Kard." He scanned the buildings and seemed to be noting a familiar site. "Everyone in!"

Ian went in first, and Annja handed him his camera. The cameraman switched on the lamp and tested it underwater, giving her a thumbs-up. She tossed out the red and white dive flags.

"You have any weapons on this boat?" she asked as she and Scout prepared to jump into the canal. "A harpoon might not be such a bad idea to bring along."

"I don't, but you're thinking smart now, Creed. I'll pick one up tonight."

If someone was also searching for the treasure, a shopping trip tonight could prove too late for their safety. But she wasn't willing to change and make a quick run now. Yesterday had been a fluke. She hoped.

"Later, then." She pulled down her mask and slipped into the water.

Five minutes into the murk, Annja passed the gated tunnel into which the shooter had escaped yesterday afternoon. She paused to jiggle the gate. Still locked. She studied the spot, but her headlamp didn't allow for too much detail. It was impossible to know where the tunnel led, but she was curious and wished she had a picklock.

A nudge from Scout and a gesture to the gate—he was asking if that was the gate where the attacker had disappeared—and she confirmed with a nod and a dismissive shrug. Nothing else they could do here.

She swam onward, taking the lead until Scout came alongside her. They used their head beams in tandem to sweep a wider field of vision before them.

Her headlamp swept across a small wire cage, a chebe, that must have been set down by a resident to collect crabs and small fish. Nothing inside it, and it was clean of seaweed that the tides would have draped across the wires. Might have just been set down in the water, or else it took days or even weeks to lure in a catch.

Scout pointed toward a line of closely spaced wood pilings. Annja followed him as he worked his way methodically along the base, where crevices and nooks formed an archaeologist's dream map of the city's lifeline.

The idea of living on water appealed to Annja, and she was ever amazed that the city had not completely sunk. Venice should hold its watery ground for centuries to come, even with the rising tides that slowly crept higher year after year.

A rumbling from above alerted her and she turned onto her back to look toward the surface. She couldn't see daylight from the depths they were at, so was surprised to have heard the noise. The diving flags were a signal to passing boats not to drive in the area, and

Kard should be keeping watch. If he didn't have a beer in hand.

She'd forgotten to give him that talking-to. She was shirking her babysitting duties.

Spreading her arms wide, Annja floated through the water as if on the surface, eyes upward, flippers slowly kicking. A glint cut through the waters like sun through the clouds. Surreal. She reached out to touch it and then someone swam up beside her, startling her out of the misplaced moment of reverie.

Scout signaled they surface. Annja shook her head, not understanding why he wanted to. They'd only been down about twenty minutes. But he persisted, so she didn't continue to argue. He could be having equipment troubles.

She kicked upward, but just as the daylight came into blurry view, she felt the shove of the water as a powerful wake pushed her backward against Scout's body. He reacted defensively, shoving her away. Annja kicked toward the surface, but only realized she'd swam toward a boat when the zing of metal sheered above her head. A force pushed her down through the water. She opened her mouth but closed it before the breathing regulator could fall out.

Panic-sticken, she settled her urge to scream and take in water. Unable to process what had happened, she trod water suspended in the murk surrounded by a swarm of bubbles and the body-moving *schush* of the boat's wake. She sensed an aching heat on the top of her head. Reaching up, she winced when her fingers slid through a gash in her scalp. She'd been cut?

A hand gripped her at the waist. She reacted, slapping her hand down to clutch the wrist and kick the attacker away with her heel. The water wouldn't allow for quick defensive moves, nor would her flipper serve a good kick, but she managed a knee up and jammed it against the man's chest at the moment their masks were but a foot from one another. He chuffed out his breathing tube at the force of her kick and released her.

She only registered that it was Scout at the last second. He'd been trying to help her. Maybe. She'd been disoriented by the passing of the motorboat overhead. Kicking hard and fast, Annja breached the surface and tugged off her breathing tube.

Scout appreared next to her. He ripped off his face mask and grabbed her by the head, pressing his fingers over the crown of it and her saturated hair. "It's cut. But there isn't much blood."

"I'm fine," she said, pushing away from him and kicking her legs slowly, using the momentum of her flippers to tread water.

She didn't feel the cut, but knew that oftentimes scalp injuries hurt the least yet bled the most. If it wasn't bleeding, then it was either just a graze or one of those cuts that went so deep it didn't bleed.

Thinking that if she had kicked one more time, the boat propeller could have cut more than just the surface of her scalp, Annja heaved out a breath. "That was close."

"Too close."

"I'm sorry, Scout, I didn't know who you were when you were trying to help me."

"I figured that. Or maybe you just owed me one for the attitude, eh?" His smirk returned, and Annja decided she'd been apologetic enough.

"You all right?" Kard called down from the boat.

Scout signaled a thumbs-up. Just then Ian surfaced. "I lost the two of you—" His attention turned to Annja's head. "You're bleeding!"

Now she felt the warm trickle spill over her eyelid and down onto her cheek.

Scout took her by the elbow and escorted her toward the back of the boat. "You're done for the day. Let's get you out of the water."

"I'll be fine. We need to find out who was driving that boat."

Annja dismissed Scout's assistance and levered herself up by the steel ladder rungs. Once seated, she tugged off her flippers and mask. She touched her head, felt the laceration and judged it about two inches long. She'd probably gotten a long-overdue haircut in the process.

"We should have set out buoys," Ian remarked. "Kard, didn't you try to warn the boat driver away from the area?"

"Uh..." Kard began, but then went silent.

Annja assumed the driver hadn't been paying attention, and noticing the bottle of open beer near the steering wheel, she sighed. He was a hazard to their safety. But she wasn't willing to give up now.

"We're going back down," she insisted as Scout landed inside the boat. "You may think that what just happened wasn't suspicious, but why right here, right now? Yesterday's attack on you and now this? It's too coincidental. We were close. Had to be. And whoever is coming after us knows it, too."

"Your tanks are low on oxygen," Kard said. "You two will have to wait until later to go down again."

"Why weren't they filled this morning?" Annja asked snappishly.

"That's cool." Scout tugged down the zipper on his suit. "I'm going to take the lovely Miss Creed to the emergency room. She's getting testy."

"I am not!'

"I think it's from blood loss," Scout said. "We'll drive to the hospital, then out for a nice meal, pamper her a bit. She needs it. Uh, Ian, you can come along, too. If you want to."

The cameraman raised a brow at the crummy invitation. "That's okay. I'm going to help Kard fill the tanks, and then I'll edit yesterday's footage. Will you give me a call after you've had your head stitched up, Annja?"

She nodded that she would and signaled for Ian to follow her belowdecks. Annja tugged the wet-suit zipper down in the back.

"Annja?"

She quickly caught the wall to avoid falling down the stairs and realized she was not quite right. Maybe she did need medical care.

"Talk to Kard, will you? He's dangerous."

"That was my intention of staying on board. I'll take care of it, Annja. You let Scout get you to a doctor."

"I'll be up in a minute."

"One minute. If not, I'm coming back down after you, whether you're half-dressed or— I'm worried, Annja."

"I'll be fine. I'll be right up."

ANNJA RECEIVED TWELVE stitches from a chatterbox of a physician's assistant who recognized her from reruns of *Chasing History's Monsters* he'd seen while visiting friends in the States. He recounted half a dozen episodes, detailing Annja's exploits as if she hadn't been there.

She was content to let him talk. Seemed to focus him for some reason, and she'd prefer the stitches small and tight. They only had to shave a narrow line in her hair, so afterward Annja had but to pull her hair to one side and tug it into a ponytail to disguise the cut.

Scout waited in the hospital reception area. When they released Annja an hour later, he announced to her he'd made reservations for supper. Though she wasn't inclined to dine with him, Annja didn't refuse. She needed carbs.

THE ANICE STELLATO RESTAURANT was located not far from Annja's hotel. It was a cozy place to relax at day's end. The hostess seated Annja and Scout at an outdoor canal-side table. The salty wood smell from the water was overwhelmed by the delicious savory scents wafting out from the restaurant.

While they waited for their meals, their waitress brought wine and a basket of bread. The Madonna dell'Orto church stood nearby, and now the bells for compline sounded.

Annja loved church bells. She preferred the Gothic architecture of the medieval cathedrals, trimmed with layer upon layer of ornamention, buttressed and arched, and not a single spot of stone left undecorated. Such precision and attention to detail never ceased to amaze her. And to know that all the building materials had been transported onto the island of Venice with ancient means made the local monuments even more impressive.

Across the table from where she sat, Scout's smile told a tale. His blue eyes had probably netted him more than his fair share of women with no more than a wink and a teasing grin.

Despite the romantic atmosphere, Annja wasn't in the mood. She'd almost been scalped by a boat motor, and Scout seemed ever oblivious to danger. Or rather, he anticipated it, which was almost more disturbing. She always expected danger and kept a keen eye out for it. Yet she had been complacent on the dive. Floating in the water as if in a dream? She had no one to blame but herself for the injury.

"Your head still numb?" he asked.

They'd shot her up with painkillers before stitching her scalp. "It's tingly, but I'll survive."

"So you think this business will prove good fodder for your television show?" he asked. He stretched his legs out from under the table, propping them on the stone curb just beneath a wrought-iron railing that edged the canal. "I suspect Leonardo da Vinci would garner you a big ratings boost. And yet, doesn't your show track history's monsters?"

"It does. And we've already discussed this."

"I know, but I do like to beat a dead horse. Since when does Leonardo da Vinci fall into the 'monstrous' category?"

"He doesn't. The show steps into other territory every now and then by featuring historical figures. I don't know if this dive will produce anything worthy of the show, but I'd rather be safe than sorry and have footage rather than regret having nothing later."

"I'll give you that. No monsters rising from the depths or winged creatures swooping down from the heavens to carry off the pretty archaeologist. Did you know Leonardo actually sketched a dragon?"

Annja did remember reading something about that and finding it fascinating when compared to his other subjects, most of them depicting religious topics, such as the Last Supper. The man's mind must have been a vast repository filled with all sorts of ideas. She wondered now if he had slept much. Most geniuses did not.

What she wouldn't give to have a chat with the master. Ask him, *Who was Mona Lisa, anyway?* Historians posited she was the wife of Francesco del Giocondo, a wealthy Florentine silk merchant who may have commissioned the portrait for their new home and to celebrate the birth of their second son. Others theorized it was Leonardo's mother, Caterina, painted using his own likeness.

The next best thing to talking to Leonardo could be Roux. Where was the old man, anyway? He should have arrived in the city by now. Apparently, he wasn't too concerned about this dive.

"My major was medieval studies," she said. "And I do recall a dragon sketch by Leonardo. He had done so much, I'm sure we'll be discovering works by him for a long time to come. All those dukes and lords who may have acquired a sketch or notebook at auction thinking it pretty and intriguing, and having no idea of its value or origin."

"Yes, and then when bored of it, stuffing it away in some old musty castle. I love considering how many great treasures are yet out there to be uncovered. Makes a man's heart jitter."

"A good jitter?"

"A very good jitter. Like this cross we're searching for. I love how it seems to bring together René d'Anjou and Leonardo da Vinci. History is truly incredible. More people should put the time in to study it."

"It's the conspiracy theorists who bother me," Annja offered. "People searching for hidden symbols and codes supposedly left in artistic works makes me a bit crazy. Although I have to admit I've had to follow a clue or two in the past."

Annja was starting to relax. Chatting with Scout was...nice.

"So tell me all you know about the René d'Anjou connection and how he gifted Leonardo da Vinci with Joan of Arc's cross," she prompted, hoping to compare his knowledge to what Roux had already told her.

Their dinner arrived, and they began to eat while Scout explained.

"Just so you know, I'm a fanatic when it comes to Joan of Arc. Or Jeanne d'Arc, as I prefer to call her."

"Is that so?" This could either prove a fascinating conversation or a dangerous one. Annja guarded her secret well and wasn't about to reveal her connection to Joan of Arc. "Jeanne had been dead twenty years before Leonardo was even born."

Scout offered a number of facts and theories, and finally got to Leonardo and his father.

"His father was the one to recognize his son's talents, I believe," Annja said.

"Can you believe René d'Anjou, or Good King René, as his followers labeled him, wasn't even a king? Talk about some great press, eh?"

"He was king of many small lands. His mother, Yolande, a powerful woman in her own right, was one of Jeanne's tutors."

"Right, which is how René might have known Jeanne. There is speculation that they had an affair, but I don't buy into it. I doubt Jeanne had time for love affairs when she had God speaking in her head."

"That does challenge any romantic notions, doesn't it? God or the guy? Hardly a choice at all."

"If you're into stuff like communicating with the divine," Scout said.

"You're not?"

Scout shrugged. "I'll stick with having the usual love life. And wouldn't you guess a teenage girl might be a little more interested in the guy?"

"You said you didn't buy into them having an affair."

"I don't. But that doesn't mean she didn't pine for a wink from someone."

Annja rolled her eyes. The man had a weird romantic flair to his storytelling. He'd romanticized the story of the thieves as well.

"So how's your love life, Creed?"

A graceless conversational switch if ever there was one. "None of your business. So back to this cross René d'Anjou gave Leonardo."

"That diversion was not even subtle."

"You started it."

"Touché. The world-traveling adventuress keeps her personal life under wraps. I can dig it." Scout had a sip of water and continued, "Love doesn't come easy doing what we do. We take it when we can get it, right?"

She would not dignify that one with a reply, although he was close to the mark. Annja had no great love affairs, but she would never deny herself sex when she was in the mood. As handsome as Scout was, she wasn't feeling it. She was more interested in the man's brain than what he could do for her physically. Besides, she still didn't trust him. And he was kind of flaky.

"Doing what *we* do?" she repeated. "I'm not completely sure what it is that you do, Scout. Treasure hunter? Archaeologist?"

"Former. You checked me out, I'm sure."

"Right. Fell out with the University of Columbia over a dig in Peru."

"That's what it says."

"And what do you say?"

He swallowed a forkful of pasta and smiled as he chewed. "No comment."

"Uh-huh. You're very young for a professor, you know that?"

He emptied his water glass and gestured to the waitress for a refill. Once the waitress had left them, Scout picked up the conversation. "Back to the topic we can both manage without spilling secrets or alluding to our sex lives. Leonardo da Vinci!"

She'd drop the age question for now. Annja found the garlic-and-chili-pepper-laden pasta much too good to spend the time talking when she could be eating. "Agreed."

Scout set down his fork and wiped his lips with a napkin.

"Some accounts report that d'Anjou and da Vinci were friends," Annja offered. "I fall more on the side that they were acquaintances."

"That's where we get to the conspiracy theorists versus the purists. Could Leonardo have been involved in the Priory of Sion or the Order of the Crescent? Two secret organizations d'Anjou was known to have participated in."

"Who knows?" Annja bypassed her glass of water and took a drink from her wine goblet instead. "No definitive evidence has been brought forth to verify Leonardo was ever interested in the occult," she continued. "And frankly, if you want to find something in a drawing or painting, you will, if you are determined and believe in it hard enough. There are so many crazy theories, I remain a skeptic until proven otherwise."

"Fine." Scout rapped his fingernails on his goblet. The waitress removed their dinner plates and brought another bottle of wine.

The last rays of sun turned the waters of the Cana Reggio golden as they softly beat against the dock. Times like this, when she had a calm moment with no looming deadline or dig to consider, Annja found she had to remind herself to enjoy them. And yet, even when she'd found such a quiet minute, things always seemed to be happening. Best to stay alert.

"How long have you known Roux?" Scout asked from behind a swallow of wine.

She shrugged. It was never wise to divulge too much information about her relationship with a man who shouldn't exist in this century. "Awhile. Why do you ask?"

"He seems to have been around," Scout tossed out. "Seen a lot."

"You said you had met him at an auction?"

"Yes, I introduced myself to him. Took the risk in bringing up the Lorraine cross."

"I'm surprised you got to know him all that well. He keeps his personal information close to the vest."

"That he does. Nothing about him on the internet, you know that?"

She nodded. Roux was careful. Yet it did surprise her he was able to have no mention of himself online, what with all his traveling and antiques buying.

"So you think we're simply diving for a decorative cross?" Scout asked, a tone of intrigue tracing the question.

Annja blinked. "Aren't we?"

The man's laughter echoed across the patio. The people at the next table paused from their quiet conversation to peer over their shoulders at them. Annja shushed him and the couple resumed their meal.

"Is there something more in the attaché case?" she asked.

"No. Just a cross. Or so I expect, according—"

"—to the police reports," she finished.

She really should get ahold of these police reports. Could Roux have gotten the information, but failed to pass it on to her? No, Scout had gone to Roux about this dive.

"There's something more? Knock my socks off," she challenged.

"Oh, it will knock your skeptical socks right into the canal." Scout leaned forward, the eagerness in his eyes inexplicably drawing Annja forward, as well. "The cross isn't just some pretty little object to hang on a wall in a dusty old museum. It's actually—" Scout dramatically performed a curious scan of his surroundings "—a key."

Annja smirked and assumed a wondrous tone. "A key? Do tell."

Scout exhaled and sat back. "I don't think so. You don't have the ability to set aside your skepticism. It's all dry history to you, isn't it? Or in this case, wet. Find the case, discover the missing artifact, hand it back to the museum. Then it's on to the next dig or dive, or whatever, resulting in yet another chipped pot or broken vase."

She laughed and poured herself a final serving of wine. "So it's a key. To what? A safe hoarding millions in fifteenth-century gold? Stacks of Leonardo's lost notebooks? The map to the Holy Grail? Do you know how many Holy Grail maps I've seen, Scout? They are a cottage industry in and of themselves."

"To which I have contributed my fair share." His grin was smarmy, so much so that Annja almost checked the ground to see if a snail had crept by.

"It's people like you who give people like me—"

"The upright, upstanding, stick-in-the-muds who never have any fun?"

"Legitimate archaeologists who care about provenance and historical value," Annja corrected. "You do realize that, once found, you have to hand the cross over to Roux, yes?"

"He is the guy writing the check. But let me guess—you're not going to let the old man waltz off into the sunset with his prize."

"Roux knows where I stand with things. It's best you get that into your head, as well."

"Creed, now you've gone and spoiled my fun. I don't even want to tell you about the key." He crossed his arms high on his chest.

"Yes, the key to a mysterious something that most certainly will possess great power. Great enough to rule the world, or at the very least, a small portion of said world."

And yet, she couldn't deny she'd come across some amazing finds over the years. The Skull of Sidon had been rumored to possess all power to whomever held it, and she had witnessed—something—in the moments it had been held before the holder had been slain. Solomon's Jar had bound the world's demons. And many other myths and legends, some that she hadn't been able to discount and could believe because she had witnessed the truth.

Though a selkie losing her pelt and being enslaved by a domineering mortal? She had to admit Sirena worried her. Maybe she would give her a call later.

Annja had learned so much since taking Joan's sword in hand. It was as if the sword wanted her to experience the marvels this realm was capable of producing.

"You're thinking about it," Scout said. "Excellent. A crack in the woman's tough skeptic armor."

"I haven't been told what the key opens, so there's nothing for me to believe or disbelieve right now."

She held his gaze, waiting for him to back down from his pout. With a conceding exhale, he did.

Scout motioned to the waitress and borrowed her pen. He then scribbled a diagram on his napkin. Annja divided her attention between the man's drawing and the canal; some activity across the way alerted her that she should be on guard. After nearly being taken out twice while diving, she wouldn't be surprised if she and Scout were being followed.

"So this is the Lorraine cross." Scout turned the napkin toward her.

"Yes, I'm familiar with the double-barred cross. You've drawn it with the bars equally distributed along the main bar. Others push up the parallel bars to keep it more in the form of the Christian cross."

"Right, but the one Jeanne d'Arc was reputed to have given René was like this."

"Did you ever see the cross when it was displayed in the museum?"

"Yes, er, no, not displayed in the museum. So, uh, here's where the story takes a slightly science-fiction turnabout." Scout tapped at the napkin drawing.

Annja grimaced. And yet, she kept her ears wide open. For as much of a skeptic as she tended to be, she was the first to jump when the idea of proving a myth to be real was presented. Because how cool would that be?

"Hear me out," Scout said, making a few more notations on the cross before him. "René d'Anjou was all about the occult and stuff like that. And the connection to Leonardo—who knows? Still, I'm going to guess or assume that there is one between the two men."

Maybe. Maybe not. Whether there was a connection by association between symbols and da Vinci's works through d'Anjou was pure speculation

"I'm not saying any of this is true, but if it were…"

"Just spit it out, Scout. What magical properties does the Lorraine cross possess?"

"The cross isn't magical. It's a key. But what that key fits into is truly remarkable." Scout glanced across the canal, then averted his gaze along the outside tables, before leaning closer and saying in a whisper, "There's a couple of suspicious-looking men standing at the corner of the entryway. Don't turn around."

Signaling to the waitress to bring them the check, Scout tucked the napkin inside his shirt pocket.

"Wow, you do the avoid well," Annja said. "Tell me what it is the key to."

"No time." He signed the credit-card receipt for the waitress and stood up. "It's time to get out of here. You still in on the project or not? Because my feelings won't be hurt if the babysitter decides to pack up and head home after getting her skull cracked open."

"It was a scratch." She'd dampened his excitement and he was pouting. Treasure hunters. "I'm in. Tomorrow morning, same time as today?"

"Ten. See you at the boat. I'm going to head east. Why don't you leave through the restaurant to give them the slip? Ciao, Creed."

She turned as Scout took off, and eyed the two men standing in the corner. Thugs in suits. Her favorite kind. But were these goons really stalking her and Scout, or were they merely businessmen waiting for a table?

Deciding to give Scout the benefit of the doubt, she exited through the restaurant and noted one of the men did indeed follow Scout in the direction he had left, while the other...she could no longer see.

7

Annja sprinted toward a courtyard, hoping that if she could attract the thugs' attention by running, maybe the one guy wouldn't follow Scout. Why she was feeling so chivalrous, she wasn't sure. But she had a weapon and Scout probably did not. Both men were following her now and were gaining on her because she was only jogging, allowing them to catch up. There were only two of them. A number she could easily handle.

A line of hedges blocked her view of the courtyard that she knew of behind an old church. She wasn't sure if the church was still in use, but she hoped the court-yard would be empty and provide a private place for whatever the thugs had in mind.

She sped up and leaped over the hedge, stretching one leg before her, and landed on the loose-pebbled grounds on the other side. She quickly tilted her body into a roll to compensate for the momentum. Coming up to stand, she waited for the thugs to follow suit.

The first veered right, while the second made the jump, landed right on top of the hedge and rolled off it into an ungraceful splay on the ground before her. But he was quick and hopped upright, displaying an agility that should have seen him over the hedge no problem.

He slashed a flat hand toward her neck. Annja bent backward, avoiding the strike. She let her shoulders drop and swung up to kick both his knees. That put him off balance and swearing a stream of Italian curses.

Standing, she stepped over him as he rolled on the ground, and kicked the back of his knee, ensuring the damage was painful. Jumping over him, she clutched his collar and punched his jaw. Blood spurted from his mouth. She dodged to avoid it. This time her boot toe landed at the side of his ribs, targeting the kidney. He yowled and begged her mercy.

"Really? Big tough guy running after a woman isn't so sure about that move anymore? Sorry, but guys like you don't deserve mercy."

Another kidney shot reduced his ridiculous pleas to silence.

Annja turned, and though the night was dim, she saw every detail on the man who approached, holding his coat sides out to reveal a leather holster strung across his broad chest. And along that holster a line of throwing blades glinted menacingly.

"Not good," Annja said under her breath.

The first blade soared toward her, and she dodged it, but felt it fly past her ear. While bent to the side, she called the sword to hand. Three feet of battle steel emerged within her grip. Energized by its presence,

Annja blocked the next flying blade with the flat surface of her sword.

Two more blades soared toward her in rapid succession. She tilted the sword blade downward, preventing a blade from lodging in her calf. The next she felt cut through her sleeve at the shoulder, skimming her skin.

Not willing to stand there as a target, Annja charged the knife thrower. Even as he released another deadly weapon, she managed to deflect it to the side with a slash of her blade. She rammed into his chest with her shoulder, knocking him to the ground.

He, too, recovered quickly, but Annja also didn't waste any time. Drilling her elbow into his ribs, she slid her sword down his arm, not cutting through his leather jacket, but at his bare hand she sliced skin and blood spilled out.

He yelled and cursed her.

"Who do you work for?" she asked.

He said something in a language she didn't understand. It wasn't Italian. Likely, he didn't understand her, either.

She felt a blade cut along her wrist. How he'd gotten hold of one of his weapons, she wasn't sure. Releasing him and pushing him away, Annja swung around, drawing her sword across his chest. It didn't go in so deep she worried he'd die, but it was enough to drop him to his knees and stop his next move.

Striding away from him, Annja looked around but didn't see the first thug she had too easily knocked out. He must have come to and was either hiding in the nearby hedges or had hightailed it out of the courtyard.

After taking in her surroundings, she determined it was only she and the blade man left. "Really? And here I was in the mood for a challenge."

Not that the thug without a weapon would have offered her a challenge anyway.

Hearing the blade man's body shuffle on the pebbled ground, Annja swung, gripping the thrown blade near her cheek. "Good one."

She whipped it toward the thrower, landing it in his throat.

Striding off, knowing she wouldn't get any information from the guy struggling to keep his voice box inside his body, she swept out an arm, releasing her sword into the otherwhere.

IT WAS A GOOD THING he hadn't had an opportunity to reveal what the key was for back at the restaurant. Scout had sensed Annja Creed's anger over not being told the whole story by Roux. That gave him a secret thrill. And proved that he'd successfully nudged a wedge between Roux and Annja. Or at least, he was beginning to.

When he'd accepted the job from Roux, he had not been told Miss Creed was going along for the dive. The surprise had not been welcome. To him or his other benefactor.

Now he had to think fast and smart. Which he could do. By nature, he was an obstacle jumper. Always prepared to leap when something came at him. There was nothing he couldn't jump over or climb under or even slither between and out the other end.

Nothing but a woman scorned. He'd have to avoid Creed's questions when next they met. She was curious. Though if she didn't ask for details, that might bother him even more.

He opened the package he'd gotten in the market after ditching the thug and sorted through the contents in the palazzo kitchen where he was staying. He wasn't hungry, so he tossed the carrots and yogurt he'd also bought in the fridge. He wasn't sure why he'd bought the things. He preferred to eat out; much easier than actually having to prepare a meal.

Opening the cupboards, he browsed through the clear canisters of pastas and rices and spied a few boxes of loose tea stocked by the resident.

"Excellent."

Now to revoke Annja Creed's babysitting privileges.

8

After three days of no contact, Roux finally answered his phone. Annja didn't bother castigating him for his inattentiveness. It was the man's style. And it could be a means of exerting his control. Likely that was the reason, so an argument wasn't worth the wasted breath.

Foregoing niceties, she asked, "Tell me everything about the Lorraine cross. Everything that you, a man who possesses intimate details from the time period, would know."

Clearing his throat, Roux complied. A refreshing change from his usual dodgy tactics.

Roux had known René d'Anjou since the Jeanne d'Arc days, but hadn't spent any amount of time with him until decades later when d'Anjou had been in the midst of his quest to further the Renaissance. They'd initially hit it off, as Roux had noted the man's genuine interest in promoting education, which at that time had only been available to the clergy and wealthy, privileged men. They had become enemies only after d'Anjou was thought to have been hiding important valued items, possibly for his own gain.

"So you're telling me René d'Anjou may or may not have been entitled to the cross from Joan of Arc?" Annja asked.

"Whether he was or not, I don't think it matters now. What does is returning the cross to the proper authorities. In this case, the museum from which it was stolen."

Annja couldn't stop her laughter and she almost felt bad as it continued to roll out. Roux was not this man talking to her on the phone right now. He was a collector who cared not for a thing's origins, only that he owned a specific treasure and had trekked the world to obtain it.

"Fine, you want to do good?" she asked. "I'll let that selfless admonition hang out there for you to consider. But Scout seems to think the cross is a key to something."

Roux was the one laughing now, which was more a gentlemanly chuckle. "A key? To what? Did he say?"

"Actually, he didn't have time. We had to split ways and divert the thugs who were after us."

"That's my Annja Creed. Always attracting the riffraff."

"You joke about it, but who else knows about this dive for the cross? There have been two attempts on my life in two days. Not to mention the close brush with a harpoon Scout had the first day of the dive."

"Annja, really?"

She sensed his concern, which surprised her. "Did

you think you were really sending me on a mere baby-sitting mission?"

"Yes. I mean… Well…" Caught in a lie. Roux sighed. "Yes. I don't know Roberts. And I do trust you. It was necessary. But you were able to get rid of the tail?"

"Yes. But I wasn't able to have a chat with them between punches to learn their intentions. Do you think they could be following the bread crumbs from the museum heist? Of which, I have yet to receive the police reports. Can you fix that?"

"I…will get my hands on them. Scout said he'd gleaned a few details from them, but that none were helpful. The exact location of where the attaché had been dropped was not noted by the police. But it did place you in the correct canal, yes?"

"Yes. I'd still like to look over the actual reports, though."

"I'll get on it and will email them to you."

"I'd appreciate that. Do you know what the key is for, Roux?"

"I'm looking for a cross, Annja."

"Yeah, well, I'm surprised you brought me in on this project. The cross was stolen from a museum. You know what I will do as soon as I get my hands on the thing."

"Yes, you'll see to returning it to the museum."

"If and when it is found, the cross remains in my care at all times. Can you agree to that?"

"I will need to examine it, look it over. Else what worth is this expedition?"

Annja sighed.

The man was not going to make this easy, and she knew his agreement to let her deal with the cross would be null and void as soon as the old man had control of the artifact. She was stepping into dangerous territory with this one.

"I'm okay with that," she said. "But I will be standing right there when you look it over."

"Excellent."

"It doesn't end here in Venice, does it, Roux?"

"Let's just stay en pointe, shall we? You've yet to find the cross, so until then, every promise toward future actions is only conjecture."

"Spoken like a man who has a plan. I need you to help me by listing any names of persons you believe could also have an interest in the cross. Scout seems oblivious to the danger."

"He is a rather cocky sort. I'll give it some thought, Annja, but I honestly have no idea. Scout came to me—"

"Yes, I'm glad you mentioned that previously. Here I thought this dive was your idea and that you had hired him. So you joined forces with a random treasure hunter who knew you had an interest in Joan of Arc? Did you bother to look into how Scout Roberts learned so much about you?"

"It was after an auction featuring a sword from Joan's army. Nothing of hers, unfortunately. Roberts approached me and made an assumption that was correct. Are you going to fault him for that?"

"Hey, I'm just the babysitter. You're the one with the reputation, and history, to protect. I'm due at the dive site in half an hour. If there's nothing else you can give me now, I'll talk to you later. Oh, uh, weren't you going to meet me here in Venice?"

"I find that I am detained at the moment."

That could imply any number of situations, of which more than a few could be illegal. Annja did not want to consider the options.

"I should be there by Friday, at the latest."

"That's two more days. If we find the cross, you know I'll get itchy sitting on it."

"I do know that. But I also know that you are a curious woman. Oh, I got a text from Scout regarding the cameraman."

"You okayed Ian's coming along."

"Right, but I don't want this expedition showing up on your television show."

"I'm not going to make any promises."

"You know I can confiscate any and all footage."

Yes, and he'd do it without her or Ian being aware until it was too late.

"I know of your need for privacy and to keep out of the media's spotlight. Your name will never be mentioned, I can promise that."

"Not good enough."

"Well, it's going to have to be. Goodbye, Roux."

She hung up and guessed what she wasn't hearing right now were Roux's curses. The only one who could tell her what she could and could not film for the show was Doug Morrell, and he was only ever concerned with the bottom line.

Annja wasn't sure this fruitless hunt was going to provide that ratings jolt Doug loved so much.

She checked her email and found Bart McGilly had replied.

Hey, Annja, long time no type. We need to get together soon. Tito's? Let's make a date for next month. Okay?

She would try her hardest to make that date. Tito's served up the best Cuban cuisine in the States. And Bart's company was always fun and interesting. They were both members of the gym not far from where she lived in Brooklyn. They boxed a few rounds on occasion. He was a good guy.

Sorry, but I wasn't able to access the case files you requested. They belong to Interpol. Out of my jurisdiction. You in trouble?

She replied that she was not in trouble and was, in fact, chasing mermaids in Italy. Close to the truth was always best with Bart. He knew she hosted the show about "weird things."

She signed off with a See you next month.

Milan, 1488

FOLLOWING THE AUSPICIOUS meeting in the tavern, Roux observed Leonardo da Vinci's comings and goings for days. Prior to that night, he had not known that man was the painter and inventor so many talked about, but Roux had certainly recognized his genius in the few sketches he'd shown him in the little notebook he'd kept at his belt.

Roux's travels had taken him across Italy the past month, and so a few days' rest was opportune. His horse had taken a stone in a back hoof, which required the farrier to fit him with new shoes. The beast would require a day or two of rest if the stone had wedged in deep. Beyond that, he had no pressing business in Milan besides ensuring he not leave without the piece of Jeanne d'Arc's sword Leonardo had mentioned.

Could it possibly be? If it had come from René d'Anjou's hands, there could be little doubt of its authenticity.

Since the execution of the Maid of Orléans, Roux's life had changed dramatically in so many ways. He admitted that there were some things he simply knew he must pursue, such as collecting the sword pieces. He must gather them all until— Well, he wasn't sure what would happen when finally he did have all the pieces, but he understood it would be important.

His future stretched long and far ahead of him. He felt it in his soul. He had no explanation for it beyond that, yet he could accept it as a strange destiny that had befallen him that heinous afternoon of Jeanne's death.

Now he slipped around the corner of a butcher shop buzzing with big black flies and hastened his steps to follow the man in the velvet tunic who marched away from the city. Nothing but wheat fields and hovels stood outside the gates. And the burial site where new mausoleums were erected daily.

Leonardo rarely left his studio, usually only for food or drink. Roux had found a convenient, discreet post from which he could keep an eye on things.

This morning, Leonardo had purchased paint from the color man—a bit of verdigris and a pale yellow Roux hadn't a name for—and now, with dusk falling on the town, the painter walked along its busy streets.

Roux had decided wherever the man kept his treasures it was not in his studio, which was open all day to the public and his students. It seemed everyone was allowed to browse among the students at work or look over finished pieces for sale. Leonardo's sleeping quarters were merely sectioned off with a curtain; no privacy whatsoever. Certainly no place to keep valuables.

Perhaps tonight Leonardo would lead him to the spot? It wasn't long before Roux discovered the man's destination.

The cemetery was eerily quiet and Leonardo did not look back as he wandered down a wide aisle toward a mausoleum on the north end beneath a copse of oak trees.

Roux held off, squatting between two gravestones, one frosted in verdant moss, the other new, for the name carved in its surface held a sharp edge. The fetid air did not agree with him, and he wished he'd brought along a clove sachet but then dismissed it as another foul situation he must endure. He was tired and hadn't eaten since morning.

The man's whistling echoed through the air. The

painter was jovial and frenetic, always jumping from one idea to the next. As he'd explained, the notebook he kept secured at his hip with a length of braided leather provided the means to catalog his stream of creative ideas and thoughts.

Roux didn't think he'd ever need to worry about having so much on his mind he must write it down to make room for it all. Despite his lacking position in a military or a royal court, he did have a focus. And he would not waver.

Moments passed, and the painter strolled by Roux's hiding spot, which wasn't concealed, yet Leonardo did not notice him, for the shadows had fallen over Roux's brown tunic and pants. The painter jingled coins in his purse. A jingle Roux had not heard previously. For as sought after a painter as he was, he didn't seem to reap many rewards for such work. Roux suspected the man was in debt.

When Leonardo reached the edge of the cemetery and silence hung over the place as if covered by a shroud, Roux snuck down the aisle to the mausoleum that the painter had visited. The narrow building that but a single man might stand inside was fronted by an iron door featuring a cut-out cross in the metal.

Roux pushed against the door and it gave. Not locked. But then, he didn't see a means to secure even a padlock. He entered the dry, dirt-tainted air of the small chamber. The walls boasted burial drawers, something new he'd not seen until now. The darkness would not allow him to read the inscriptions, so he ran his fingers over the words and names carved into the stone.

Well, that didn't help, either. Didn't matter. He cast his gaze about the dark room, but didn't see any handles or rings to open the sarcophagi. He tested the floor with some bounces on his boots. Oftentimes there was a chamber beneath for more burials. Felt solid.

A sweep of his hand along the front of a stone bench revealed a keyhole.

Roux cursed.

Stepping outside the mausoleum, Roux pulled off his hat and cast a glance at the starry sky. Now he would be forced to pinch the key from Leonardo da Vinci's home.

He was not a thief.

Until he must be.

Roux made his way back toward the city, well aware of the shadowy presence that tracked a number of paces behind him. He didn't have to wonder if it were a footpad or cutthroat. Some devils were impossible to shake. And this one in particular had been on his backside for years.

9

Annja had only stepped out for a quick meal, but for some reason all the thugs in Venice seemed attracted to her.

Behind her hotel, Annja felt the intruder stir the air before actually hearing the footsteps that quickened to gain on her. She spun swiftly and caught a dark-clothed figure advancing. The attacker put his weight into the lunge and growled, attempting to push her down. She countered by bracing herself and leaning into the person. A forceful shove managed to disengage their sudden, surprising tangle.

The man was dressed in black; even his face was wrapped, ninjalike. He bounced on his feet, clad in black athletic shoes, ready for another lunge or even a kick. Seeing no weapons in either of his hands, Annja reacted with a roundhouse kick that skimmed her attacker's shoulder just as he tilted his hips and bent backward to avoid the connection.

Her opponent kicked out a leg and connected with the side of her knee. Pain vibrated up her thigh and down her shin, but she didn't buckle. Leaning forward, she bent to avoid a return swing from the man, and coming up at his side, she turned and clawed her fingers down the attacker's face, gripping the black mask. The mask did not give way, but she used it to manipulate him. Annja used the momentum to hoist him from his feet. She tossed the guy aside, and he rolled away, coming up onto his feet.

He immediately charged, head bent and aiming for her torso. An intense tobacco scent permeated the air. Annja swung a fist that was expertly blocked with a high forearm. She kicked up a knee and hinged out her leg, catching him at the jaw with her boot. He huffed out a groan, then toppled backward against a wall.

Using his brief incapacitation, Annja punched him in the kidney. He was still bent over to breathe through the blows, so she caught his cheek with her elbow. Swinging an uppercut toward his face, she smashed her fist into his nose. Blood bled over much of the mask.

"I just wanted a sandwich," she muttered. "You, *signore,* have spoiled my appetite."

Gripping him by the wrist, she swung him around. A foot jammed against the back of his knee buckled both legs, and she was able to slam his body to the ground. Kneeing him in the spine to pin him down, she rotated his arm at the shoulder, wrenching it backward to bring on the pain. His shout indicated extreme displeasure.

"Who are you and who do you work for?" she asked.

He swore at her in Italian.

So Annja switched to Italian, demanding the name of his employer. With a brutal twist of the arm, tweaking the muscles at his shoulder, she forced out a few bits of information from his tightly clenched jaws. His employer sought the lost Leonardo treasure. Her attacker had been ordered to divert her from the dive.

"So you could dive for it?"

"I do not even swim!"

"So there are others already searching?"

"I don't know. I do not go in the water. I don't know any details."

"What about Scout Roberts?" she asked. Because shouldn't both she and Roberts be on this nameless thug's hit list?

"I do not have that name," the man said.

"The other man I'm diving with? You were sent only to attack me?"

"Yes, the woman archaeologist with the long hair and pretty face."

Flattery would not gain him any favor. He struggled and managed to twist his body over, screaming as Annja wrenched his arm out of the socket. It had been because of his move that she'd been able to do such a thing. Stupid man.

Releasing his arm and stepping back, Annja watched the man drag himself up to sit against the wall, clutching his injured arm. A dislocated shoulder was a nightmare; she knew that from experience. He spat at her and cursed at her in Italian.

"Originality always impresses me. Not. I don't believe you don't know the name of your employer."

Rising against the wall, he again spat at her. Annja had come to expect no manners from thugs, but this was completely uncalled for. She stepped back, hand to hip. The man staggered off, and she let him leave. Wasn't as if she would get anything else from him.

And when you let the sheep go, they usually returned to the flock.

Tailing the man, Annja passed the sandwich shop. It was dark; must have closed for the night. She should have expected as much. Now she was angry and hungry.

She followed him through dark alleys, over two city bridges and finally to a gondola parked a block away from the canal where she had been diving. He didn't get on the gondola; instead he exchanged words with the gondolier. They spoke so rapidly, and in low tones, that she couldn't make out any of it from her position two houses away.

A peek around the corner of the building where she was seeking cover and she spied the gondolier looking in her direction. He made her and pointed. The man who had attacked her made a nasty gesture at her. He got into the boat, gripping his wounded shoulder, and the gondolier pushed off from the dock, heading away from her and across the canal to the opposite side.

She was inclined to follow—gondolas were not speedy getaway vehicles—and so she took the sidewalk away from the direction they traveled, to a wood bridge with wood railings that allowed her to cross the canal without being seen.

She waited, concealed by the bridge as the gondola

stopped and both men got out. They scanned the area before walking down an alley. A car waited at the end of that alley.

Annja raced down the alley but by the time she'd reached the street the vehicle was no longer in sight.

Retracing her steps to the gondola, she hopped in and looked around. No clues.

"Back to the police," she said. But again she wondered why *she* was drawing the rogue pseudo-ninjas and outboard propellers, and Scout was not.

IAN TATE SCROLLED through footage he'd filmed the past two days and couldn't help but feel disappointment. He'd gotten much better footage out by the San Michele island years ago. Certainly there was a difference between the open seawaters and the canals snaking through the city. The waters flowing through Venice were much too murky to provide anything more than muted shots. His headlamps had shone on sediment and abandoned refuse and concrete and wood pilings.

A few shots of Annja and Scout gliding through the water illustrated their underwater quest.

"Nothing usable," he said with disgust.

He liked working with *Chasing History's Monsters* and appreciated the credit for his résumé, but he wasn't going to get any more jobs with the program if he couldn't make the film look half-decent. He knew the producer, Doug Morrell, liked the sensational stuff. But how to make a quest for a lost artifact sensational? If a sea monster were to swim by, he'd be in the money.

Hell, he'd celebrate if there was a stray octopus. There was a lot Photoshop could do with tentacles.

Laughing to himself, Ian tried enhancing the shots from day one and decided the technique improved the light depth markedly without washing out the picture too much.

"Wait."

Suddenly noting something out of the ordinary on one of the slides, he zoomed in on the clip. Something shiny glinted from between a closely spaced row of wood pilings. It wasn't an engine part or tin can, either.

Ian tilted his head, trying to discern the shape of the thing, but it was only a segment he saw between the two wood pillars. "Is it possible?"

He wasn't expert at knowing what to see in the waters on an expedition. He just filmed. But he suspected Annja and Scout would want to see this, so he cued it up and then headed out for the morning dive.

10

Annja leaned over Ian's shoulder to view the laptop's monitor. He'd arrived just as she'd been climbing top deck after suiting up. The gleam in his eye had spoken more than he'd said the past two days. When he'd excitedly told them about his find while going through the footage this morning, she had felt the same familiar hum of excitement. It was comparable to dusting off the edge of a deep-buried bone and not knowing what lay beneath. Just an old bone? Or a complete piece worthy of much study?

Scout joined them as Ian cued up the shots.

"It just flashed at me," Ian explained enthusiastically. "I don't know why I didn't recall seeing it while filming. Sometimes you have to look at something twice or more before you see what's really there."

Scout met Annja's gaze, and she had the distinct feeling she should take Ian's words more personally. As in, why could she only see what was on the surface where Scout was concerned? What was really going on with him? Did she need a few more times to look before she saw his truth? And why hadn't she found out more about him yet?

Perhaps because she'd been fighting a thug on an empty stomach? She hadn't mentioned the encounter to Scout. Would he even be concerned? She doubted it.

"There." Scout tapped the screen and leaned in to get a better look. "Can you increase the size without losing the resolution?"

"A little." Ian tapped a few keys, blowing up the shot to 200 percent, which, in the process, lost some resolution, giving it a grainy appearance, but the object was apparent. Definitely silver and with a smooth edge to it.

"That's got to be it," Scout said. "The Halliburton case. This was taken on the first day? So that was right back where we started, south from where we are now."

"Yes," Ian agreed.

Scout told Kard to fire up the engine and motor down the canal to their starting point. Within twenty minutes the dive flags were out and the crew dived.

The water was warm this afternoon, and Annja sensed had she not been diving for treasure, she could have spent some leisurely time picking through the underbelly of Venice, exploring, mapping out the unique footprint of a city that had grown up from the water. There was so much to discover.

For some reason today the water was less murky. The tides were high; that could be the reason. Her head-lamp beamed twice as far. As she swam, her gloved fingers traced over jagged concrete and seaweed-coated rocks. She avoided a snarl of fishing line not for fear of getting tangled but rather snagging a flipper or part of her wet suit on a rusty hook.

Behind her Ian had been following closely—he suddenly came forward and gave her the signal that he was moving ahead. He didn't stray far; he was required to document what she and Scout discovered, but he was growing bolder in his explorations and that didn't bother her. He had been the one to make a breakthrough.

Scout's flashlight caught her attention. She and Ian veered and followed his lead. They had swum about twenty feet when she saw the glimmer of silver under Scout's roving light beam. Keeping his beam steady, the light illuminated the entire underside of the structure and the concrete pilings that had crumbled measurably.

Not a secure structure by any means. The case was wedged in about three feet beyond the wood pilings. Just far enough to make it out of arm's reach. Scout again pointed upward, twirling a finger to indicate he would surface. He swam upward, leaving Annja and Ian behind. Likely going to find something to assist them in retrieving the case. An oar would be perfect, she thought, though it was difficult to discern how wedged the case was.

She swam over to Ian and gave him an underwater high five. Deserving, for he had been the one to bring them back to this spot. They might have never returned to this area, having already marked it off their list.

Scout returned with a handheld spear about five feet long. The rubber strap was wrapped about his hand,

and the opposite end sported five stainless-steel barbs. He might not be able to hook the barbs into the metal case, but if he was lucky he could snag the handle.

Annja stayed out of the way while he finessed the barbed end through the wood pilings. Ian filmed. What she was really doing was keeping an eye out for falling debris from the building overhead. And she was keeping another eye toward the water's surface. In their position, they were tucked far enough away from the surface, so she didn't expect a motored boat to get close enough to scalp her again, but she wasn't about to take any chances.

With his face mask pressed right up to the wood pilings, Scout fished for the prize. When he retracted the spear with the case dangling from the end of it, he turned to them and pumped his fist. He swung the spear around toward her, and Annja carefully removed the case from the barbed end. It wasn't as heavy as she'd expected the case to be, so that gave her some hope that it was indeed watertight.

It was a great prize. Immediately, she imagined them opening it right away, although the digital code had likely been destroyed after being in the water for so long. A thin steel chain was wrapped twice about the case. Annja wasn't sure why. If it didn't slip off easily, it could be cut away in seconds.

She exchanged the case for the spear with Scout. He patted his find and then, guiding his light beam across the low ceiling, they navigated out to the open water and surfaced thirty yards from the boat.

"This is it," Scout said. "We found it."

"Race you to the boat," Annja cried.

"Race you to the champagne!"

SCOUT HAD KARD bring them to the San Marco *sestiere*. Ian had wanted to return to his hotel room to properly clean his equipment, but promised he'd be with them in about half an hour. He made Annja promise they wouldn't attempt to open the case until he got there, and she did. She wanted the reveal on film.

The San Marco *sestiere* featured the Doge's Palace and Saint Mark's Square, which was currently packed with tourists. Annja followed Scout to an eighteenth-century palazzo hugging the inner curve of the canal opposite the San Polo *sestiere*. Scout strolled into the palazzo, tossing his gear to the floor by the door. Annja couldn't help but stand in the entryway and marvel at the non-hotel-like decor. No cheesy reception area. No nosy tourists humped over piles of battered luggage. Not even a snotty bellman who would ding your suitcase if you didn't tip him correctly.

"If this is Roux's idea of a hotel," she said, "I've been going about it all wrong,"

Scout, who carried the titanium case, which was still dripping canal water, paused at a door on the right at the end of the vast stone-tiled foyer. "Not a hotel, Annja. Roux offered, but I refused. I've a, er, friend who travels a lot. We trade houses when we're in each other's respective hometowns. Dude owns a ski lodge in Vail and a little fishing cabin in Wisconsin."

"And what do you offer him in exchange?"

Scout shrugged as he opened the door. "A pied-à-terre in Paris."

"Nice," Annja muttered. Maybe she could try being a little nicer to the man. She traveled a lot, and hotel rooms tended to get old after a while.

A halogen light lured her gaze to the room to the right.

"Check it out," Scout commented as her eyes fell upon the artifact under glass.

A gold pendant about the size of her palm featured a lion's head surrounded by flames detailed in fine gold granulation. Gold wire spiraled around the edges. "Fifth century," she decided. "Etruscan?"

"Yep. An original, too." He rapped the glass. "Not even wired. Do you know how easy it would be to nick this little beauty? This place is filled with valuable artifacts."

"But your friend would know who to come after."

"There is that."

He gestured for her to precede him into an adjoining room. Annja could smell the musty dirt and dust before she was all the way through the door. An archaeologist must live here. Or else a collector.

The dark room grew brighter as Scout pulled aside the heavy, lined draperies to let in the sun that glinted off the canal just outside the window. This side of the canal didn't sport a sidewalk, only the narrow, foot-wide ledge up against the buildings. She suspected it must have a drive-in dock, and couldn't wait to explore the palazzo's layout if given the chance.

Scout laid the case on a massive granite-topped

desk, which also displayed an intricate 3-D–printed globe that Annja recognized. She hissed as the case almost knocked the globe off its polished maplewood stand.

"Chill, Creed. I saw it."

Also on the desk were thick volumes with faded gilding on the spines. She spied a few titles and wondered if they were first editions. Couldn't be. The owner wouldn't keep them stacked, unprotected, on the desk like that, would he?

"You should set the case on a towel," she commented. "I'm sure the owner, no matter how good friends you may be, would appreciate you not getting water on the valuables sitting so near."

Scout winked at her and headed out the door.

"Take a look around," he called back. "I'm going to put on some tea. It's a bit chilly this afternoon, what with the rain coming in." He rubbed his palms together briskly. "Then we'll open the case."

"Take your time," Annja called after him. "We do have to wait for Ian."

She could spend all day in this room.

Running her fingers along the balding emerald velvet edge of a coin tray, she quickly determined the coins sitting within were medieval. Gold and silver. They were not pristine, either, which lent to their appeal, at least to her. Meant they'd been dug out of the ground. Most likely hadn't been bought but rather found and handled often. Pored and preened over. They were a personal treasure to admire whenever the owner wished.

It then gave her pause…. Had the proper authorities been contacted regarding the find? Likely so, if the coins were sitting here on someone's desk. Of course, she had no idea who owned this home; could be an archaeologist who worked at a university.

Or he could be a treasure hunter. He was friends with Scout, after all.

Disregarding the niggle of frustration over a treasure-hunter's booty, Annja strolled to the bookshelf that lined the entire back wall of the spacious office. Artifacts were nestled among books in need of dusting and re-covering. A volume of Shakespeare stood out, but only because it was leaning against an ancient Greek mask styled in leather and depicting a rabbit with one broken ear and pinholes for which the wearer could look through.

"Nice."

With the proper care, the mask could be oiled and perhaps the ear restored to nearly its original state, but Annja was getting the "leave it as is" vibe from the room's eclectic collection.

Her fingers strolled over a large collection of DVDs. Travel guides, it turned out, of various countries and cities. The disks must be viewed often for the lack of dust.

Scout returned with a plate of sandwiches, one of them shoved in his mouth. "I was hungry," he said around a bite. The sandwich dropped into his free hand. "You like egg salad? Made it yesterday, but it still tastes fine."

Annja was hungry, so she didn't hesitate to consider the shelf life of egg salad. She grabbed a sand-

wich from the plate and bit into it. Lots of mustard and
onion, just the way she liked it.

"If you come down with food poisoning, I'm not
responsible," Scout added.

Grabbing the towel he'd tossed over a shoulder, he
lifted the case to wipe away the puddle of water beneath it, then spread the towel out neatly and set the
case on top of it. He'd put on a pair of black thick-
rimmed glasses, and they changed his face remarkably. They gave him a geeky edge to his look. As he
sat before the desk and finished off the sandwich, he
moved the case to face him.

"If I get food poisoning," Annja said, chewing
through another bite, "you'll be suffering right alongside me. So." She leaned over the desk and rapped on
the case gently. "You going to unlock it? It's digital,
you know."

"I'll do my best." He opened the desk drawer and
shuffled the contents, producing a screwdriver. "When
in doubt, force it."

"What about Ian? I promised him."

"If he wanted to film this, he should have come
along with us. I can't sit and wait."

"You *can* wait. And besides, I suspect you won't be
able to crack that lock for a while anyway."

"Well, actually, I'm quite good at this. Sorry, Ian.
I'm sure he'll understand."

Annja fumed, but started on the second half of her
sandwich while Scout worked at the digital lock. The
teakettle began to whistle and she offered to go tend
to it.

"Bring the tray I set out. And cream!" Scout called after her.

The kitchen was bright with white plastered walls and homey red-and-white-checked curtains. A little kitschy for this grand palazzo, but she liked it. Taking the kettle off the burner, she poured the hot water into the waiting teapot and set it on the tray Scout had set out, which sported a lone cup and saucer and a few cubes of sugar, along with a spoon. Serving for one? Hmm… She checked the refrigerator for cream and found a small glass pitcher and selected a bottle of water for herself.

Back in the office, she set down the tray on the desk, then went after another sandwich.

"You want some?" he offered. "Guess I wasn't thinking when I only set out one cup." Scout poured a cup and sipped at it. He'd gotten no further with the case.

"I'm good with water. Maybe later. What is that flavor?" she asked of the tea. "It smells kind of bad to me."

"Dandelion root. Made by a local. It might not be to your taste. It's very earthy. There are bags of black tea in the kitchen cupboard."

"Thanks. I'll probably go with one of those later, but I'm happy with possible food poisoning at the moment. There's probably a locksmith somewhere in this city that might have a clue about digital locks."

Scout sat back in the office chair and brushed his gaze over her. He didn't strike her as a man who liked to let others do things when he could make them happen—or force them to happen.

"We could also wait for Roux and you could hand the case over to him," she suggested, "since you do work for the man, and this case is, for the most part, his property."

"For the most part?"

"If it indeed contains a stolen cross that once belonged to Leonardo da Vinci—"

"And Jeanne d'Arc."

"Yes. If it is inside, then you know we have to return it to the museum."

"I'm sure Roux has that all under control. But I'm not passing anything over until I've taken a look at it. And what if it's someone's rotten egg salad inside? There is the possibility we may have found the wrong case."

He winced and swallowed, then pinched the bridge of his nose as if to fend off the sudden need to sneeze.

"I would suspect rotten egg salad might tear this case apart if left to sit too long," Annja joked. "But I'll fall on the side of finding a valuable artifact within."

Scout blew out a long breath. He removed his glasses. "Is it hot in here?"

"No. It's started to rain, just as you predicted."

"Why don't you crack the window open, please?"

"You were just complaining about the chill." She did as he'd asked and the breeze brought a salty odor from the canal. She turned to find Scout bent over the desk, his hands pressed to his temples. "Scout? Are you okay?"

"I think the food poisoning is setting in."

"Seriously?" She assessed her own stomach. She didn't feel weak or even woozy. Maybe the breeze was a bit too cold to leave the window open for too long. And she did have a strong stomach from traveling so much and having to survive sometimes on whatever she could find. But shouldn't Scout be the same?

Sweat beaded on the man's forehead and he had begun to shake. The glasses tumbled from his face, falling to the floor.

Annja rushed to his side, pressing a hand over his forehead. His skin was boiling hot. "You need to lay down."

The man pushed the chair back, but instead of standing, Scout tumbled forward onto the rug.

"Not exactly how I'd intended you to do it."

Annja lunged toward him, helping him onto his back. His clammy skin disturbed her. Food poisoning didn't occur so quickly, did it? She couldn't recall how long a reaction had taken the few times foreign foods had disagreed with her.

"I should call for help. The emergency number in Venice—what is it? It's not 911, I know."

"For an ambulance, 118" Scout muttered. "Phone's in…" He turned his head and vomited. His body began to convulse.

11

Milan, 1488

The piazza at the Santa Maria delle Grazie cloister was bustling with many who followed the ringing of bells for matins. The convent had been expanded and a chapel added for public services. Services were now complete for the morning.

Roux pushed through the crowd of parishioners questing toward homes and a meal with family, sliding a hand over his hip as he did so. He tied his purse inside his tunic and high up under his arm against his ribs. Cutpurses looked for victims in the least suspecting places.

Laughter echoed from nearby. He spied Leonardo da Vinci's shoulder-length curly dark hair. The man was dressed in his usual tunic—much shorter than the typical style that dropped to the knees—and high leather boots. A green jasper ring drew attention to his long fingers. A painter's hands.

Leonardo spoke to a man whose back was to Roux,

yet Roux would recognize that deep, guttural chuckle any day.

"Garin Braden," he said softly. He hadn't seen him in a while, but he'd sensed him the past few days as he had followed Leonardo about the city.

"Bold move." He admired the man's audacity to talk directly to the painter. "But do you know what you are after, Braden?"

He must know. And if he did not, then he was merely making a show, expecting Roux to witness his interaction with the painter and suspecting it would dig into his gut and pick at his competitive nature.

He wouldn't fall into the man's game. And yet, he would not be able to shake Braden now that he had infiltrated Leonardo's trust.

If he had.

Garin Braden did have a way about him. Despite his gruff manner and superior physicality, he had the ability to charm practically anyone with a few sentences. It frustrated Roux that the insolent young thing—whom Roux had trained as a solider earlier in the century—could so easily assimilate himself into any crowd, situation or even a private conversation.

As the twosome wandered off, Braden put his arm across Leonardo's shoulders and again the men chuckled.

"I won't let you win this one," Roux vowed.

Braden had attempted to sabotage his quest for the sword pieces before. The man could have no idea what might occur should Roux collect them all, so why was Garin so worried about said collection?

"Obstinate bastard," Roux muttered.

LATER THAT AFTERNOON Roux observed as, outside his studio, Leonardo da Vinci spoke with a uniformed guard whose livery marked him from the castle Sforza. Ludovico Sforza, a man who had seized control of Milan's government despite his many vocal and often-times violent naysayers, also had an interest in artists.

Roux had been doing a bit of sleuthing. Apparently da Vinci was owed quite a bit on a recent commission he'd agreed to complete for an altarpiece in a chapel here in Milan. He'd been paid in parts and had yet to receive the entire sum. Supposedly Sforza had attempted to appeal for payment on Leonardo's behalf, but still no luck. Roux would never accept a fee being split into payments, but then, would he ever have to take on a job? Likely not. His was more a cause.

On the other hand, with some of these painters and sculptors… The more he learned about their lackadaisical habits in completing projects, the more he understood the buyer's need to ensure the artist be kept to heel and not be given any payment that he would then spend before he even touched paintbrush to canvas.

"Geniuses," Roux muttered. "Impossible children, if you ask me."

He should simply accost the man while he walked the dark streets, cut his purse strings and be gone before he realized who had knocked him over the head. But he didn't need the aggravation of becoming a hunted man. And the city guards walked everywhere in this, the closest district to the Sforza castle. He needed to do this in secrecy and without Leonardo being the wiser. Roux did not want Leonardo to gain knowledge of his crime until it would prove impossible to locate him.

So he waited as the night grew long. Waiting, waiting for that single candle flame in the window of the man's studio to finally extinguish.

"Does he ever sleep?" Roux pulled his wool cloak over his shoulders against the fall chill. He sat wedged between two buildings farther along the street, squatting against the wall. "Perhaps he sleeps with the candle lit?"

His horse had recovered and was ready to ride. And frankly, Roux was tired of Milan. Time to move on. But not without the prize.

Roux pushed up from the wall and stretched out his back muscles. Time to take action. He strode across the cobbled street, using darkness as his cloak.

The studio door was unlocked and creaked as it swung inward. Roux popped inside, his eyes slowly adjusting to the dim light that crept from behind the curtained sleep area. The studio was small and littered with canvases in all stages, from sketch to partially colored to completed work. All must have been done by Leonardo's students, though Roux suspected the maestro put his touch to the canvas when needed.

The man's bed was behind the curtain. Not a lot of space to maneuver. The painter was snoring. He sat at the head of his bed, boots still on and blankets pushed into a heap at his knees. His head tilted forward onto his chest, a canvas with charcoal sketch but a hand's reach away. The candle on the low table near his bed had guttered and would soon blink out.

Knowing a wrong footstep could startle the painter instantly, Roux scanned the room while keeping one eye on Leonardo. The man was wearing his pants and a tunic, but his belt had been removed, so the purse should be—right there, beside the plate of half-eaten bread and the small chunk of cheese.

The cheese had attracted a fly, and Roux shooed the insect away as he lifted the purse. No coin inside to jingle, but he felt the distinctive shape of the key. To take the whole purse or simply to slip out the key? Either way, the painter would realize the theft as soon as he either lifted the purse or saw that it was missing.

Roux stuffed the purse into his waistband and slipped out through the door as silently as he'd entered. He shut it behind him and listened but heard no shuffling about inside the studio. Then he strode down the street.

12

The hospital emergency room was located close by in the Cannaregio. An ambulance boat had arrived and whisked Scout away. Two hours later, Scout's stomach had been pumped and the nurse had reassured Annja it had not been food poisoning, but perhaps instead the tea.

Stale tea? Or perhaps tea that one suspected was dandelion root but instead was something far worse? The weed could be potentially toxic, the nurse had suggested. Annja was thankful she hadn't drank any. And to look at Scout now, whose skin was white and lips were a chalky shade as well, she was doubly thankful.

Annja had called Tomaso Damiani at the police station when she and Scout had arrived at the hospital and told him about their find in the canal and that Scout was ill. The police officer said he'd be there soon to talk to her further about the situation.

While Scout weakly answered the nurse's questions so she could fill out a file on him, Annja waited by the door, wondering if she'd had the forethought to lock the palazzo doors as they'd left. No, she hadn't. And inside were many valuable artifacts. In her panic to get Scout medical help, she'd forgotten about the case. She needed to return and lock up shop.

Or better yet, Ian should have arrived at the palazzo by now. She was surprised she hadn't run into him while they had been carrying Scout out. She dialed his number, but it rang through. Must have turned off his phone. She'd have to return to the palazzo, and soon.

The nurse left the room, leaving the door open behind her. Scout moaned, which prompted Annja to his bedside.

"And here you were warning me about the egg salad," she teased.

He laughed, but just barely. "If only it had been the sandwich. Nurse said the tea could be the culprit. I need to stay in this place for twenty-four hours for observation."

"The police will want a sample of that tea for testing," she said. "I didn't see any bags. Was there a canister in the cupboard?"

"I'll take care of that when I return. You don't need to worry about it, Creed. Oh, man, I feel like a truck hit me."

"You should rest."

"Already on that," he said, his eyelids fluttering. "We found it, Annja."

"Yes, but what do we really have? A cross? A key? Or a poisoned pot of tea?"

"It could be something so much more."

"Yes. You never did get a chance to tell me the big

secret about the cross before we were intruded upon by thugs."

"Hmm…"

"I should leave you to rest," she offered. "We were in such a rush to get you to the hospital I didn't have a chance to lock up. Is there a key for the palazzo? I'll bring it back once I'm sure the place is secure."

"In the office desk drawer. But I'm sure the place is fine. You needn't rush out, Creed."

"What? You want me to sit here and hold your hand?"

The man cracked a half smile. "Would you?"

"Are you serious?"

"No. But a guy has to try, you know? Gorgeous woman like you…"

He was delirious. And he did look pitiful. Annja patted his hand. "I'll stay a bit. And if you feel inclined to chatter aimlessly about the truth behind the cross, don't let me stop you."

"Just want to be quiet," he murmured, "and know someone is here with me."

Great. Annja hadn't much of a bedside manner. Her thoughts raced to the unlocked palazzo. Surely the owner would be inconsolable should a theft occur. But she didn't have to wait long. Within minutes Scout's snores echoed in the private room and Annja couldn't force herself to remain any longer. If anything happened to the palazzo—or the case—she would blame herself. And she felt sure Ian must be wondering what was up.

When she returned to the palazzo to find the front

door slightly open, she struggled with her memory. Had they left so quickly she hadn't closed the door properly? It was possible. Scout's attack had come on so suddenly it had startled her and she hadn't been thinking straight.

"I didn't leave through the front door." She'd been allowed to accompany Scout in the ambulance boat, and they had all left by a rear door.

Could it be Ian?

Pushing the door wide open, she entered the foyer cautiously. The hum of the sword tickled her fingers. Sometimes she could sense it in her grip without even calling it to hand, as if it knew when she was in a dangerous situation.

Shadows darkened the foyer—it was well past nine in the evening—and her boots softly thudded on the stone floor. The office door was wide open, which made sense to her. The emergency workers had carried Scout out on a stretcher, she following close behind to the garage dock tucked at the back of the palazzo.

"Ian?"

No reply, but she hadn't expected one.

As she turned to enter the office, she saw the curtains were fluttering in the breeze and the window was open. Her gaze immediately went to the granite-topped desk. The stack of old books had been pushed over, a few of them on the floor. The silver case was open and empty.

Annja put her hands on the case, noting the screwdriver beside it, the one Scout had been using earlier.

No signs of trauma on the case or the digital lock, the display was flashing.

"Interesting." Had someone known the code or been able to crack it?

If she'd had her backpack with her and the ever-present camera inside, she would have snapped some shots of this apparent crime scene. As it was, she had best not touch anything.

A smack outside the window startled Annja and instantly she was on alert. She raced over to the window. A man had just landed on the narrow ledge hugging the building. He'd jumped out of the kitchen window. Must have heard her calling out for Ian.

He adjusted his backpack, looked up at her, grinned and ran away.

13

Climbing through the open window, Annja stopped with one leg dangling over the ledge when she heard Ian's voice calling to her from the foyer.

"In here!" she hollered, keeping an eye on the man who now sprinted over the bridge fifty yards away from the palazzo.

"I stopped in earlier, and the door was open but no one was here," Ian said. "You didn't answer your cell phone. I wasn't sure if you two had gone out somewhere to eat, so I grabbed a bite myself. So weird."

Ian strode into the office and looked about the dim room. When he saw her sitting on the window ledge, he sputtered and gave her a confused look. "Annja?"

"Scout was poisoned. The attaché case was looted. I think the thief just left. I'm on him right now. The palazzo key is in a desk drawer. Lock up, please, and I'll call you as soon as I can!"

Annja prepared to jump off the ledge, admonishing herself for not having considered any security before dashing off to the hospital.

Now she couldn't let the thief out of her sight. She

saw the silhouette of the man on the opposite side of the little pedestrian bridge down the canal.

Inching along the narrow ledge, her footing was sure. Behind her, Ian's head appeared out the window, along with his video camera. She wasn't sure the chase was necessary for the show, but then again, Doug would love this footage. Leaving Ian to his pursuits, Annja dashed along the ledge and jumped onto the bridge. Soon, she was within yards of the thief. Whatever had been in the case they'd recovered was now in that backpack. And she'd lay bets it wasn't an egg-salad sandwich.

Gripping the railing at the end of the bridge, she leaped and made the cobbled sidewalk. The thief had dodged left, down a narrow stretch between buildings too close for anything larger than a bicycle. She moved along the passage, her elbows scuffing the concrete.

The thief had spotted an iron ladder clinging to one wall; he grabbed the bottom rung and seemed to defy gravity as he pulled himself up each side of the ladder with his hands. Employing amazing upper-body strength, he only pushed off a rung with a foot every so often. With an audible *ouff,* he landed on the top of the roof.

Making a running leap for the ladder—the bottom rung was about seven feet from the ground—Annja gripped the lowest rung and used the momentum of her body to boost herself up and clasp the next rung, and the next, until she could steady herself using her feet. It took her mere seconds to breach the roof.

The curved terra-cotta shingles were at a low angle,

so balancing was easy enough. Gaining speed, though, on the smooth shingles still moist with rain, proved a challenge for her hiking boots. Still, like the thief, Annja ran as best she could, bent over, stabbing the tiles to steady herself.

The thief paused at the edge of the building to look back at her. Yeah, she was on his ass. He leaped to the next building, his silhouette disappearing from her view. On the street below a clatter of tiles had broken and fallen as the thief had jumped.

"A little parkour on this cloudy evening?" Annja eyed the lower rooftop. "Just what I was in the mood for."

She'd learned from one of the best, a parkour trainer in Paris, and enjoyed the physical challenge. She estimated the drop to be about fifteen feet with a six-foot gap between buildings. The missing tiles could either provide a foothold or a nasty slip off the edge.

The thief was already halfway across the other building.

Retracing her steps, then turning, Annja sprinted and took a running leap, pushing off from the edge, causing tiles to loosen and fall. Her body soared through the air, but she didn't enjoy the unhampered feeling of flying; instead, she ducked and leaned into a roll as her feet touched the tiled roof. She came up to a crouch, balancing with fingertips to the tiles, but didn't pause to celebrate the jump.

The thief had already leaped, landing on another close building, she presumed. She could see his head, and he was running along the edge of the building that paralleled the one she stood atop.

They were two stories aboveground. The thief balanced with arms out, tracking something—he disappeared. The thief dropped over the side of the roof.

Annja quickly arrived at the edge of the next building and saw the bus. Vehicles in the city were rare, so it must be a tourist bus. It wasn't open on the top with seats for people to sit and take pictures, but instead the roof was flat, offering a nice landing platform. And there, the thief crouched without looking back and up to see if she would follow.

Annja tracked the bus to the farthest edge of the building, gripped a steel bar positioning power lines or cables, and swung out over the gap below, kicking hard to get the most momentum. She released her hold and landed on the building opposite. The tiles had a greater curve than the previous roof and did not offer good footing. She slipped, grasping at the closest tiles. A leg slid over the edge and dangled in the air.

She wouldn't go over the edge, but the time lost had allowed the bus to get a good distance away. Two buildings away, the bus turned right, out of her view.

Scrambling up to a squat and scanning the area, Annja spied a ladder hugging the building across the street the bus had passed, but to attempt the twenty-foot jump was suicidal. She raced around the edges of the building, seeking a ladder, some way down. Instead of risking more time lost, she ran for the rooftop door. It was open and the stair access was not blocked.

She raced down the two stories and landed in the

lobby of a private apartment building. The concierge lifted a hand to question her as she ran for the front doors, but she was out and gone before he could voice his dismay.

Now on the street, she veered around the corner and didn't see the bus. That didn't stop her from running north in the direction she had last seen the bus traveling. The neighborhood was mostly residential, yet there must be a tourist site close by. Why else would the bus be in the area? And so late? The sun was setting behind the buildings. Maybe it was a night-time tour?

She couldn't see above the buildings to check for landmarks to gauge her position. The city wasn't that big, though the Cannaregio was a large *sestiere*. If she didn't stay close to the bus, she'd lose the guy.

Feet swiftly tracking the tarmac, she neared an intersection. The *ting* of bicycle bells announced their approach, and Annja veered widely to the right to avoid the duo of bikers, yet she had to stop abruptly not to collide with another biker bringing up the rear. She grimaced in reply to the man's effusive curse at her, but took it in stride and resumed her pace.

Ahead, a bus approached the intersection. Pumping her fists, Annja ran onward, thankful that the vehicle stopped before driving through the intersection. That gave her a good look at the bus roof, and she didn't see the thief clinging to the top. Was it even the same bus?

Arriving at the bus as it crossed to the next street, she ran alongside it, seeing no heads in the windows. It wasn't a tourist bus. Inside, the seats were not arranged in rows but rather pressed up against either side of the vehicle, facing one another. Not that she could be sure the bus the thief had dropped onto was a tourist bus; she hadn't seen any logos from her position above and looking down. But the fact remained: the thief was gone.

She swung around behind the bus, managing a good view inside the back window. She confirmed there were no occupants.

Grasping a light pole at the following corner, she huffed and puffed to a halt. Pressing her cheek to the pole, she scanned where she had come from and all other directions. She'd lost the thief and, with him, possibly the Lorraine cross. Scout wasn't going to like hearing about this. Nor would Roux.

It had been because she'd not locked up the palazzo— Annja stopped the self-blame. If the thief had wanted access to the palazzo, a door, locked or unlocked, would not have stopped him.

But now that she considered it, how had the thief known there would be something of value inside that particular palazzo? And if so, surely other things might have been taken. The Etruscan disk alone had to be worth tens of thousands. She hadn't noted that it had been missing. Whoever had entered the palazzo had sought only the contents of the case. Had they been followed from the canal by the thugs who had been interfering with their dives?

It seemed a possible option. But who were *they* and who did they work for?

A gunshot sounded close by. Annja jumped and ran

toward the noise, backtracking down the street in the direction from which she had come. She wasn't able to judge which canal had been the source of the noise because she'd lost track of her location.

Suddenly, a man wearing a baker's apron, white pants and tennis shoes ran across the street. His gestures were exaggerated, hands going to his head and then splaying out in dismay. Annja figured he must have seen the shooter.

Had someone been shot?

Gaining on the baker, she passed him by and he called out that he would contact the *policia.* A body lay sprawled in the alleyway next to the bakery. The dead man was dressed head to toe in black. He'd worn a backpack as Annja had pursued him across the rooftops. Now the backpack was gone.

Someone had beaten her to the prize. Had the thief been on his way to hand off the stolen goods? Had his contact been instructed to shoot him after receiving the goods?

A pool of blood formed beneath the body's shoulder. She didn't need to press her fingers to his neck to confirm death. And though she was compelled to rip off the head mask, she didn't want to disturb the crime scene and didn't expect it would actually be a face she recognized. Yet, what was that?

The distinctive scent of tobacco lingered on the man's body. The same smell she'd noted when battling the knife thrower in the church courtyard.

"Interesting."

Frantic, the baker arrived beside her, waving his

cell phone. He explained in Italian that he'd called the police. Annja could already hear the sirens and judged they would arrive via the nearby canal.

The baker asked if she knew the victim. She shook her head. "Just walking through the neighborhood and heard the gunshot. Did you witness this? See anyone run away from the scene?"

The man crossed his arms over his rotund girth, the epitome of the plump baker dressed all in white. Flour even dusted his cheeks. He rubbed his jaw and shook his head. "I don't think so," he replied in Italian. "Was in the shop. I heard the sound and ran out."

The man fidgeted and shifted his weight from foot to foot. Annja didn't believe him. But whether or not she believed him, the shooter could still be in the vicinity.

The police sirens neared. She put a hand on the baker's shoulder and met his gaze. "Tell the police everything you saw. It's important. I'm going to take a look around."

She'd call Tomaso Damiani with all the information she had, but right now, she had to scope out the surrounding area. Guessing that the thief had fallen forward after taking the bullet to his chest, she looked across the street in the direction the thief had been running. Toward the canal.

Taking off, she headed toward the water. The police boat was docking, and two officers had already disembarked, hands to their holstered pistols as she passed them. She considered calling out to them, but she had no solid information to provide beyond what they would see for themselves.

If the shooter wanted to make a fast escape, he would have hopped into a boat. Annja reached the dock and looked both ways. The wake from the police boat still rippled against both sides of the canal. A few gondolas were parked nearby, and one slowly floated away from where she stood, but it was occupied by a kissing couple.

Scanning upward and around behind her, she noted the rooftops were clear of people. No one raced away on the cobbled streets.

Following along the canal, Annja focused on the alleys between buildings and ran another quarter mile farther along, hoping to glimpse something out of the ordinary. It was well past 10:00 p.m. and getting more difficult to see in the darkness.

Stopping at a bridge peopled with a dozen tourists taking photos, Annja decided she'd given it her best shot.

Pulling out her cell phone, she called Ian. He'd locked up the palazzo and was now back at the hotel. She was walking there now, she explained, telling Ian that she'd lost the thief, only to see him killed. He agreed they should go to the hospital to check on Scout.

At her hotel room, Annja took a quick shower, combed her wet hair into a sleek ponytail, and slipped on black leather pants and a gray T-shirt. She gave Tomaso a call and detailed finding the man on the street with a bullet wound. She'd also told Tomaso about her chase across the *sestiere*. The thief had taken whatever it was they'd found in the canal.

Tomaso had been pleased she hadn't touched anything at the palazzo and she hoped Ian had the forethought not to touch anything, as well. Tomaso intended to make arrangements to investigate the palazzo with a team to take photos and fingerprints. He said he'd try to meet Annja at the hospital, but when he realized how late it was, he said they could talk in the morning. And if Scout was resting, he probably wouldn't be in a talking mood right now.

She signed off by agreeing to meet him at the police station at ten in the morning; meanwhile Ian met her in the hotel lobby. He handed her a slice of warm pizza. She wasn't even going to question its origin. It was warm and smelled like oregano and spicy sausage.

"Cheers," she said and bit into the oozy goodness.

14

The hospital was quiet this late at night; still, Annja checked with reception. Visiting hours were open until eleven, so she had a few minutes to spare. Ian had mentioned how much he disliked hospitals. It was the smell. He'd spent a lot of time in a hospital as a child with a heart condition. He was fine now, but he had inhaled sharply upon entering the facility, and Annja had looked at him to make sure that he was okay.

He was chatting amiably to her as they navigated the hallways in search of Scout's room. Specifically he wondered if she'd been shot at while pursuing the thief.

"Nope, not a target this time," she said. "I'm in one piece."

He patted the wound on her scalp, his expression relieved. She'd forgotten about the cut. It was almost healed. Since taking Joan's sword in hand, she healed just a little faster than normal. It wasn't as though she'd been bestowed a superpower, but it was still pretty cool.

Annja nodded to a cleaning woman who pushed a cart of linens and supplies out of Scout's room.

"Are you sure this is right?" Ian asked as he entered the private room before her.

The space had been cleaned. The bed was empty, the fresh sheets folded down and tightly tucked, in wait for the next patient.

Annja checked outside the door for the identifying chart, but the slot that held that information was empty. She checked the next room, feeling sure she had the right one, and found it was occupied by a woman with her arm in a sling.

Turning, she walked right into a nurse wearing pink scrubs who wielded an armload of charts and a questioning yet weary smile.

"I think I must have the wrong room," Annja said. "I'm here to see Scout Roberts."

"He left earlier."

"Oh. I understood he was supposed to stay for twenty-four hours for observation."

"We can't force a patient to stay, *signorina*. I think he left just after your previous visit. I remember you were in here earlier. Is he your husband?"

"Oh, no. Just a friend. Did he, uh, mention where he was going?"

She shook her head. "Sorry."

"That's fine. Thank you."

Joining Ian, they exited the hospital. He exhaled noticeably once outside.

"A guy forgets that smell after a while," he said. "It's very powerful."

"Come on, we'd better head over to the palazzo."

He nodded. "Scout must have returned not long

after I locked up there. That was less than an hour ago."

"I called Tomaso at the police station and explained everything to him. The Venice police should be there now. You didn't touch anything?"

"No. Except the front door pull." He fished in his pocket and handed her a key. "I had intended to return that to Scout. He can't even know the cross was stolen, can he?"

"I'm not sure."

Annja was too curious over Scout's quick escape from the hospital. Was that what it had been? An escape? He'd left immediately after she had left him snoring in bed? She'd told him she was going to check the palazzo and lock it up. He'd told her where to find the key. Without the key he wouldn't be able to get inside the palazzo. Unless he had another key.

Or he had no reason to return to the palazzo.

Something felt very wrong.

"Let's hurry," she said and sprinted down the hospital steps, picking up to a brisk pace in the direction of the palazzo. "You're sure you didn't walk by Scout on the way to or from the palazzo?"

"Positive. And if had walked by, why wouldn't he have called out to me?"

"You could have passed each other on opposite sides of the street."

"He doesn't like me."

Yes, she knew Scout did not like Ian for reasons that were unclear to her. Did he have something to hide?

"He was just surprised about having a cameraman following him around," Annja offered.

Digging out her cell phone, Annja called Roux while she picked up her stride. The phone rang unanswered, so she shoved it into her pants pocket.

Ian led the way to the palazzo. Tossing him the key, Annja wondered where Tomaso and his crew were. Perhaps he'd decided to wait for morning? Might not have had a full team working this late at night. It was possible.

She went inside, into the foyer after Ian and rushed into the office. Ian had secured the window shut earlier.

"You said you didn't touch anything?"

"Nope. Even pulled a sleeve over my hand before closing the window."

"Let's stick with the no-touching rule," she said. "The police haven't been here yet."

She looked around. The open, empty attaché case still sat on the towel on the desk. If Scout had been in here since, he would have likely moved the case.

She swept her gaze around the room, ill-lit by a low-watt bulb in a table lamp. The dusty bookshelves were as before. The plate with the sandwich crumbs still sat on the desk. Scout's glasses lay on the floor near the desk leg.

Why did the scene of the crime feel wrong?

Her phone rang. Annja's pulse spiked as she pulled out her phone and offered a quick hello.

"You called at an awful hour, Annja."

"Roux. I thought you were on your way to Venice?

Where are you that the hour is awful? No, don't bother telling me. There's been a hitch."

"Scout."

He stated the name; it hadn't been a guess. A feeling of dread scurried up the back of Annja's neck.

"Roux, how well do you know Scout Roberts?"

"Not at all. I did tell you I had just met him at an auction when this expedition came to light."

"Well, he's a treasure hunter for starters. And maybe a lot more…"

Annja sat on the corner of the desk, and just when she was about to touch the edge of the open case, she retracted her hand suddenly. Instead, she peered at the case, looking for some aggravation to the edges that only another object could have created when attempting to force it open. Nothing. Had someone actually cracked the digital code?

Nudging the case with her knee to better study the lock, she caught Ian's hiss. She pointed to her knee and whispered, "Didn't touch it."

"What's that?" Roux asked.

"Nothing. I'm at a crime scene, looking over the evidence. A crime possibly perpetrated by your treasure hunter."

"He's not my treasure hunter, Annja. Do you know *why* he is a treasure hunter?"

"Why does any man sink to such low levels?"

"Some do it for the thrill. You know a thing or two about the thrill, eh, Annja?"

She didn't have time for this conversation. But the more the man kept talking, the longer it would be before she'd have to reveal the contents had been lost, at least temporarily. "So why does Scout do what he does?" she asked.

"According to the online trail, it seems he fell on hard times a few years ago. He was discredited for writing a paper on the Peru expedition that put the blame for his crew members' deaths on another man on the team."

"Completely false."

"Exactly."

"So he was disgraced?"

"First, forced out of the University of Columbia. Then he bought a new home and quickly spiraled into bankruptcy."

"So now he'll do anything for some cash," Annja guessed.

"Right. Except, the paper trail ends because…"

"Because?"

"I've turned up a coroner's report for Scout Roberts. He died by hanging two months ago in Miami Beach, Florida."

15

Annja was stunned. She hadn't seen that one coming. She glanced to Ian. With his arms crossed, he stood as if waiting for information.

"So our guy is not really Scout Roberts," she said, trying to fill Ian in.

Roux exhaled heavily.

He sounded exasperated with her, these circumstances and, yes, even himself, she thought.

Hey, these things sometimes happen. The background material on Scout had been solid. Most would only check his résumé. Possibly go further and read any published articles. But she was surprised the coroner's report hadn't come up earlier in the research.

"How much did you pay him to locate the Lorraine cross, Roux?"

"He won't receive a dime until I've got the cross. I'm funding all the equipment and the hotel."

"He's not in a hotel. He's staying at a friend's palazzo."

"Ah. So I wonder who is staying at the hotel right now. I've received a summary of the bill. In fact, I had assumed he'd another on his team for the large amount of food and extra towels charged to the room. There was also a charge for cigars."

The tobacco-scented thug? Annja guessed so.

"I might have a clue who has been staying in the hotel. But it won't take us far. I'm beginning to wonder if Scout—or whoever he is—hasn't jumped ship for another team."

"What makes you say that? Where is the man? Have you found the cross?"

"A lot of questions, and you won't like the answers to any of them. We did find the cross. Rather, we located a Halliburton attaché case, rumored to have been the case the thieves tossed into the canal, which is rumored to have contained the Lorraine cross."

"Did you open it?"

"Someone opened it. We didn't have the chance to since Scout—or whoever he is—was poisoned."

"What?"

She explained about Scout drinking the tea.

"You didn't drink the tea?" Roux asked.

"Hadn't time. And Scout was kind of possessive over it."

She hadn't thought anything of it at the time, but now it struck an odd note. Why not provide an extra cup for her? Had he planned something in advance? But to poison himself? Didn't make sense. Or did it?

"Did you touch the tea service?" Roux asked.

She glanced to the tea set sitting on the table. "I did. I brought it in for him."

"So your fingerprints are all over it."

"What are you getting at, Roux?"

"You said Scout disappeared, as well as the cross. Doesn't that sound suspicious?"

"Very suspicious. But I don't believe he was the one who stole the cross. I'd just left him in the hospital and I arrived not ten minutes later at the palazzo to find the thief slipping out the window."

"Just because he didn't slip through that window doesn't mean Scout didn't arrange the theft. He may have known you'd be away, tending him in the hospital. In fact, that was probably the plan. Did he try to keep you at the hospital?"

Annja thought back to their conversation. Scout had been tired, but had asked her to sit with him until he fell asleep. She felt so foolish.

"Scout must be working for someone else. The someone who's been staying in the hotel room you paid for, and also the someone who snuck in and stole the cross while we were out of the palazzo."

"A someone who offered Roberts—we'll have to call him that until we learn his real name—much more than I did. And now he's implicated you neatly in the heist."

"Right…"

It would make sense to implicate her in the poisoning, if not the theft. Took eyes off Scout—a suspicious person who had assumed a dead man's identity.

"I suppose you have contacted the authorities?"

"Of course."

She didn't tell him about the dead thief who smelled of tobacco or the new thief who'd done the shooting.

"Would Scout have taken measures to steal from himself twice to blur any complicity falling on him? That's a whole lot of planning for a person who seemed pretty casual about most things. Although he sure wasn't pleased to have me on board, or Ian."

"Get out of there, Annja."

"I don't think the cops are coming tonight."

"You can't be sure."

"Yes, but…" She had been the one to alert the police. What a mess.

Annja gestured to Ian to get moving again. "I think we're grasping here, Roux. Scout could have gone back to the hotel room you rented for him. I think I should head there."

"You do that. But don't say I didn't warn you when the police want to talk to you. And don't mention my name."

"You know I never would. I guess now is as good a time as any to tell you I've already spoken to the police this evening—I called right after losing the thief, who, I should mention, was shot midchase."

"The thief who stole the cross? Where is it now?"

"Not sure. I wasn't able to track the shooter. He had a black backpack. I assumed the cross was in it. But this feels wrong."

"You don't normally dally on the wrong side of the law."

"No. Not normally. Though—"

"I would beg you to learn more information about your partner in crime before speaking with the police, Annja."

"He's not my partner in crime, Roux. He is, or was, your employee. I was just the babysitter."

"And a fine job you did at it. Remind me never to call you up when I've an— Oh, forget it. We both know that will never happen."

Did they?

"You have any idea who your competitor might be?" she asked. "Anyone at all, besides Scout, who might be interested in the Lorraine cross?"

"Few know about the cross."

Roux's tone was the oddest thing. He did know of someone else. Annja sensed it. But she also sensed he wasn't going to toss out any names and risk her taking that information to the police.

"I'll think on it," he said. "We need to meet."

"That's a good idea."

"If Scout knows what to do with the cross and he has it in his possession, then I know where he's headed."

"What do you mean, 'what to do with the cross'? What do you know about the cross being a key, Roux? Scout didn't have time to tell me—"

"Nor do I. I'll arrange for transportation for you. Can you be ready to leave in an hour?"

"Sure. I only have a few things to collect."

"The police are already at your hotel room, Annja. I'm sure of it. Things can be replaced. Go directly to the train station. I'll send a car to take you to Milan."

"Milan," she said. "And will you have a replacement laptop and camera waiting in that limo, as well?"

"As you wish. A change of clothing and anything else?"

"Gloves, notebooks, ziploc bags, everything I usually carry with me. My cameraman is with me."

"It's time to part company with him, Annja."

Yes, it probably was. This expedition had just become something much more than a search for a lost treasure. She didn't want to risk Ian getting hurt.

"Roux, when will you enlighten me on this mystery of the missing cross?"

"Over breakfast."

He hung up, and Annja heard a knock at the front door. Stepping over to exit the office, she paused in the doorway. The police?

"Should we answer?" Ian asked.

She did not want him caught up in any of this. And Roux was right: from here on, she didn't need his services anymore. No matter that the cross may have historical value and prove an interesting episode for the show—circumstances had become too dangerous to have him tagging along.

"Job's over," she announced. "The cross is gone. But it seems I may be questioned—or even worse—about poisoning Scout Roberts. I don't want you involved. But I'll give you a choice of answering the door, possibly to the police, or slipping out the window with me right now."

She glanced back to the tea things, still on the desk. Seriously? Scout had planned that one a little too well if he'd thought to drag her into his poisoning. But she wasn't willing to take chances. She had no time and nowhere to store any evidence of the tea.

Ian pointed toward the office window. "Ladies first."

Slipping out onto the ledge, she retraced the initial steps she'd taken when following the thief until she'd crossed the canal on the foot bridge. There, she shook Ian's hand, thanked him and promised she'd be in contact. She apologized for the abrupt ending to the adventure, but he took it in stride. The artifact was missing. There was no more filming to be done.

He brought up Sirena. In all the commotion, the woman who claimed to be a selkie had slipped her mind.

"We won't forget about her," she reassured Ian.

"I might drive that way. Take the scenic route. I just want to see how she is, you know."

"Sounds good, Ian. I'll be in touch with you soon."

Luckily for Annja, the train station wasn't far. As she walked, she called Tomaso. She wanted to feel him out and see if she really was running away from being arrested or if that was merely Roux's imagination. Tomaso didn't answer.

She didn't mind. In either respect, she'd had enough of Venice for a while.

16

The driver didn't show for hours. Annja considered taking a train, but the guy was also meant to be delivering a few necessities, which she had to admit she would appreciate. So she had opted for sleep and found a comfortable bench until she was eventually woken by an apologetic guy in a crisp black suit. She yawned and followed the driver to the limo.

The ride from Venice to Milan would have proven a shorter trip; however, the autostrada was a slow go. She estimated it would be a while before they got to Milan.

Browsing through her own brand-new backpack that had been waiting for her in the backseat of the limo, Annja found a laptop—fully charged and all accounts to be billed to Roux—as well as an iPod and earbuds, and a top-of-the-line digital camera. A change of clothing was, naturally, the right size and her style: cargo pants and a sleeveless T-shirt, along with some lightweight running shoes. There was a notebook and pens, latex gloves, tweezers and small plastic bags.

The man had thought of everything. As well, a note

informed her that her things at the hotel were being shipped home. If she'd known the wait for the limo was going to be so long, she could have swung by the hotel and claimed her stuff.

Oh, well.

Annja settled back, put in the earbuds, found some favorite tunes and was thankful for Wi-Fi so she could do some additional research on da Vinci.

The fascinating thing about Leonardo was his range of skills and interests, and that for a man who was known to have put out an amazing quantity of sketches, ideas and models, it was believed there were many more of his works still to be discovered.

It was no surprise to Annja when someone stepped forth claiming to have found a work believed to have been created by a famous artist, although disappointment often followed. Authentication processes could be long and arduous, and many times the excitement over finding a supposed masterpiece turned into a letdown when it was learned it had been done by a student, for example, instead of the master himself.

She glanced over a story that featured a restorer who used to authenticate famous lost paintings, such as by Picasso, Rembrandt and da Vinci. Seemed the person had a successful business in validating—or not—discovered lost works. The only thing wrong was the works that were authenticated were also tampered with—by the authenticator. Fingerprints claiming to match the great artists had been created by the authenticator, so when comparing a found print on a painting, the match was perfect. But since the original fingerprint had been a forgery…

The lengths some people would go to for fame and a small fortune never ceased to amaze Annja.

The driver called back that he was stopping at the Autogrill, a restaurant and gas station that arched over the busy highway, for gas. It was a midpoint between Venice and Milan. Annja used the opportunity to run inside and purchase some bottled water and, seeing the diner offered some yummy sandwiches, ordered two ham-and-mozzarella panini to go. She and the grateful driver broke their fast at the roadside before heading on to Milan.

Resuming her research, Annja tried to connect the Lorraine cross to Leonardo da Vinci and found no articles online. If this was an item Roux believed only a few people knew about, then it wasn't difficult to also believe there would be no information available.

There were a few short articles regarding the original heist earlier in the year. She already knew nothing had been captured on the few security cameras placed throughout the museum, though two sets of shoe prints—standard size, nothing remarkable—had been found in the mud near the building. It had rained torrentially that evening, though it was suspected the heist had occurred as the storm had dissipated, thus the reason the footprints hadn't been completely washed away.

That there were no photographs of the cross in the museum was a curiosity.

"It's just a cross," she said, scrolling through a list

of Leonardo's paintings to familiarize herself with his works. "The cross was valuable for sure, but not world-changing."

Generally Roux went after the world-changing artifacts. Yet, the connection to Joan of Arc was enough for Annja to believe the cross would have real importance for him. The man's history with Joan complicated his reality. It must have been an event that would haunt him forever, too. And to be haunted for over five centuries?

"Can't even imagine."

Skepticism tended to blind her at times when she wanted to be more open in her outlook and set aside her doubts until the truth was revealed.

She tapped her fingers impatiently on the lid of the laptop and considered how easily it had been for Scout to slip out of the frame. Had he planned to steal the cross from under her nose all along? Roux had hired him and then, at the last minute, let Scout know she was also on board for the dive. The babysitter. And a cameraman must have surely thrown a wrench in his scheme.

But would that have given Scout enough time to arrange for the theft? To arrange a self-poisoning? Had he really done all that? What a desperate act to throw suspicion away from him. Risking poison and near death?

Unless he'd consumed a sort of antidote before taking the tea. That would have lessened his reaction and countered the poison. It may have also allowed him to suffer just enough that an emergency-room visit was required and that the doctors would believe he had been poisoned, while ensuring he wouldn't die, but merely suffer a horrific stomachache.

She'd obviously been through a lot on her adventures to believe there was an antidote for every poison out there and that something like that could actually work. Annja wasn't up on various poisons and their countereffects. She'd leave that to the police investigation. The authorities would surely take a sample of the dandelion-root tea Scout had consumed.

"Good thing dandelion tea offered no appeal to me," Annja muttered.

And to have someone else steal the cross while he was infirm in the hospital had been genius. The theft while he was sick pushed the blame further away from him. Scout appeared the victim no matter what. He checked out of the hospital and later met up with the thief—most likely his partner in crime—and now he had the prize.

The scenario felt...almost right.

There had been two thieves: the one who'd taken the cross from the case in the palazzo and had smelled of tobacco, and the one who'd shot the first thief and left with the backpack. Planned that way? Or a coincidence?

She was missing something. It felt as though she'd uncovered a good portion of the strata, yet the main part of the piece was still hidden beneath the compacted dirt and required more intense dusting to remove fine particles and debris.

She should have wiped the teapot of her fingerprints. At least she had called Tomaso with her side of the story. Roux's idea that she'd been implicated wouldn't hold water if Tomaso trusted her. And she hoped that he did. Of course, he had no reason to.

On a whim, Annja typed in the address of the palazzo where Scout had been staying and, with minimal browsing, was able to track down the owner's information. Alessandro Mattadori owned a half dozen rental properties in Venice and Italy, all featuring pictures of the bright interiors and offering top-notch maid service, along with discounts to local restaurants. The palazzo where Scout had stayed wasn't listed as a rental. Possibly because it was his private residence?

Dialing the listed number for the rental office, Annja got a secretary and decided to play it by ear.

"I'm calling regarding Scout Roberts. He wanted me to check in with Signore Mattadori about the palazzo in San Marco. He may need to stay a few more days."

"I'm sorry, *signorina,* that is not one of our listed rental properties. Do you have the correct address? I don't have a record of Scout Roberts renting from us. Perhaps you are mistaken?"

"Perhaps it was a friend-to-friend thing," she said. "He mentioned he was friends with Alessandro. In fact, I believe the address may be Signore Mattadori's personal residence?"

"I cannot confirm that, *signorina.*"

"Of course, I'm sorry to ask. Could you have Signore Mattadori call me, please? It's regarding the palazzo and Mr. Roberts."

She gave the secretary her number and, suspicions rising, guessed Alessandro Mattadori wouldn't have a clue who Scout Roberts was. But then again, the man wasn't actually Scout Roberts. She didn't know who the cocky American treasure hunter was. And she wasn't sure where to begin the search on him.

She closed the laptop and tilted her head back against the leather seat. The driver, noting her relaxation, said they had another hour before they arrived in Milan. Might be a good time to catch a few more winks.

ANNJA THANKED THE driver and waved him off. Hooking the full backpack with her new supplies over a shoulder, she stood at a main intersection in the center of Milan. Roux had asked her to meet him there via a text during the journey. Since she seemed to be early, she decided to purchase another bottle of water from a shop she spotted nearby. The day was hot, and she wasn't sure when she'd have a chance to eat again.

A plain sedan pulled up before she could take a step. An elderly man with long white hair gathered in a leather bind at his nape, and a beard that needed a trim, gestured she hop in.

"Good to see you, Annja," he said out the window. A wry smile crinkled the aged skin at the corners of his bright blue eyes. "Have a pleasant drive here?"

"Drop the niceties, Roux." She slipped into the passenger seat and he shifted into gear. "What's up with the cross and where are we headed?"

"You know more about the location of the cross

than I do. As for where we're headed, the destination is not so important as the maneuvers and dexterity of your driver. We're evading a tail."

Annja turned and spied the usual traffic one would expect at this time of day. Horns honked and buses cut off smaller vehicles. Bicyclists swerved between the harrowingly close jagged lines of traffic. A group of tourists attempting to cross the street with arms linked cast fearful gazes toward the oncoming traffic.

Then she spotted the black SUV with the darkened windows. It was two cars behind Roux's vehicle and she thought there were no plates, but she wasn't certain.

"Annja! I haven't time to win your trust right this moment. You'll just have to go along for now."

"I presume it's not me they're after," she said, "since they must have been following you. And no one knew I was arriving in Milan except you. So, what did you do this time, Roux?"

"Not fair, Annja."

"Completely fair, and you know it."

Roux swerved around a parked car and gained two car lengths on the SUV. "I believe the men in that car are under the false impression that I may have cheated at our poker game last night. I never cheat. I'm just that good."

"I make no judgments. I suspect you have centuries of experience behind your full house."

"Poker is a more recent game, Annja. I believe it emerged sometime in the early 1800s."

"That still gives you a couple centuries on the guys behind us."

"The *guys* won't be a problem. What is a problem is that I haven't got a better handle on the Lorraine cross. I've come to believe that I may have been duped."

"By Scout?"

"Scout Roberts is dead, Annja."

"Right, but until we know his real identity… You know, I hadn't pinned the guy as clever, but he did set me up nicely."

"He's working for someone else. Someone who knows me all too well."

She swung a look at the man whose hands gripped the steering wheel tightly. He didn't give her the answer she was waiting for, and her cell phone rang before she could ask him.

Scout Roberts had the audacity to call her. "Sorry about that mix-up in Venice, Annja."

"Mix-up? Don't you mean setup?"

"Possibly. It's all in how you define things. I didn't see how to get you off my back. Had to be done."

"Because your employer insisted?"

"Roux? Nah. I've moved on to a higher bidder. I thought you'd be en route to rendezvous with the old man right now. Did you tell him to take a hike?"

She gritted her teeth, trying to maintain her control.

"He's greedy, Annja. I don't believe Roux ever intended to return the museum's cross once found. And you know, it's not about the cross anyway."

"It's not?" She glanced to Roux, who now whistled

softly while keeping an eye on the rearview mirror. Classic avoidance technique. "Do tell."

"I've already told you, it's a key. A key to the un-imaginable."

"That's how it always works in fairy tales and legends. Are you living in a fairy tale, Scout?"

"That I am. And getting richer every second I have the cross."

"So you haven't passed it on to your new employer? Good to know. Were you the man who intercepted the thief last night?"

"I don't know what you're talking about, Creed."

"Right. You certainly recovered from that poisoning swiftly."

"I work out and eat right."

Garbage, all of it. "You in Milan?"

"Er, yes—so, you are with Roux. Well, then, it's a race. See you at the finish line."

The phone clicked off. Annja barely resisted screaming. But next time she saw that man...

"What exactly is this cross, Roux? A key? To what?"

She tucked her cell in her pocket and turned to Roux, who had stopped whistling and now held a keen interest on the rearview mirror.

"We'll talk later. Right now? Hang on," he said and jerked the car sharply to the left.

From what Annja could determine, they were still in the northeastern part of central Milan. They cruised past modern skyscrapers in a business district. Roux deftly avoided a pedestrian who stepped out on a red light. The SUV followed closely.

"Do you have an intended destination?" she asked.

"Not at the moment. Just trying to discourage our friends back there from following us. Watch your head."

At that warning Annja instinctively ducked. A bullet pinged the car's passenger-side mirror.

Roux tsk-tsked and at the nearest side street wrenched the wheel to the right. Alone apart from the vehicle still following, Roux produced a pistol from below his seat and handed it to her. "Do show those idiots who they are dealing with, will you?"

She did not like to fire in the city, whether there weren't any people visible or not. Still, when the next bullet shattered the back window, Annja turned to eye her target, using her seat as a shield. She aimed at the vehicle's hood.

Direct hit.

But the bullet hadn't done any real damage, since the vehicle kept advancing on them.

One of the vehicle's passengers leaned out the window, gun arm extended, and fired another round. Annja ducked low behind the seat. The bullet pierced her headrest.

"He's an excellent shot."

"They're not trying to slow me down," Roux said. "Which riles me. They want to kill me."

"Yeah, well, I've no intention of bleeding all over your car today."

"Thoughtful of you. But don't fret over it much. It's a rental."

"Your compassion really touches me," she replied.

"I'm turning right…now."

As Roux swung the car around a corner, Annja aimed, both hands clasping the gun, at the SUV's front tires. Firing twice, she succeeded in hitting the driver-side tire. The SUV swung out of control and crashed into a lamppost.

"You hungry?" Roux asked casually as he turned onto another street. "I'm hungry. My hotel is nearby. Let's go in for a nice meal."

"And then we'll talk, yes?"

He nodded, not verbally committing to a reply.

"We'll talk," Annja said. "Or I walk."

17

The hotel Roux was staying in was a fifteenth-century convent that had been converted into a luxury respite in downtown Milan. The moment he handed the keys to the valet, Roux was treated like a king. A hotel employee escorted them into the restaurant and to a private table overlooking the luscious garden. The chef immediately arrived to introduce himself and describe the day's special, which Roux opted for. Roux then ordered a four-hundred-euro bottle of wine.

As Annja sipped the wine, she decided that the expensive stuff was definitely worth it. Much as her budget didn't allow for such extravagances, she was grateful when it was on offer. Roux was well-off financially and sometimes she had the impression that he enjoyed spoiling her. On occasion they seemed like a father and daughter. However, she was always quick to correct the relationship. She never forgot that Roux could treat people ruthlessly at times, especially if his wants were under threat.

The first course, featuring zucchini ricotta, was so creamy she thought she'd gone to heaven. But she wasn't about to let the food distract her from finding out what she wanted to know.

"You said you would tell me everything," she prompted between bites. "So tell."

"Not going to allow me to enjoy my meal?"

She shook her head, leveling a stern gaze on the old man who always knew how to manipulate a person.

"I still don't understand what it is we're after," she said. "Is it something beyond the Lorraine cross?"

"It is."

"Then what is it? Something supposedly invented by Leonardo da Vinci? Does it possess destroy-the-world power or is it a cozy painting to hang over the fireplace?"

"Annja, I can't believe you'd suggest hanging a da Vinci over a smoky hearth." He mocked a shud-der. "Sacrilege."

She smirked. There was the playful side to the man she enjoyed seeing. Though Roux could also appear as fierce and strong as a man thirty years younger. His ability to switch personas at the drop of a hat both comforted and bothered her.

"Very well." He finished his first goblet of wine and poured another. "The cross is a key."

"That's what Scout said. A key to what?"

"Why, a time-shifting device, of course."

Upon Roux's casual announcement, Annja almost choked on her wine. Instead, she pressed the linen napkin to her mouth so she could awkwardly swallow.

"When the key is placed in the device I seek—

which is a music box, by the way—the user shifts in time with another person."

"Time travel?" she managed to gasp. "You are kidding me. Of all the crazy gadgets and things I've chased over the years, they have all, at the very least, been real."

"It's not time travel but time *shifting*," Roux insisted. "Big difference."

Annja couldn't prevent a chuckle. "How so?"

"Apparently when you place the key, which is the cross, in its lock in the music box—yes, supposedly designed by Leonardo—the bearer shifts places in time with another person."

Annja knew her jaw had dropped open, but she couldn't find the words to counter that explanation. He'd spoken it so plainly. And with total belief.

"Fine, Annja, it isn't real. Time shifting is not real," Roux admitted.

"Glad we agree on something."

He promptly shook off her admonishment. "But the idea of shifting time is appealing, you have to admit that."

"More appealing than having a sword in the otherwhere? More appealing than being able to live through the centuries?"

"Well, yes."

She wasn't completely convinced by his reply. Still, he was more of a hopeful believer than she would ever be.

"It is unique in its power. And a curiosity to me."

"How are you even sure what this device is and what it's supposed to do?"

"Annja, trust me when I say I know of what I speak."

"Did somebody show it to you? Demonstrate it? Have you already time shifted, Roux?"

"No, no and no. Annja, really?"

She shrugged and dragged her fork across the plate, cleaning up the last traces of food.

"I saw the device," Roux said. "And I saw the drawings in the notebook that detailed its use."

"Right." Annja set aside her empty plate and immediately a server appeared to whisk it away. "So this is all speculation based on a drawing made by a man who is known for having sketched thousands of intricate and fantastical devices that were never built because of their impossibility?"

"Exactly." Roux's glee added a lilt to his voice. And that worried Annja. Did she need to have the old man committed?

"Let's say a person really could shift places with someone from another time period—for example, you," she said. "How would the person ever get back?"

The man had no immediate reply to that one.

"And would that person you'd switched with suddenly appear in this time to replace you? How would *they* return? Would your atoms collide in the process and destroy you both?"

She waited for his eager response, but he only remained silent.

"Exactly. And what's to say there is a return lock

and device in the other time period?" Annja chuckled. "Was more than one device created? There can't be two at any given time. Or can there?"

"Annja, all time revolves on a continuum."

"I've heard the theories. If you're going to launch into hypothetical notions of imagined outcomes, then I'm out of here. But I will grant that the idea of someone having made a time-travel device is a good one."

"A time-*shifting* device."

"Semantics."

"We'll never see eye to eye on this."

"And that makes me one happy skeptic."

"You could go back and meet Joan of Arc," he encouraged, as if it was something easily arranged.

"Swell..."

"Sarcasm isn't your forte, Annja."

The next course was delivered. A fancy plate of pasta, mushrooms and peppers. Annja stabbed a fork into the dish and tasted. Not bad.

She leaned forward and said in a low voice, "Do you want to travel back through time to see Joan, Roux?"

"I've already met her. Nice gal. Tragic ending."

"Then I don't understand your quest for this device."

"It is a relic wrapped in a fascinating concept possibly constructed by one of the great Renaissance masters. Isn't that enough?"

It should be, but Annja sensed Roux's reasons for obtaining it were more than mere fascination or historical significance. If it wasn't at all related to Joan of Arc, would he have been even slightly interested in the far-out legend?

"Don't you want to discover if it holds an iota of truth?" he asked.

"No, I—" She forced herself to stop the diatribe and blew out a long, relaxing breath. She took another few bites before she said, "If the cross wasn't of some importance, I'd walk away from this project right now."

"That's not the enterprising young archaeologist I know."

The man was right. Why was she having such a tough time with this? The idea of time travel was crazy. But merely finding the cross would be accomplishment enough for her. It was a link to Joan, after all.

And it was stolen property. She'd been close to it. She was closer than most and gave herself good odds of finding it and returning it to the museum.

"If and when the cross is located," she said, "and whether or not it is a key to shift time…"

"Leonardo knew man could fly. And he had the science to back it up. Do you think it's so *out there* that we board tin canisters and soar across oceans nowadays?"

Annja sighed.

"I stand by what I've said about the device," Roux huffed.

"Which you got from whom?"

"Personal knowledge,"

"Well, someone else knows what it is, because

Scout is hot on the trail, as well. He's already got the cross—"

"Unless," Roux said.

Annja set down the wine goblet. "Unless?"

"Da Vinci kept extensive notes on everything. He always carried a notebook with him. Was scribbling in one on the night I first met him."

"And…someone out there has that notebook. It's possible. And the only probable answer to some of our questions."

"Whoever has that notebook is a thief," he said. "Wouldn't you say?"

"Yes. Unless they don't know what they have."

"But what if they did? What if the notebook for the time-shifting device was paired with the cross?"

"You think there was a notebook in the attaché case we brought up from the Venetian canal?"

"Roberts must have the notebook *and* the cross." Roux sounded half angry, half peeved. "Who is that man?"

"And who is he working for now?"

"You have to ask?" Roux smirked and raised his goblet to his lips for a swallow of wine. Finally, he said, "Garin Braden."

18

"There are only two people in the world who know exactly what the device may be capable of doing," Roux said.

"Two people?" Annja started to think about it, but she didn't have to think long. He'd just told her the man's name. "You and Garin. So you both saw the sketch for this music box back in the day?"

"We did. And actually, Garin was the one who had a conversation with Leonardo about the box. He didn't mention it to me until much later. Couple hundred years, maybe."

To exist in a world in which conversations were ordered by which century they had taken place stymied Annja.

"As usual," Annja commented.

"What is that supposed to mean? We are not always at one another's throats. We've worked together many a time."

"Then why not work together to locate this particular artifact?"

"I don't want to share, Annja. A man is allowed that right, isn't he?"

"You've moved beyond turning it in to the rightful authorities, haven't you?"

"I didn't say that. I want to look at it. Hold it in my hands."

"Time travel?"

He shrugged and quickly sipped more wine.

The man actually thought he could travel through time? Perhaps the centuries had not been kind to his brain after all.

"So you think Garin is the one who hired Scout away from you? Or maybe he hired Scout to press you into funding the dive?"

Roux flashed her a look that told her he hadn't considered that underhanded switch. He turned his attention to the windows that lined the restaurant and looked out over the sharply carved hedges and trees. "Anything is possible."

"Anything indeed. Did you and Garin spend a lot of time with Leonardo?"

"I spoke to him on a few occasions." He frowned. "Garin I can't vouch for."

Annja read the man's stiff, defensive body language with ease. This was a sore point between Roux and Garin. And that would make this quest all the more dangerous if they were pitted against one another. "So the two of you weren't speaking at the time in history when this item was revealed to you both?"

"Is that your best guess?"

"Yes. It makes sense."

"It does?" He leaned his elbows on the table and gestured for her to continue.

"What better reason to be on opposite sides now? Is there more to the lock on the music box besides the key?"

"The cross somehow fits into the lock on the music box and…I'm not sure how it works, exactly. It is what I remember Garin telling me."

Hmm. What she wouldn't give for a little hard data and findings her scientific mind could appreciate.

She had always known Roux to be sharp, wise and smart. He used common sense and his vast wealth of knowledge to keep one step ahead of the usual in life's game.

"Have you heard of the devil's chord, Annja?"

Interesting change of topic. But she could go with it. "It was a tritone of musical notes that in the Middle Ages the Catholic Church banned from being played or used in musical scores because it was thought to be evil and of the devil. When played, its quality is dissonant."

"Diabolus in musica." Roux recited the Latin term.

"The devil in music," Annja translated. "It's certainly not worthy of excommunicating someone or even worse, wherever it may have been used. So what does the devil's chord have to do with a cross that once belonged to Joan of Arc? And time travel?"

"Nothing. And everything."

Intrigued, Annja waited patiently for Roux's answer.

"The Lorraine cross is the key to activating the devil's chord."

"If you're going to try to explain how this is tied to time travel—"

Again, Roux flashed her a startled look. "Is Roberts aware the key works with a time-shifting device?"

"I don't think he had any idea what he was really looking for. However, he clearly knows some of the details. He's bested us at every turn."

"Yes, but I can't imagine Garin would have provided Roberts with the full picuture. Doing so would expose his position, make himself vulnerable, things Garin would never do."

"But…Roux, really? Time travel? It's all fun and games until someone actually does it only to realize it's a one-way ticket."

"Annja, please, can you set aside your skepticism for one moment?"

"Sure. I'm doing it right now. What you've said is now in the past. Me sitting here is the present, but my words— Oops, there they go, fading into the past. And the future is right after my next words."

"Touché."

"Why would you want to time travel anyway? What's the draw? It must be important, since it's compelled you to seek this fantastical music box that will play you back to another time."

"I'm not at all concerned with revisiting the years I have already walked through."

"Then what is it?"

Roux checked the wine bottle. Empty. He tapped

the base of his goblet a few times. Seconds later, the waiter appeared with profuse apologies and poured a fresh goblet for Roux. Annja refused. She'd had enough to drink but she wouldn't argue against more food. She'd inhaled the main course.

When the waiter had gone, leaving the new bottle of wine at the table, Roux leaned forward to confide.

"I saw the device once. In the fifteenth century. At least, I'm pretty sure that what I saw was the time-shifting device. I was in a hurry and didn't have a chance to really examine it. Garin almost stole it."

"So Garin was with you when you saw the device? Interesting."

"Yes, well, I do recall a fistfight and much arguing. He didn't leave with the thing. It wasn't what I was there for."

"There? Where was *there?*"

"I intend to visit the mysterious *there* quite soon. After we've finished dessert, in fact."

Dessert? Yes, more food!

"And what will we find at this mysterious *there?*" she asked. "The time-travel device?"

"We can hope. Although, I wouldn't place any bets on it. It's been centuries."

Roux gestured to the waiter, who, seeming to know the old man's wishes, appeared with the dessert tray. He chose for them both.

"It's not important. It's the past, Annja. And as you've said, there is no reason to venture into one's past."

He was obviously eluding the question. Now more than ever Annja wanted to discover what it was Roux had been "there for."

AN HOUR LATER, they pulled up to a graveyard tucked within the southern interior of the city and parked outside the black iron fence. Roux didn't seem interested in leaving the vehicle. He scanned the visible tombstones and the backs of mausoleum walls that edged up close to the fence.

"How will we find what we're looking for if we don't go in?" Annja asked carefully, as if addressing a reluctant child.

Roux merely nodded toward the cemetery.

Annja's gaze landed on a person exiting a four-by-eight mausoleum. He bent to brush dust from his jeans, then clapped his hands, and as he did so—his eyes fixed on Annja.

The man using Scout Roberts's name smiled that ridiculous charming smile of his. He strode toward their vehicle, stepping over tombstones that lay flat on the ground and squeezing between two stone statues. He grabbed the fence posts near the pointed tops and peered between the iron bars.

"Annja! We meet again."

Casting a questioning glance at Roux, she received a nod from him. The teacher directing the student.

She got out of the car and stepped up onto the curb. "Last time I saw you, you were close to death by tea," she offered. "You recovered nicely."

The man patted his abs to indicate his fitness. "Sorry about that. It was necessary."

"To foist the blame on me and make me a suspect of a poisoning in Venice?"

"Sounds like the plotline from a medieval thriller, eh?"

She reached between the iron bars and gripped his T-shirt. "You've got some nerve smiling like that. If you wanted to get away from me so badly you'd risk poison, then what's up now? Why the casual conversation? Where's the cross?"

He put up his hands to show his palms. "What cross?"

She tugged his shirt, and just when his forehead would have connected with the bars, he managed to get his hand in front of it. He yelped at the pain of his skull pressing into his fingers.

"The cross your guy stole from the palazzo while you were in the hospital," Annja clarified. "The same palazzo that you stole."

"You checked into that, eh?"

"The owner had never heard of you."

"It was a sweet place, Annja. Much better than that cheap old hotel Roux put you up in. Hey, Roux!" He waved to the immortal waiting in the car.

"You should be thankful you're on the other side of this fence," Annja said. She released his shirt. "You know your thief is dead?"

"I do."

"That means you either never got the stolen goods,

or you sent someone else to claim them to further obliterate the trail that leads back to you. Or—"

"Give it up, Creed. It'll just make your head spin."

Annja grimaced. She couldn't help it; she wanted to vault over the fence and knock the truth out of him. But would that really get her any closer to the music box and Lorraine cross? No.

"Who are you?" she asked. "Scout Roberts died two months ago."

"I was nervous you'd catch on to that sooner than I could ditch you. Roux wrecked my original plans by sending in the babysitter."

"Happy to make your life miserable."

"Not so much miserable as challenging. But I met the challenge with style. You know I've always been allergic to dandelion? Had a few close encounters with the emergency room as a child. Whew! I nailed that one."

"Risky."

"I was pretty sure it wouldn't kill me. Mostly. But how awesome was that when I suggested poisoning to the doctor and he picked that one up and ran with it?"

"You're avoiding the question about your identity."

"I'll leave that for you to figure out. Apparently you still haven't researched all the paperwork related to this situation. I'm disappointed in you, Creed."

Annja gripped the iron bars and bowed her head. She hadn't been briefed on everything, including the infamously ungettable police report. Was that the key detail she was still missing?

"Braden knows," Scout volunteered. "Sent me here,

expecting the two of you would show. Said this would be the first place Roux would check. I didn't see anything inside the mausoleum beyond dusty old crypt drawers, but you're welcome to take a look."

Annja glanced at Roux. The old man could hear their conversation, but he kept silent and gave her no indication. "What was supposed to be in the mausoleum?" she asked Roux.

He ignored her and turned forward, resting a wrist on the steering wheel.

It had to be the time-travel device. But how would they find anything here now? Surely the graveyard had been built up and remodeled since Roux had been here. Possibly some graves had been moved or even destroyed in the process.

"Well, I've a good idea what the old men are after. And they are very old, aren't they?" Scout offered. "At least, Roux is." He winked at Annja.

"You'll hit seventy soon enough," Annja said. "And I sure hope you drink the wrong tea then."

"Seventy." Scout grinned. "I think Roux has gone well beyond that age. But then, you don't know him all that well, so I won't bother you with the details. You figure out what the key is for yet?"

"I have. Roux's explained it to me."

"So my work here is done." Scout stepped back and slipped between the two closest mausoleums. "Catch you later, Creed!"

"Track him," Roux called to her. "I'll follow in the car. We need to tail him to Braden."

Taking a moment to vacillate with her own warring need to chase the villain or reach inside the car and twist the other villain's neck, Annja quickly took off in the direction she'd seen Scout turn.

Dodging around an ancient oak tree with bulging roots that had cracked the curb, she managed a look between gravestones and mausoleums and spied Scout's blue shirt. The cemetery ended just farther up the road. She stopped at the next corner and peered around to see a black SUV waiting at the front gates.

She glanced backward. Roux was driving slowly toward her and she gestured that he pick up speed, but he did not.

Scout got into the SUV and it took off, gliding away like the last car in a funeral procession, and not much faster.

Annja jumped into Roux's vehicle. "He's leaving in a black SUV, just around the corner."

"We'll give them a head start."

"Fine. Wouldn't want him to think we're following, when that's exactly what he expects."

"Annja, I know what I'm doing."

"Well, since you're not in a rush, now would be the perfect time to tell me what we're doing at a cemetery and what, exactly, should have been in the mausoleum Scout just checked."

"It was once a hiding place used by da Vinci. He kept valuables in the mausoleum. Had fashioned a nifty safe, which I'm sure Scout destroyed in order to get it open."

"If it was even still there. I realize he could be lying, but he said he didn't find anything."

"And it is possible the safe was long ago removed or destroyed."

"What was in it?"

"Nothing, apparently."

"Before," she insisted. "In the fifteenth century. You must have known about this from when you knew da Vinci."

"He used to keep the device in there. I assume he must have moved it to a safer location."

"Safer location? Why? For what reason, if he'd initially thought the mausoleum a safe hiding spot, would he have reason to then move the object?"

Roux shrugged. "Does it matter, Annja? It's been five centuries. Of course it wouldn't still be there."

He was talking in circles.

"Well, where is it now?"

"That will prove the interesting part."

"Because you don't have a clue? What about Garin?"

"I'm not sure what he knows. But we'll stay on his lackey, won't we?"

He turned the corner and slowly drove before the cemetery gates. A quarter of a mile ahead, the black SUV turned right.

"I'm beginning to question how worthwhile this goose chase really is," Annja said.

Annja rubbed her hands over her face. She rarely got headaches, but the semantics and double-talk involved with this crazy device could prove capable of giving her a migraine.

"Where's your imagination, Annja? Consider all

the unexpected people and things you've uncovered over the years. Some could be explained, while others could not.... What if that's the situation this time?"

"You do have a point."

"Da Vinci was a remarkable man in so many ways. Historians often remark that, and I can personally vouch that his peers did, as well. I'm sure you would agree."

"I do." Still, could there really be a time-travel device? The skeptic in her shouted against it, but the other side of her brain toyed with the idea.

"Let's suppose the device does exist and can work. Again I ask, what use have you for it? What is it about all this that's pushing you so strongly?"

He turned right. The black SUV was no longer in sight, so Roux picked up speed.

"The historical significance, of course. Nothing more."

"And is that Garin's reason, as well?"

Roux didn't answer, now focusing on the tail.

Annja sat back and closed her eyes. The historical significance? That didn't feel right coming from a man who had lived the history. He wanted it for other reasons.

Could he possibly want to time travel, or "shift" through time? To when? Did he miss a certain period and wanted to go back and relive it? Supposing that a return trip to the present was impossible, he'd be trapping himself in the past. Forcing himself to relive decades, possibly centuries. And that wasn't Roux. The man was too clever.

Too clever to believe in time-travel nonsense.

So there was something she was missing. And Annja was now determined to learn what it was.

19

Roux ducked around the corner of a high mausoleum, pressing his shoulders to the stone wall. Though his pursuer was stealthy, the man couldn't disguise the swish of his long leather coat as he made his way down the aisles among the tombstones and statues.

Resting his hand on the knife he kept at his belt, Roux knew it would serve no good. It would make the man angry, perhaps slow him down a bit, but it wouldn't kill him.

This living through the centuries was quite the experience. He only wished he could live it alone and not with the added hassle of Garin Braden ever following as if his shadow. The man had been his squire and he'd taught him how to be a soldier. He'd been proud of Garin, of his strength, his learning, his ease with handling a broadsword. Roux had been like a father to him and at times even a friend.

But since Jeanne's death? They'd been enemies more often than friends. Garin's nefarious methods always bothered Roux. So, they would endure one another's company, and yes, even work on the same side from time to time, but that was it.

Roux was aware that Garin did not hold his belief that if all the sword pieces were collected, something great would occur. Garin sought to thwart Roux. The bastard had almost dropped a piece in the ocean had Roux not been quick with the grab. That the man possessed such insolence!

Well, he was close now and he wasn't about to let his young upstart get in his way this time.

Roux waited, listening to leaves nearby crinkling. His pulse raced and seconds later he leaped out from behind the mausoleum. His body collided with the brute strength of his larger and stronger pupil.

Taking an elbow to the rib cage, Roux huffed out a breath. Garin did not relent. He wrapped an arm about Roux's neck and jerked his body downward, smashing his face into his knee, before shoving him to the rough ground.

As Garin lunged for him, Roux kicked out and caught his toe up under Garin's jaw. The oaf grunted and stumbled away. He crashed into a mausoleum, and leaves and twigs sifted down to decorate Garin's head.

Spitting away the refuse, Garin growled. As Roux stood and Garin followed, they met each other in a swift exchange of fists. The blows were expert and no energy was wasted, as each time Garin struck a vulnerable spot on Roux, Roux returned the favor with equal force.

Blood scented the air. Roux spat and swung hard,

knocking Garin from his feet. Crouching on top of him, he gripped his tunic and smashed his head against the cobblestones.

A leg twisted about Roux's, flipping him over to land on his back with arms splayed. The key he'd been holding clattered across the cobblestones.

Garin grabbed the key and rushed into the mausoleum. Roux rubbed at his jaw. The man had learned a few new tricks, he thought.

Inside the stone building, his former protégé grunted and cursed. "How does this stupid thing work, Roux?"

"It's a key. You shove it in and turn it, idiot." Roux propped up on an elbow and frowned. Were there no means to be rid of the man? Though best he was close to the prize when finally the safe was opened.

"Get in here."

"Patience. I'm an old man, and the bones are creaky."

"You're agile, swift and dangerous. I know that better than most. Now, come help me before I get so angry I take down the whole place."

Roux stood and wandered into the mausoleum. Garin bled at the eye and the corner of his mouth. Just so.

"I imagine should you beat down the walls, the safe would remain standing," Roux said. "We'd be no closer to the prize. Or rather, I would be no closer. Why do you insist on thwarting my mission? It's nothing to do with you."

"It's everything to do with me."

"How so?"

The man paused and then gestured as if Roux already knew the reason and understood. Maybe he did, since there hadn't been a feasible explanation thus far. Neither Roux nor Garin knew what awaited them should all the pieces of Joan's sword be found. Would they go on? Would they suddenly dissipate to two piles of dust? Ashes to ashes and all that?

Garin feared the latter, Roux suspected. But Roux wasn't so sure. He felt something grander awaited them when all the pieces had been reunited. And he would not rest until that moment had been delivered.

"Hand me the key."

Garin slapped the needed item into Roux's palm. In the darkness he could barely make out the lock and, using his fingers, fitted the key into the small port.

"I did that. Nothing happened," Garin said.

"It probably requires a strong turn." Roux tried to twist the key left and right but it didn't budge.

"Uh-huh. Tried that too, old man."

Roux bashed Garin under the jaw. The connection sent the burly man reeling, head rocking backward. He landed across the threshold, arms overhead and eyes closed, jaw open.

"That'll grant me the silence I crave," Roux said. "For less time than I desire, unfortunately."

Bending over the stone safe, he wriggled the key in the lock, feeling if it would give in one direction or the other. The painter was known to experiment with devices of all sorts, so certainly this one could prove a puzzle.

He pushed the key upward and it moved. Downward, it slid as if on greased wheels. Then at an angle to the left and...right.

Some inner mechanism clicked. The safe door popped open.

"One of these days, old man," Garin muttered as he came to.

"Stand back and give me some light," Roux ordered. If only to get the brute as far out of the mausoleum as possible.

Garin complied and moonlight beamed in and highlighted the opened safe. Inside the safe were two notebooks, a curious wooden box fitted with metal parts, gears and arabesque designs, and a small silver chunk of steel. Roux grabbed the piece that looked as though it could have once been part of a blade that had melted under intense heat.

When he made to close the safe door, Garin's hand clamped over his. "You got what you wanted. But what's in it for me? What's that?"

Lying before the box was also a small iron cross. It was in the style of the Lorraine cross Leonardo had once shown him.

"I am not a thief." Roux struggled to close the safe door.

"You are, and you just proved it. I, on the other hand, will take whatever can fill my purse with coin. And what is that box? It looks like it's bejeweled. Let me in there, old—"

He was fast tiring of knocking Garin out cold. And his knuckles ached. But persistence would not win the brute the prize this time. Closing the door and moving the key in the opposite direction to relock it, Roux then carefully replaced the key in his purse, along with the steel. He stepped over Garin's sprawled body and hurried away down an aisle of tombstones.

A quick stop into da Vinci's studio to return the key and then on to claim his horse. He would ride out of Milan before sunrise.

20

"You have a laptop?" Roux asked as he cruised Milan's streets.

"Yes, thanks to you." Annja kept all her documents and research records in a cloud account online, so she didn't have to worry about losing data, but ultimately, having her laptop back in hand would be optimal. "What do you want me to look up?"

"I'm not familiar with modern-day Milan. I can't recall where Leonardo's studio once stood."

"You think that's where Scout is headed?" Annja nodded. "Give me a minute."

She tugged the laptop out of her backpack and powered up. It wasn't long before she had a Wi-Fi connection and typed in a search for Leonardo's address while he'd stayed in fifteenth-century Milan. She thought it might be a good idea to check the location of the Duke of Milan's—Ludovico Sforza's—castle, or else very close by. Her eyes wandered over the search results. The plague had struck the town for three years during this era, and there was the start of work on the dome of the cathedral.

She repeated these details to Roux, who appeared annoyed.

"Are you looking for a location or getting lost in research?"

"Ahem."

Annja read the last bits of a bio. After Sforza's fall in 1499, Leonardo left Sforza's court for Mantua and Venice. She clicked on to the next listed URL.

"Anything?" Roux asked.

"I'm not sure. Sforza's court could place him in the actual castle or still possibly somewhere else. There are no addresses that I can find, but give me a minute."

"I never went inside the castle," Roux said. "His studio was not far from there. I remember a big, wide doorway opening to his studio. No stairs. Slabs of marble against the walls and canvases stretched on frames."

"Yes, I know he had his own studio in Milan…." Annja spent another ten minutes searching online. "I've found nothing. There's got to be— Hang on. I have an idea."

She signed on to archaeology.net and posted a question in one of the forums on Renaissance art.

Currently in Milan and am looking for original site of Leonardo da Vinci's studio. Anyone know the location or the vicinity? Thanks.

"I've posted about the location on an archaeology site. I usually get replies within twenty-four hours," she explained, closing the laptop. "So what did you have in mind? You think the device was transferred from the safe in the cemetery back to his studio?"

"It's only a guess. The music box could have been destroyed for all we know."

"Certainly, if there were items left behind in Leonardo's studio they've been cataloged and recorded. Maybe I can find out once I get settled somewhere. I assume we're staying in Milan?"

"Until we figure things out, yes. Braden is likely staying here."

Roux pointed out the window. Annja hadn't realized he'd parked. The hotel was on the opposite side of the street. A liveried doorman helped a sophisticated-looking woman out the back of a limo.

"How do you know it's this hotel?" she asked.

A black SUV pulled away from the drive in front of the parked limo.

"Scout just walked inside before that lady," Roux said. "I'm inclined to believe Braden will know we followed his lackey and, as you said, expect us to drop in on him. So what do you say?"

"I'm in."

"Excellent." Roux adjusted the rearview mirror. "You go first. I'll just park the car. I believe the entrance to the lot is behind the hotel, actually."

"Sure."

Annja got out, and Roux peeled away from the curb. Startled by his quick retreat, she spotted a new car, a sleek black sedan. Roux drove past the sedan and that car stopped, made a U-turn and followed him.

Annja shook her head. "That old man and his gambling."

Once inside the hotel, Annja bypassed the sophisticated-looking woman who was chastising the bellman, and looked around the lobby. No sign of Scout.

Her reconnaissance was distracted by thoughts of Roux's hasty escape. It had been an escape of sorts.

She tapped a valet on the shoulder and asked, "Which way to the parking garage?"

ANYONE WHO HAPPENED to see the old man with the white ponytail and beard would expect he was on his way home, where his lovely wife waited with a roast in the oven and an apron tied about her ample hips. Or perhaps he was off to spend some time with the grandchildren in the park.

Either assumption would be dead wrong.

Annja approached the scuffle in the parking garage with caution. Roux stood against three thugs. He was holding his own. And she expected him to. He wasn't an old man. In years, he was, but in terms of the ability to fight, and to deliver a choking throat chop with blinding speed—ouch, that had to hurt—he had not wavered over the centuries.

She winced as the thug who'd taken the throat chop went down. She guessed from his lean build and the biceps his muscle shirt revealed that he wouldn't be out of the fray for long.

With one man down and yet another reaching inside his jacket to produce what Annja suspected was a weapon, she decided now was a good time to make her presence known. Going straight for the man who flashed a gun, Annja gripped his wrist and directed the pistol downward, while using the heel of her opposite hand to smash up against the base of his jaw. His fingers loosened and she took away the gun and tossed it under a parked car.

"I can handle this, Annja. Thank you." Just then the second man lunged at Roux, who easily deflected the incoming punch.

Meanwhile, Annja exchanged blows with her opponent. Dressed in a sleek black shirt unbuttoned to the waist to reveal tattooed abs, he was agile. He bent to avoid a right hook and went to kick out her legs from underneath her. She jumped high and used the momentum to inflict a roundhouse kick on him.

"You want me to leave?" Annja managed.

"Suit yourself! Watch his blade!"

Sure enough, she spotted the knife and dodged backward, feeling as though she was going to lose her balance. She immediately steadied herself and prepared for another onslaught. As he approached, she slammed into his chest, landing on top of his body. The blade clattered across the concrete floor, spinning within grabbing distance of the first thug Roux had left on the ground.

The opponent got a hand on the weapon.

"Sorry!" Annja said.

She leaped up and off the bruiser. Gripping the side mirror on the SUV behind her, she swung up and caught the man in the chest with a forceful kick. He stumbled backward, connecting with his buddy, who currently swung the knife toward Roux. His aim went skyward, missing Roux's nose by inches.

Roux pressed his hands together and performed a grateful bow to Annja.

"De nada!" she called.

Now she gripped the collar of her thug and kneed him high in the kidney. Once, twice, she effectively moved around to pummel the blows directly to his side. He began to wobble. Arms reaching out before him, he huffed out a breath and spat blood. Annja continued the punishment until she felt his body grow heavy in her grip. She dropped him, but followed through with one more kick to the ribs.

Roux walked up behind her, dusting off his hands. "I think he's down for the count."

"He is now." She stepped back to look over the three fallen men. "How much did you win off these guys, anyway?"

Roux smiled and moved on toward his vehicle. "One point two million," he called back. "And I've suddenly developed an extreme aversion to this hotel."

"But we tracked Scout here. What if Braden is here, as well?"

"He'll keep. You want to come along, or are you staying put?"

Annja turned back to the men lying on the concrete. They were out cold.

"Staying put. They weren't after me. I think I'll do some investigating."

"Suit yourself. I'll be in touch."

"Wait!"

Roux slid behind the wheel and cast her a glance. Annja advanced and got her backpack from the car. Some online research was necessary before they could make another move.

"You don't know for sure that Garin is staying here?"

He shook his head.

"Okay. I'll wait for you to get in touch. I'll check in and see if anyone replied regarding a possible location for da Vinci's studio."

"Excellent." He revved the engine and Annja stepped aside as he backed out of the parking space and drove away.

She waved, but knew he wouldn't bother to look back. "You're welcome!"

Annja strode inside the hotel. The thugs wouldn't complain about their rough treatment in the parking garage. And if there were security cameras, no one could blame her for jumping in to help out an old man, right?

ASKING AT RECEPTION for Scout Roberts didn't merit recognition from the desk clerk. The man shook his head.

"He's a friend. I was supposed to meet him here," Annja tried. "He was just in here about twenty minutes ago?"

"Oh, that gentleman. American?"

"Yes. Blond hair. Killer smile?"

"Killer smile?" The desk clerk frowned.

"Uh, not like a killer." Bad translation. "Kind of

sexy in a charming— Forget it. Could you give me his room number?"

"He is not here with us, miss. He merely came by to pick up a package from one of our former guests. Sorry."

"Oh." *A former guest? Could it have been Garin Braden?* She needed to think about this, so without a place to land she checked in.

Once in her room, Annja decided a sauna was well deserved. The spa was gorgeous and soon the sweat was rolling down her skin. Twenty minutes later, she felt like a wet noodle when she exited the intense heat, but oh, what an awesome feeling. Quickly wrapping a towel around her as another woman entered the sauna, she covered the bruises on her shoulders and thighs and made a swift exit.

Roux was probably enjoying a fine wine at his four-star hotel. He hadn't offered to cover her expenses now, although he should have. She was, in essence, working for him.

And she was not. She wanted to serve history. To save pieces once stolen and have anyone be able to view them and learn from them was what she was working for. Adding the music box as a possible new find would prove phenomenal. And then to convince the world it was a time-travel device? Uh-huh. Make that a time-*shifting* device. She hadn't gotten her hopes up about finding it for exactly that reason.

She tightened the belt on her terry-cloth robe provided by the hotel, then wandered down to her room.

Did Roux actually buy into his fantasy about Leonardo having been a time traveler himself? No, he did not. He was just trying to make fantasy meet reality, as people often did when they wanted to believe in the impossible.

Yet she believed in men who could live beyond a normal age, so Annja wouldn't dismiss everything entirely.

Depositing her backpack on the end of the bed, she dropped the robe and sorted through the new clothing that had been provided for her by Roux. Very basic, but everything fit, so she couldn't complain. The gray cotton T-shirt and olive-green cargo pants were actually comfortable. She pushed aside the curtains and scanned the metropolis that had grown up into an amazing city.

A major economic and financial center, Milan was also famous for a number of cultural and architectural sites. La Scala, the opera house, was one of her favorite places to hang out. She easily recalled the building's sumptuous auditorium. The red velvet, silk and gilded stucco always caught her eye and the chandelier was a dazzler. The revered venue was just one of many in the city. She guessed tourists must flock to Milan almost as much as they did Paris.

And what about when Leonardo da Vinci would have strolled the streets taking in every detail? She imagined herself in an elegant gown with her hair done up and decorated with a beaded headdress and rich gold trimmings on her sleeves and hems as she strolled beside him. Obviously, she imagined herself someone from the court.

Annja laughed. "Why not? If I'm going to dream, I might as well have been rich."

Where rich was concerned, the de' Medicis and the Sforzas popped instantly to mind. Annja powered up the laptop and typed in a search on the nefarious families. The de' Medicis had ruled over Florence and accumulated much wealth to fund their influence and standing.

Ludovico Sforza was Duke of Milan from the end of the fifteenth century until he died early in the sixteenth. He had commissioned *The Last Supper* from da Vinci. He had been big into taxation to support his artistic and agricultural ventures. An alliance with the French king Charles VIII turned sour and resulted in the French laying claim to not only Naples but Milan, as well. He had been responsible for starting the Italian Wars against the French, yet was eventually driven out of Milan by the French because he had no allies. He'd died in a French prison.

Time travel was starting to lose its appeal.

Annja shook her head, unwilling to make that leap. "It's just a pretty music box that still holds historical value. And I will find it. I've come this far."

Because once set on a mission, she rarely abandoned the quest. Even when attacked by natives—or threatened by thugs miffed about losing 1.2 million dollars—she never gave up. It wasn't in her DNA to surrender. And someone had to remain the calm, rational one who would see to bringing any found treasures to a local museum or university for authentication.

Her cell phone rang. The No Caller ID flashing on the screen annoyed her. "Hello?"

"Annja, I'm surprised you didn't catch me. I think you let me get away, yes?"

"We needed to follow you back to your home base."

"Which you didn't find."

Yes, well, stating the obvious.

"What do you want now, Scout?" She had to stop calling him by that name. While she spoke, she opened her email program. Roux had said he'd sent her a copy of the files she hadn't seen.

"I have this keen notion that you don't know everything there is to know about this whole search for the missing music box slash time machine. Am I right?"

"I know as much as you do, Scout."

"I think not. And I'm willing to divulge my secrets if you'll meet me for coffee sans the white-haired old man."

Annja sighed. Playing into the enemy's hand, allowing him to lure her to his choice of meeting place, was never wise. But he did have more knowledge than she did. And if he was willing to share?

"I saw a bistro near the Parco Sempione that sported a pink pig hanging over the door," she said. "I'll be there in half an hour."

"I'll have the coffee waiting for you. You take cream? No, wait. Black. You're one tough lady."

She hung up, thinking she did like it black. Coffee that bit back was the only way to go.

A message from Roux sat in her email inbox. Attached was a pdf scan of the police report filed by the antiquities museum in Poland after the heist. It didn't tell her anything new. But the second page was a Milan police document regarding the arrest of Lisa Phelps and the subsequent arrest of her partner, Evan Merrick, a few days later in the States.

The thieves who had stolen the Lorraine cross.

"So Phelps must have squealed on her partner, since he was caught a few days later," she said as she scrolled through the document. "In his New York apartment."

"They admitted to knowing some details of the crime, but were never convicted. In fact, they didn't even receive a court date. Lacking evidence." She read the notes.

Annja leaned back against the padded headboard, and dragged the laptop up onto her thighs. She glanced out the window.

"Of course there was no evidence, because it had been dumped in the canal. I'm surprised they didn't authorize dredging the canal."

Her eyes scanned the report and saw that the canal where Evan Merrick admitted the case had been dumped by his companion was listed as the Rio di San Vio. A canal positioned completely opposite in the city from the Fondamenta della Sensa, where they had recovered the attaché. It couldn't have drifted from the southern edge of the city to the north. There were too many canals, too many twists and turns, and the tides didn't move that way.

"He gave them false information."

So how had Scout Roberts known to look in the Fondamenta della Sensa? Weird.

She still found it hard to believe both thieves had been let off with nothing more than a slap on the wrist. No fingerprints had been found at the scene of the crime, so...

Thinking back to that first day she had met Scout—or whoever he was—Annja recalled his tale of a lovers' quarrel in the gondola floating down the canal. The woman had dumped the attaché case while her lover's attention had been distracted.

So that must have been the big breakup. And in an attempt to get back at the man who had scorned her, had the woman purposely dropped him in hot water by partly confessing to the crime? She had to have known going in that they couldn't charge her with the theft without evidence. But a confession should have been sufficient.

The details of Lisa Phelps's interrogation were not included. Someone on the inside had to have been helping the thieves. A dirty lawyer? Or judge?

Annja suddenly didn't care about the woman. There were only two people who knew the exact canal where the attaché case had been dumped overboard—Lisa Phelps and... "Evan Merrick."

21

True to his word, the man who claimed to be Scout Roberts sat waiting for Annja. A steaming coffee cup awaited her and she sat down before it and had a sip. Nice and dark. She didn't want to get too cozy and start trusting the guy again. And she kept one eye on her surroundings as she sat there. He could have backup, and she wasn't about to be tricked by this one again.

"I also ordered some cookies," he offered.

"Cookies will not erase the double-crossing you've done, Merrick."

"Ah?" Stretching out his legs beneath the table and leaning back in an open come-at-me posture, he winked at her. "Well, look at you. Took you long enough to figure that one out, Creed."

"Like I said before, I didn't have the police report going into this."

"Roux just sent it to you now? Are you really his employee or maybe something more like his errand girl?"

"You should stop trying to bait me, Merrick. It won't work."

The waitress appeared and set down a plate of iced cookies. Evan ate one in a single bite. "Sweet."

"Clever," Annja said, "the way you orchestrated the dive and your ultimate escape with the cross."

"After you arrived, my plans required some last-minute changes. I impressed even myself with my quick thinking."

"Glad to be a problem. So why involve Roux? Why not just dive for the case yourself?"

"Creed. If I could afford a boat and the equipment, I would have gone down weeks after losing that stupid case. But Lisa, my vindictive ex-partner—"

"And lover?"

"She expected me to propose to her that evening, Annja. I thought we were going to have a nice meal, hug, then take a break from each other for a few weeks like our normal routine. *Marriage?* I did not see that one coming."

Annja shook her head, noting the man's genuine dismay.

"She took everything from me," Evan explained with clear disbelief. "I called ahead to New York. My good buddy who lives down the hallway in our high-rise reported she—or someone she had hired—had cleaned out the apartment in less than two hours. The walls were bare, and the safe door was hanging open. Light fixtures were even missing the bulbs. Can you believe that? I was incarcerated wearing tennis shoes. That is so not my style, Creed."

"I'm having trouble shedding a single sympathetic tear."

"You women are all the same."

From behind another sip of coffee, Annja lifted a brow. She did not like being cobbled into the category of "you women." But it wasn't worth the argument.

"Totally erasing herself from your life. That's a gutsy female. And she had every right to do so."

"Yeah? She had no right to erase *me*. She emptied all our accounts."

"You didn't have separate bank accounts?"

"We did. But one of the reasons we worked so well together was that she was the fingers—" he waggled his fingers, then twisted them around as if manipulating a safe dial "—and I was the logistics and get-away man. But as well, Lisa was the computer geek. Could crack a digital code in seconds. Bank accounts? No problem."

"Sounds like she was doing most of the work."

"Not fair, Creed."

"Which is why you confessed, to get back at her, which resulted in her arrest in Milan."

"I had to go for it, Creed. I knew they didn't have any evidence. I made a plea bargain and walked out of the police station that day."

Annja slid back against the wicker chair and sighed. "Listen, I'm an archaeologist. I'm not an expert in personal relationships. Or theft."

"Here I thought you wanted the whole story?"

"I guess I do. How did you get the attaché case open if she was the digital-code cracker?"

"I knew that code all along. I mean, it was my case. But I couldn't have used it with you watching. Right?"

"Right. So what do you think you know that I don't know?" she asked. "And will you tell me why you have so much information on this music box? I know Roux didn't give you details on how it works. And you have no reason to know of its existence."

"Roux didn't tell me anything." He sat back now, crossing an ankle over his knee and gripping his calf. "But then, do you think Roux understands how it works? Maybe the old man's slipping. Did you ever consider that?"

He wasn't making sense. Perhaps his intention had been to lure her into the open and waste her time while— "If you've sent men to my hotel room to—"

"I haven't. I've no reason to. You're not the one with all the clout around here. You're just the baby-sitter." A protest stung her tongue, but he continued, "I know things, Creed. Things that you don't, but certainly that Roux does."

The only way Scout—Evan—could know about the music box was if Roux or Garin had told him, yet she hadn't seen Garin, so had no proof Evan was even working with him.

No, he'd mentioned Garin's name. Garin must have given up the details or else Merrick was bluffing, trying to get information out of her.

"You have the notebook," she suddenly guessed. The one in which Roux presumed Leonardo da Vinci had drawn sketches and schematics for the time-shifting music box. Perhaps it also detailed the Lorraine cross and its use in relation to the box.

"I do. The notebook is sort of a partner to the Lorraine cross."

"You found it in the case we saved from the canal? Unless…"

She sipped the coffee, letting her mind sort the timeline of events since she'd met him. He sat there with that annoying little smirk on his face waiting for her to work things out. The guy was not an archaeologist. What he was, was a confessed thief. And thieves could put their hands on all sorts of things others weren't even aware existed.

"You've had the notebook all along," she decided. "Before diving for the cross."

Evan whistled in appreciation. "You are not stupid, Annja Creed."

"Why wasn't it in the case along with the cross?"

"Because it wasn't in the museum. The only reason I pinched the Lorraine cross was because I'd been led there by studying the notebook. The notebook was a bonus item from a previous heist a few years ago. Can't give you details, naturally."

It hadn't occurred to Annja that the notebook would be separate from the cross, but of course, the museum would have listed the missing notebook in the police report. And surely anyone who took a moment to glance through the notebook would have matched the cross to any drawings that may have been done of it.

"So the notebook was…in a library? A bookstore? Your mother's attic?"

"Found it in a dusty old tin box in the back of a

safe," Evan said. "The museum, or possibly bank—or it might have even been a dusty old castle—hadn't any idea what they owned. It was never reported missing. I knew what it was immediately. Good old Leonardo. That guy was amazing, you know that?"

"Are there drawings of the Lorraine cross and the music box in the notebook?"

"Yes, and very detailed. Everything a guy needs to know to operate the music box is found within the pages of that notebook. Er, mostly. I'm still a little iffy on locations and such. I even took a trip to the Pinacoteca Ambrosiana right here in Milan. Did it as soon as I arrived yesterday."

"What's in that museum of interest to you?"

"Da Vinci's *Portrait of a Musician*."

Annja was familiar with the portrait. It was supposed to be the only instance Leonardo had depicted a male in his portraiture. The painting featured a gentleman in black and brown robes with a red cap holding a piece of sheet music. His focus was not on the music, but off in the distance. Often considered one of his least important works—since it seemed it was semi-unfinished—some even debated whether or not it was truly da Vinci's.

"Part of the musical score has been cut off at the bottom of the painting," Evan said, "but I'm pretty sure there's a tritone in there somewhere. I'm no musician. But don't you think it makes sense? The devil's chord having been banned?"

"Possibly."

"Come on, how clever was that to maybe add the musical score when the notes were banned?"

"Clever? I don't see how."

"It's the map to operating the device, Creed."

"But if there's a key, what need have you for a map?"

Evan scoffed and grabbed another cookie.

Annja refused to get distracted by Evan's twisted theories. "You're diverting the attention from your criminal dealings," she said. "What's to stop me from notifying the authorities right now and having them arrest you?"

"What proof have you besides a confession no one else has heard?" Evan grabbed another cookie and popped it into his mouth.

"Do you have the Lorraine cross?" she asked. "The notebook? You said Garin Braden had the cross."

He grinned, but only chewed the cookie.

"Nothing you've said to me has been true. You haven't handed the cross over to Garin. And you don't intend to."

"Of course not. You're good, Creed. What I'd like to know is more information about Roux, because you know what?"

"Dazzle me."

"Roux is proof that the time-shifting device works."

"Absurd—"

Evan's gaze darted to something behind her. He stood and grabbed a handful of cookies. "Suspicious characters at the side door. Could be Braden's bullies. I'm out of here. Nice talking to you, Creed. See you in Rouen."

He took a step, and Annja reached to grab his wrist. He'd done this disappearing act on her once too often. She would not let it happen again. Evan shook off her grasp.

Annja was prevented from going after him by a hand slamming down on her shoulder.

22

"Let's take a walk outside," a gruff voice said with as little joy as Annja had ever heard.

Evan had already rushed out the back door. Not wanting to cause a scene in the crowded bistro, Annja stood. "Sure. Feel like a little exercise anyway."

She turned and aimed for the restaurant's main exit. The man behind was twice her size, and the man in front of her was more slender but a head taller. The slender guy was dressed in leather motorcycle pants and a T-shirt that did not reveal any hidden weapons stashed at his waistband, for instance. He flexed his fingers into a fist.

Outside, the slender guy turned immediately right, down an alleyway that was about four feet wide and had three-story buildings on both sides. Not optimal for swinging punches or getting her back clear so she could keep both men in sight. But she would make do.

Where had Evan gone? Frustrated that he had a knack for continually giving her the slip, Annja mentally prepared herself.

The fist she didn't want to meet swung around toward her. Annja ducked and reached up to grab the larger guy by his forearm. Dropping into a forward roll, she managed to tug him off his feet and slam him against the other man. The impact surprised them both.

Now she had her back clear. The men staggered to their feet, and the larger one again took the initiative and reached inside his jacket pocket. Annja called the sword to hand from the otherwhere. It fit with a smart landing against her palm. A knowing warmth surged through her arm and made her stand taller. Yet she didn't have the freedom to swing in a wide arc, so would have to compensate with smaller stabs and defend herself.

"He said she might have a sword," the tall one said to the other.

Not many people on this planet would be able to warn their henchmen that she wielded a sword.

"Braden," Annja suggested. "Yes?"

"I've got no idea what you're talking about, lady."

"So I'm a lady, eh? If this is the way you treat ladies, your father needs to be admonished."

"Don't bring my dad into this," the thin one spat.

Annja was losing her patience with these guys and so ran toward both men. She leaped sideways, pushing off the wall to her left, and swung down hard to knock the first guy off-balance. He yelped and dropped a knife he had drawn from the inside of his jacket.

Annja landed and quickly slashed the other man's thigh. Shoving the tip in deep, she ripped the seam of his pants open and, behind that, scored his skin in a crimson slice. He fell to his knees, yowling.

His partner reacted, scrambling for the knife. He speared it toward Annja. She caught the blade against her sword hilt and dashed it away with a flick of her wrist.

Stepping up onto the fallen man's shoulder for added height, Annja jumped and spun in the air, striking the sword across the man's neck as he lunged again for the knife. Midair, blood spattered her gray T-shirt.

She hit the ground perfectly balanced and assessed the damage. Both men were alive and would remain so with the proper emergency medical care.

"That's going to leave a mark," she noted of the thigh wound she'd left on one of the goons.

Not wanting to stay for a chat, she ran down the alleyway. Releasing the sword to the otherwhere, she cursed Garin Braden's need to exercise his muscle from a distance.

If the man had an argument with her, she preferred he address her face-to-face. Or had it been Evan that Garin was ultimately after? She hadn't seen if Evan had gotten away without luring a henchmen after him.

Evan...Garin... Who was working with whom?

BACK AT THE HOTEL ROOM, Annja assessed her injuries. Minimal. A few scratches to her arms and wrists, and another bruise on her shoulder—it was beginning to look like an interesting tattoo with the green-and-purple tinting.

She gathered up the laptop and stuffed her dirty clothes into the backpack.

She rang up Roux but he wasn't answering, as usual. Where had he gone? Had the thugs following him tracked him down yet again? For 1.2 million dollars? Most certainly that tail would be difficult to shake.

"Supposedly, he can handle himself," she muttered and tucked her cell phone into a pocket as she exited the room.

She didn't check out of the hotel, but rather decided to keep her room as backup should she find herself staying in the city one more night.

She guessed Evan's choice of hotel after scanning the offerings online. The place was centrally located, so easy to get to. At the reception desk she asked the angelic-faced blonde to see Evan Merrick, not expecting that he'd actually used that name. Getting a headshake and a reply that no one under that name was registered, Annja nodded. She made up some story about being Evan's fiancée and missing a train connection, describing him as the sexy American with the pulsating blue eyes. Yeah, pulsating eyes, she repeated. It killed her to say that, but the receptionist nodded in kind. She'd seen him and knew he was staying at the hotel. But she refused to give Annja his room number.

Annja sighed. "I understand. You might lose your job. Oh, is there a bathroom here in the lobby I can use?"

The receptionist pointed it out and watched Annja walk across the marble floor and enter the unisex bath-

room. The space was small, offering only two stalls
and one sink. She wasted as much time as she could
thinking of a means of escape that would get her past
the blonde at reception. Nothing useful came to mind.

When a handsome, mature man walked in, she nodded and made a show of washing her hands. He did his
business, and she quickly grabbed a paper towel and
wiped at her shoe to buy her some more time.

"New," she said to him as he stood at the sink washing his hands. When he left, she peeked out after him.
The man had been just handsome enough…

Yep, the receptionist's head whipped around, following the man with tufts of gray above his ears. He
wore the Armani suit and leather shoes like a fashion
model. The distraction allowed Annja to slip along
the wall behind a palm frond and around the corner
to the elevator bay. Fortunately an elevator was just
arriving. She slipped inside and pressed the button for
the second floor. A good thief would choose a lower
floor, she mused, for an easy and fast escape. Though
a higher floor would allow for a better vantage point
of the surroundings. but he was the getaway man, so
there you go.

There were only four rooms on each level. The first
two rooms she dismissed given the food trays sitting
outside the doors. Unless Evan was eating for two and
liked roses with his meal, she guessed rooming behind
those doors were honeymooners or traveling couples.

Two doors remaining. She stood before the first,
poised to knock and heard the television beyond the

door. Sounded like a religious program given the prayers being offered.

Annja adjusted her position and opted for the opposite door. No light from underneath the door and no sound from a TV. She knocked and didn't bother to step aside. When darkness flashed over the pinhole, she smiled and waved.

The door opened and Evan conceded her win with a gesture that she enter his room.

"Of course you'd stay at the da Vinci hotel," she said, wandering in and scanning the surroundings.

"I'll give you that one," he said. "Way too obvious."

"So we were having a conversation," she said, "before you decided to leave me to fight the bad guys."

"Was there a fight?"

"You weren't followed? Figures. Was the harpoon in the canal meant for me? Because it doesn't make sense otherwise."

"Ah, sorry, Annja."

"No, you're not."

"Nah, I'm not really. Were they Braden's men just now?"

"I can only guess. But you're not working for him, either. That's why he sent the thugs. Am I right?"

"I haven't given you enough credit, Creed. Never thought a television personality would be so smart and observant. But then, I think you know both Roux and Braden much better than you've allowed me to believe, yes?"

"Roux just hired me for this job," she replied, unwilling to detail the complexities of their relationship.

"Now, let's continue where we left off. Why is Roux proof that the music-box device works?"

Evan ran his fingers through his hair, exposing a healthy flash of ribbed abs as his shirt stretched up. Annja averted her eyes. He was working it. She was not interested.

"All right." He splayed his hands in surrender. "You've earned that much. But I'll tell you right now that the Lorraine cross is not in this room."

"I believe that. It would be foolish of you to keep it out in the open. But you've got it close."

"Very close. You want to search me?" He lifted the shirt to again expose his abs.

"Just explain about Roux."

"I can do better than that. I'll show you."

He lifted up the duffel bag from the chair by the bed and picked through the contents. Pulling out a small leather-bound book, he then tossed it to Annja.

Guessing what it was while it was midair, Annja deftly reached to catch it, but at the same time was careful not to do so roughly. She clasped it gently in both hands. The supple leather creaked and the loose leather tie rested over her wrist.

"This is…" She carefully turned the antique over and studied the plain leather cover. "You idiot!"

"What?"

"This is five centuries old! And you just tossed it across the room like it was the remote control. Have a little respect, please."

She set the notebook on the end of the bed. Evan made a move to pick it up but she blocked him.

"If you've no interest in looking at it…"

"I do." She shrugged the backpack off her shoulder and pulled out a pair of latex gloves. "I just need to do it right."

And she knew immediately it was that old when she peeled aside the cover and saw Leonardo da Vinci's writing. "This is the notebook you nabbed during—what heist did you say?"

"I didn't say. But good try. The Lorraine cross is detailed on the first page. The info about the music box is toward the end. But there's something even more interesting in the middle. Let me show you."

He held out his hand and she was reluctant to give him the notebook. This was compelling history that had been kept from the public. The first page was an orderly mix of text, and a sketch on a smaller card had been pasted onto the page—the Lorraine cross—and text written over what appeared to be erasures. Paper had been a valued commodity in Leonardo's time, so it made sense that he'd used as much of the space as possible.

Evan snapped his fingers. "You can drool over it later. Right now, let me show you what you wanted to know."

"You got gloves?"

He nodded and from the nearby duffel bag pulled out a pair of black latex gloves. The color was appropriate.

She handed him the notebook and he carefully paged through it, which she appreciated.

When he found what he was looking for, Evan

folded back the front pages against the back of the notebook, and even as Annja cringed, she saw that the papers curled easily like that. Perhaps it had been found rolled. It conformed to such a shape.

He handed the notebook back to her, opened to a sketch.

She was careful to only touch the leather cover and the very edges of the paper.

Annja gasped at the sight of a man's face drawn in red pencil on the lower right corner of the page. He was not young, nor very old. Middle-aged. Long white hair curled gracefully around his face, and a few marks crinkled out from the corners of his world-weary eyes. The artist had also illustrated a frown line at the bridge of his nose—a line with which Annja was all too familiar. The name *Roux* had been written near his ear, as if to label the face for future reference.

Remarkable. Could this be the drawing Leonardo had made of Roux that night they'd met in the tavern? It made sense.

Evan had mentioned he'd already obtained this notebook before any of this business had started. So, when he'd met Roux at the auction, he had already seen this sketch. Maybe? Had he tracked Roux down purposefully? No wonder he seemed to think he knew so much about Roux. But this was only a sketch.

Before Annja could ask her first question, her eyes noted the bottom of the page where the sketch ended at Roux's right shoulder. In black ink, written in thick angry letters, was the word *ladro.*

"Thief," Annja interpreted.

Why would Leonardo have written that? She knew Roux was a shifty old coot, but had he a deeper vein of thievery that had prompted him to steal from the famous painter? Had *Roux* stolen the music box?

No, that made little sense. He was looking for the music box now. Although, if he actually had the music box, then all he would need was the Lorraine cross.

She needed to talk to Roux.

"As I've told you, I pored over this notebook for months after obtaining it. I know every line Leonardo sketched as if I'd drawn it myself. I recognized Roux immediately at the auction. But even more interesting? This sketch is the same man I saw in the SUV this afternoon outside the graveyard. You can't deny it."

"You're really pushing to make the uneven pieces fit, Evan. If the man in the picture was Roux that would make the Roux I know over five hundred years old."

"Yep."

Annja's laugh was forced, and she knew it sounded that way, too.

"Haven't you ever heard of doubles?" she tried. "Doppelgängers? Throughout history the instances of people resembling historical figures are well-known. There is an entire subset of blogs and websites devoted to celebrity and historical look-alikes."

"You talk a good game, Creed, but I'm willing to bet you know the truth. And if you don't, now you do."

"And what truth is that?"

He rubbed his palms together in such gleeful delight Annja took a moment to consider his mental stability. He had poisoned himself—surely his sanity was questionable.

"Roux is a time traveler," Evan stated. "And," he continued, "he's traveled to our time via da Vinci's music box, the time-shifting device everyone is eager to get their hands on. And Roux is after it to return home."

Home? Annja's jaw dropped. It was a fantastic explanation. To have arrived at such a conclusion must have cost Evan a heap of brain cells.

On the other hand, he'd provided a great cover for the truth. Far be it from her to rain on the man's crazy parade.

"Aren't you the clever boy?"

Evan dropped the excited pose. "Do not condescend to me, Creed. You think I'm deranged."

"I think you're a man who will believe what you need to believe. It's gotten you this far."

"Indeed, it has."

"But tell me one thing."

"I've already told you more than a sane man should."

"Yes, well, your sanity is under consideration," she noted. "Where do you intend to *travel* once you get that device? And do you think you'll come back? I mean, if Roux traveled from the fifteenth century to here, why didn't he go back?"

"Creed, would you go back to the fifteenth century if you landed in the technologically advanced twenty-first century? I mean, the modern sanitation system alone should answer that question."

He had a point. While studying the Middle Ages was fascinating, being a modern woman living in the Renaissance would present many challenges. Computers she could manage without. But no camera to record all that she saw? And to imagine never again eating at her favorite restaurants again? And if she went there, she had to consider the friendships she would miss. Doug and Bart, and yes, even Roux, and occasionally Braden. Some things were too valuable to live without.

"I'm good with where I'm at," she replied. "I'm going to guess that you are, too. Who are you selling the device to?"

Evan's shock gave him away. Annja knew if he had a buyer, he wouldn't spill. And likely he did not have a buyer arranged just yet. He needed to have the music box before he could attract a buyer willing to lay down the millions, she estimated, he would ask for the prize. Though if he were so hard up on his financial luck, it did surprise her he wasn't using every angle he could manage to bring in bids for the time-shifting device.

"Don't think about it too much, Creed," he said. "It'll give you a headache."

Indeed.

"All parties involved know the cross is in play, Evan."

"As I've said, it's safely in my hands."

"Yes, and that it is required to activate the device. Yes?"

Again, he pointed to the notebook.

Annja sat on the bed, taking advantage of Evan's willingness to cooperate for the moment. She half expected he'd try to knock her out and make an escape. That was why she sat facing him as she pulled the notebook onto her lap.

"See how I'm still wearing protective gloves?" She waved at Evan. She couldn't stop herself from making the point.

Paging toward the back of the notebook, as he'd indicated, Annja found the part that detailed the music box. It wasn't labeled as a time-shifting device. There wasn't a label at all. But she guessed this was it. It had a particular steampunk-ish look to it. A rectangular box with a compass and a crossbar fitted to the top, and gears at either end, which rotated—with a turn of the cross key? Another crossbar fronted the long, narrow side of the box with dials placed along it, like a combination lock. The box had been fashioned from wood and some kind of metal and had ornate decoration all over it.

She did not see a revolving cylinder whose pins would pluck out a tune rumored to have once called to the devil, but suspected that was inside the box. There were no interior drawings, it seemed. She closed the notebook, looking again at the cover. Less fine forgeries had fooled many a scholar over the years.

"It's the real thing," Evan offered. "I sure didn't make up all that stuff inside."

"Someone else could have."

"Really? To have been aware of a device you've confirmed to me that only a few people should know about? Exactly one person, by my count. And that would be the man who came from that time period and who possesses such knowledge because he knew Leonardo da Vinci."

Annja tilted her head, silently conceding to his wild, yet remarkably accurate, guess. Not as far as Roux time shifting, but for having known Leonardo. Well.

But that he hadn't included Garin as a time traveler meant he knew little about his recently discarded employer. In fact, it was likely Evan hadn't even met him in person, but rather had been manipulated through calls from Garin and visits from his thugs.

"So where do you expect to find the device?" Annja asked. "The graveyard was a bust. Does the notebook indicate where it was kept?"

Evan shrugged.

She referred back to the page with the sketch, but the words around the sketch were in a strange sort of writing. She stood and held the notebook up to the mirror, but her interpretation of the Italian was slowgoing because the script was tiny and fading.

A name did stand out, though.

"Jeanne d'Arc?"

"Really?" Evan joined her and stared into the mirror, squinting. "Where does it say that?"

"At the right side of the box, see? Near that impression on the side. It's very small. I wonder if that's where the key fits. There's only the one view of the box, as if looking on it from above. No side schematics?"

"That's the only page with the sketch."

She leafed through the notebook. The pages were

delicate, yet at the same time, she didn't expect them to crumble or fall apart. There were sketches of people milling in a market square. A closeup of a cross section of a pear, showing the seeds and growing seasons. Another drawing showed the pear cut through the center belly, giving a top-down perspective of the fruit.

"Leonardo da Vinci was so meticulous," she marveled aloud.

The Lorraine cross had been drawn at the front of the notebook. Very small, about as long as her baby finger, though again, the detail was intricate. The three-dimensional drawing was drawn from the back of the cross, which wasn't flat and plain as Annja would expect from a wall hanging or a personal item one kept on the end of a rosary or tucked in their pocket. It was notched, almost like a key, but an elaborate key at that. And a few pieces looked movable, and she guessed from the directional arrows drawn beside the cross that they did indeed move. It might snap out from the main part of the cross, like an electronic key some cars boasted, or perhaps the notches were inset for a reason. The cross fitted onto a specific position on the music box.

"Interesting. This notebook needs to be studied by historians and placed in a museum for the whole world to share."

"Yeah, that's not my choice. Highest bidder gets to do as he desires with it."

"I could keep it. Not give it back to you."

The almost imperceptible *snick* of a gun safety being slid off alerted Annja. She looked up from the notebook. Evan held the semiautomatic pistol casually and then aimed it directly at her.

"Go ahead and finish browsing through the book," he said. "Since you're without a cameraman to record details, I won't deny you the thrill. It'll be your first and last chance, though, so look carefully. But understand, I have to protect my investment."

"Of course."

And instead of arguing or even lunging across the hotel room to fight for the gun, Annja switched her attention to the notebook. The historian in her was too greedy to give up this opportunity. As well, that part of her that preferred to stand up for what was right needed a few minutes to think through a plan.

The only idea that spoke to her was to stay close to the notebook. Sooner or later it would lead to the music box.

She returned to the page that had the sketch of Roux. Was he aware that Leonardo had drawn his face and labeled it *thief?* The painter may have shown him the sketch over a goblet of wine, yet to judge the ink used to write the word *thief,* as opposed to the red pencil used for the sketch and Roux's name, she suspected Leonardo had added the accusatory label at a later point.

What had Roux stolen from Leonardo da Vinci? And had it anything to do with the music box or the Lorraine cross? Again, she turned back to the first page that detailed the cross.

"You have the key all figured out?" she asked Evan.

"As best I can figure, it fits onto the music box.

There are no diagrams of the key mechanism, as you've seen. But the text that reads *Jeanne d'Arc* is now my best guess."

"But her name doesn't mean anything. It's just another detail…" That could mean something if Annja put some thought into it.

She scanned another page that looked like a list of trees and another filled with sketches of various body parts, such as knees, elbows and wrists. The music-box page kept drawing her back to it. Annja tried to fix it and the page with the study of the cross to memory in case she did not see the notebook again.

Back to the diagram of the music box. Could Joan's name be the real key to unlocking that riddle?

Wishing she had the actual object here so she could turn it over and study it from all angles, Annja traced the lines of the sketch carefully, yet her latex-gloved fingertip didn't quite touch the paper.

Evan leaned across the table and tapped the notebook with the barrel of the pistol. Annja had forgotten he was holding that. "You're done. Close it up and slide it across the table like a good girl who doesn't want a hole in her head."

"You won't shoot me, Evan. A bullet through my skull would splatter the wall behind me and drip over the chair and probably into the carpet. Too much cleanup."

"Yeah, but you must know I didn't use my real name to sign in."

"Right. But the noise of the gunshot would surely attract attention."

He smirked, shaking his head. "Why couldn't it have been you in the gondola with me, Creed?"

"You mean you wish I had been your partner in crime? I don't steal."

She closed the notebook but didn't slide it toward him. From the duffel bag, Evan produced a couple of white zip ties. He tossed them to her.

"Put two together and use them for your wrists. I'll tighten it. I can't risk you running back to Roux, can I? You know too much."

Annja wasn't at all worried that she was putting herself in a dangerous situation. Evan she could deal with. But if he was headed out of the hotel, she wanted to make sure that happened. He would lead her to what she wanted to know and possibly even Garin. So she threaded a plastic strip through the small slot of the other, then formed a loop and put it around her wrists.

"I can break out of these at any time," she warned as Evan tugged the ties tightly without setting down the gun.

"I know. But you'll play nice so you can learn the location of the music box, right?"

He was not a stupid thief.

With no reply necessary, Annja settled back in the chair and watched as Evan got out a laptop and spent the next half hour clacking away at the keys. Emailing contacts? Prospective bidders? Both notions were likely, given the fast responses he seemed to be getting only moments after he appeared to hit the send button.

Was one of those responses from Garin, wanting

to retrieve what he probably felt should have been his to start with?.

Or could it be that Garin was unaware Evan had turned against him? The thugs had not been concerned with Evan at the bistro, which led her to believe Garin might be unaware of the dupe.

That man would not be happy when he finally met the frustratingly indomitable Evan Merrick.

23

Venice, 1502

"Thief!"

Roux stopped abruptly and cast his gaze about. There were but a few people lingering in the doorway to a linen shop, and down the way a cart wobbled, overstacked with hay. Boats floated by quietly on the canal.

From behind the cart, Leonardo da Vinci rushed forward to accuse him again. "You have stolen something from me!"

Roux scoffed at the man. He was embarrassed to have been caught out like this. "I've nothing that belongs to you."

"The sword piece. You were the only one I told."

"You've lost it? Pity."

"You dare to regard me as the fool?" Leonardo stepped up before him, preventing his exit. "But you didn't take the real prize. That makes you the fool!"

Da Vinci stormed off, cursing the heavens. Roux rubbed his bearded chin. He recalled but a few notebooks and the Lorraine cross in the safe kept in the graveyard. Also, there was that curious little box.

Was it the box or the cross the painter considered his most prized possession? Well, he could have them both. A simple cross could not change Roux's life.

But the section of Joan of Arc's sword? That was his future.

Evan parked his rental car in the city center. Annja got out of the car herself. Her hands were tied in front of her. And really? She was tired of faking it. Besides, she'd gotten where Evan was going, so she was happy with the situation.

Fisting her hands, she then brought her elbows forcefully down and toward her hips. The zip ties broke apart, freeing her hands with ease. The plastic strips dropped to the ground and she fell into step behind Evan, who had bolt cutters in hand.

Given where they were parked, Annja couldn't see much over the tall buildings surrounding the warehouse they seemed to be heading for. Though they had seen the Sforza palace upon approach. It was about half a mile to the north, she estimated. Walking distance for her. Had Evan pegged a possible location that Leonardo da Vinci had once lived?

The majority of the buildings in this neighborhood were utilitarian, no historic monuments around here. Shops offered goods and services that were less touristy and more about the essentials, such as a market, a pharmacy and a type of hardware store, and she could smell the fertilizer wafting from a nearby greenhouse.

It wasn't as if they had the neighborhood to themselves. People were out and seemed occupied with their daily routine. Annja glanced around curiously. Could this be the spot where da Vinci's studio once stood?

Evan flashed her a look from over his shoulder, then frowned. "Really?"

She held up her unbound hands. "You didn't think I'd wear them like a bracelet you'd gifted to a lover?"

"Kind of thought you would." He flicked her that killer wink. No wonder his partner in crime had ditched him. "We have potential, Creed. Think about it."

"Don't waste my time. What led you to think this is the site of Leonardo da Vinci's former studio?"

"The symbol drawn at the back of the notebook. It surrounded a diagram of the Sforza castle in the background."

He pointed over his shoulder. The towers of what had once been one of the biggest citadels in Europe were visible. The back of the castle arched out like a horseshoe, and they stood out from the arch. On the opposite side of the castle was the massive Parco Sempione. And somewhere, Annja knew, stood the Arch of Peace, built during Napoleonic rule. The emperor apparently had a thing for stone arches, she thought with a smirk.

"It is a guess," Evan offered. "But I think it's a good one."

She eyed the bolt cutters. "Let me guess. You were not the safe cracker in your former duo?"

"The woman had magic fingers."

"Don't need the details."

"As I said before, I was the plotter and the logistics man. She did the delicate finessing and entry."

"Too much information. So, we're breaking into this building? I have a problem with that. What is this place?"

"An old glasswork factory. And we're only cutting a loop in some chain link. Not officially breaking in. We'll replace the chain on our way out. And if you think I'm wrong about this place, then take a look behind you."

Annja swung around. She recognized the dark hair and rugged face of Garin Braden in the driver's seat of a black SUV. And stepping out of the passenger side and around the hood of the car?

"Roux?"

24

"You and Braden are playing on the same team now?" Annja asked as Roux and his cohort approached. "Interesting."

"Not half as interesting as seeing you with him," Garin said and stabbed a finger at the grinning Evan Merrick. "Long time no see, Creed."

"Not long enough," she replied. She angled a look at Roux. "Thought you two were on opposite sides of the coin with this one?"

"The old man knows when he's defeated," Garin said, stepping toward the building. He was dressed in a business suit, expensive, and brushed Annja's shoulder as he passed her. "We both want the same thing. And this one—" he gripped Evan by the throat "—has it."

Evan raised the hand with the bolt cutters. "The cross is in a safe place. You kill me, you lose any means to operate the device."

"You believe in time travel?" Garin asked the thief, who was trying his best not to shake. "Idiot." Snatching the bolt cutters away, he shoved Evan, sending him stumbling to the ground.

Propping the cutters over a shoulder, Garin turned to Annja. "You with us or against us?"

"I prefer to remain the interested bystander. I'm not taking sides. I'm not even sure who's on what side anymore. The artifacts must be—"

Garin swept away her perceived trivial morality with a gesture of his hand. "All in good time, Creed. Roux? You think this is the place?"

The Frenchman had been scanning the area with a hand to his brow to block the sun. He turned slowly, still assessing their location with an expertise Annja imagined had been fixed into his memory a very long time ago. She couldn't imagine the city resembled what he'd once seen then.

"It's possible," he finally said. "The castle was nearby. If memory serves, the distance seems correct. There was that little bread shop not far from Leonardo's studio front."

"Oh, yeah." Garin nodded, his smile growing. "I remember the wench selling sweet pastries out front— what was her name?"

Annja rolled her eyes. The man hadn't changed much in five hundred years. Garin Braden had been and apparently would always be a ladies' man. As well, he'd mastered questionable liaisons with certain shady characters who could increase his fortunes. He was a billionaire now, so he had plied his trade well. He had friends in high places, as well as the darkest, lowest niches a person could imagine. But on occasion his hard heart did seem to soften and his conscience would win out. Briefly. Rarely enough that

Annja knew not to trust him—ever. Except for when she absolutely needed to.

Now was not that time. The only one who held the upper hand was Evan, who had the Lorraine cross and the notebook. To play the devil's chord that would dance them back through time?

"The wench?" Evan muttered. He looked to Roux and winked.

Roux and Garin hadn't been careful with their secret, which was no accident on their part, Annja knew. Now Annja held even less hope of Evan coming out of this alive.

"Doesn't matter," she replied to Garin's search for the wench's name. "If we're doing this, let's get inside before someone starts being nosy."

Garin cut through the chain link and tested the steel door. It was locked, but a firm kick from his Italian loafers pushed the door inside. Out billowed a cloud of dust that he didn't even flinch at as he stepped over the threshold and into the cool shadows.

Evan hustled in after him. Roux gestured that Annja should go next.

"So you dumped me for him, eh?" she asked Roux as she paused in the doorway.

"I didn't dump you, Annja. I've been dealing with…" He cleared his throat, obviously unwilling to complain about his gambling troubles. "Garin spotted me with those fools and offered to help get rid of them once and for all."

"Once and for all? What do you— Wait. Never mind. I don't want to know."

Because she could guess it had to do with those
thugs that had come after Roux about the gambling
winnings. And "once and for all" could entail moving
bodies to places where no one would ever find them.

She stepped inside the building. "It's still every man
for himself, am I right?" she asked over her shoulder.

"As it should be. Have you a flashlight?" Roux
asked.

"Always."

She dug out the small Maglite from a cargo-pants
pocket and flashed it inside the big warehouse. It was
about two stories high and all open space. Crumbling
Sheetrock peeled away from the timber-framed walls.
The concrete floors were coated with dust and stray
two-by-fours. She couldn't determine if someone had
been trying to fix the place up or had been tearing it
down for a DIY project. Either way, no one had been
inside this building for months, possibly years.

Her flashlight beamed across Garin's broad back
as he ran his palm over a wall. Searching for what? If
he knew the place, would he know where Leonardo
had once kept things? Hid them? Surely the building
had been torn down and rebuilt many times since then.

"This is the place," Garin decided, rapping the wall
with his knuckles. "Roux?"

The elder man had crossed to the front of the building, where, from the inside, boards had been nailed
across a single-frame entry. He scanned along the wall,
stretching out his arms as if measuring history in his
memory.

"Likely."

"You think this is the original building?" Annja asked.

"Many structures from the fourteenth and fifteenth century have survived the years, Annja," Roux admonished. "They've been stripped to the original limestone walls and fixed up dozens of times surely, but the core remains the same."

"If this was Leonardo da Vinci's studio," Annja said as she strolled behind Evan, who searched high and low, "an inventory of his belongings was made after his death."

"Yes, but he died in France," Roux corrected. "If he had left anything behind here, it would be…" He glanced across the floor.

Garin had already begun pacing methodically, his tracks in the dust dragging a labyrinthine trail back and forth.

"It's not here," Evan announced.

Both Roux and Braden stopped abruptly and gave the thief their full attention. The tension was palpable. Annja had to remind herself to breathe. Why were they being so patient with Evan? Why not force him to produce the cross and be done with it? It wasn't Garin's style at all to play nice.

"But it was worth a look, eh?" Evan's expression said too much.

Garin knew it and finally exhibited the quick strength Annja knew he was capable of. He lunged for Evan, pinning him against the closest wall. Evan croaked, but in his favor, he maintained silence and eye contact with his attacker.

"You know where it is?" Garin asked.

"I have my suspicions."

"How can you?" Roux asked.

"He's got the notebook," Annja told them.

Both Garin and Roux looked at her and said, *"What?"*

"The notebook in which Leonardo da Vinci sketched the Lorraine cross and the music box," she said. As well as Roux's face, she thought. She wasn't sure he should know about that. But there was no keeping it from him. He'd see it eventually. "I need to see the notebook again, Evan. Where is it?"

"What are you talking about, Cree—" He blew out the last syllable in a huff as Garin's fist met his gut. "Chill out, man. I'm on your side."

"You haven't been on my side since you arrived in Milan," Garin said. "You think you can find the thing on your own and sell it to the highest bidder?"

Bent over to counteract the pain, Evan managed to squeak out, "That was the plan."

Garin gripped him by the hair and slammed his head back against the wall. Sheetrock dust billowed about them. Another slam.

Roux crossed his arms, observing calmly.

Annja frowned. Evan was the one with most of the pieces they needed to complete the puzzle. Did it make sense to abuse the guy this way?

"Yes, yes, you've made your point," she said as she stepped up beside Evan and put up an arm to block Garin's next punch, aimed at Evan's face. The impact of his fist into her palm was incredible, but she held firm and defied Garin with her most steadfast stare.

"Annja, I'll have the information we need in another few minutes. Step away."

She wedged herself between Garin and Evan. The thief hung his head on her shoulder, heavily. "He was staying at a hotel, but he's packed up and left. Everything he has is in the car we arrived in."

Roux strode toward the door through which they'd entered.

Garin growled—yes, actually growled—revealing the sneer she guessed he'd probably wielded in many a bloody medieval battle against the enemy. Right before he sliced off an opponent's head.

"Looks like you're taking sides after all, Creed," Garin muttered.

"Really? Because if you ask me, your opponent has the drop on you right now."

With another angry growl, Garin shoved off from Evan and slipped away through the open doorway.

Stumbling forward and resting his hands on his knees, Evan heaved in a few breaths. "Thanks, Annja. The next fist was going to end me for sure." He moved his jaw, testing it. Standing upright, he turned and assumed a bit of the suave persona he seemed to like so much. "Does that mean you're on my side?"

She punched him in the gut, bringing him to his knees. "Never."

25

Milan, 1488

Garin ordered two steins of beer. In appreciation, Leonardo slapped him across the back. The painter had seen him strolling through the street near his studio, looking over the sweet pastries offered from a baker next door, and had invited him into the tavern. So why was he paying for the drink?

Didn't matter. But the face in the notebook Leonardo da Vinci turned toward him right now did matter.

"Do you know this man?" Leonardo asked.

Garin made a show of looking over the simple sketch that captured Roux in exquisite detail yet with surprisingly few strokes. His pale hair, the few lines radiating out the corners of his eyes. Those eyes that were rarely kind, most often judging and usually set upon a task.

"Why?" Garin asked. "You must know him if you sketched him?"

"I sketch many people. Most, I never learn their names."

"You've written his name right here."

"Yes. Roux. A Frenchman. He is a scourge."

Garin smirked. *Got it on the first try.*

"No," Garin finally replied. "I've never seen this man. But he seems to have gotten you steamed."

"He is a thief!" The painter pounded the table, upsetting the beer. He grabbed his stein and drank for a long time.

"And what did he steal? Something of yours?"

"Something I valued immensely. I know it was him." Another fist to the table. "I showed it to him but days ago. How dare he? It has no value. It was but a shard of steel."

A shard of steel? Hmm, that sounded too familiar for Garin to merely brush it off. Roux had taken a bit of steel from the safe in the cemetery? So whatever else had been inside likely hadn't the same value to Leonardo. He shouldn't have allowed Roux to get away so easily. The more pieces he gathered...

"One man's treasure can be another man's curiosity," he said hastily. "I'm sorry about your loss. You had not locked it away?"

"In a safe! In a very unusual place, even. A graveyard."

"Odd place to keep one's treasures."

"But who would think to look among the bones and vultures, eh? He must have followed me. But oh, that he did not take the real treasure."

"The real treasure?" Maybe he had missed more than just the piece of sword.

"Indeed." Leonardo tilted back his beer and slammed

the tankard on the table with grandiose flair. "There was another item in the safe that the wily old thief did not touch. It's a project I've been working on. Something of great scientific importance."

"I'm not much for science," Garin said, baiting the man. "Some sort of contraption for determining the position of the stars, I suppose?"

"An astrolabe? No, that's already been invented. I don't design the common, Signore Braden. I create the future."

"Is that so?"

"Or rather, in this instance, I may have created a portal to the future. Or the past. Whichever a man prefers. What would you do if you could switch places in time with another man? In what time would you choose to visit?"

"Uh, er..."

What an entirely unexpected conversation. And it wasn't at all interesting to Garin, until he started wondering if Roux might be interested. And he suspected he may be. Why hadn't he taken the thing from the safe? He knew they should have taken the entire contents.

But that only proved Roux hadn't a clue what the thing was they'd left behind. Nor did he, actually. There was something to move a man back and forth through time? It sounded dangerous and impossible.

"I don't know," Garin said. "What that has come before us in time would prove of interest to you, maestro?"

"Oh, I've no desire to move into the past." Leonardo settled on the tavern bench now, lifting a leg and propping an elbow on it, as if in thought, but his focus remained on Garin. "I've been trying to convince a friend to give it a test, but he refuses."

"Your young friend I've seen accompanying you?"

"Yes, he's quite a marvelous painter. Daring and adventurous, as well. He was right there to help me test my flying apparatus. But this new device? It frightens the boy."

"It is the unknown. What man would not be frightened by that?"

"Really?" Leonardo tapped the table and leaned forward. "Signore Braden, you strike me as a man who would take a risk into the unknown."

"The future may offer great wonders. But stepping back in time? No. How does one traverse through time?"

"Oh, it's all about resonance. And—" da Vinci cast a glance around the tavern, then pressed in close so only Garin could hear "—the devil's chord." He sat back, a grin of satisfaction curling his mouth.

Garin had heard of the musical chord that had been banned by the church. Although he hadn't *heard* it.

The devil and music?

It could be possible. He wasn't much for lutes and harpsichords. At one time he'd found himself in a woman's boudoir and she'd insisted on bringing in musicians to accompany their amorous liaisons. The devil indeed.

Yet the only devil he believed in was the one who might end his fun. And that man wore long white hair, an arrogant demeanor and could match Garin in a sword fight, stroke for stroke, and never tire.

"One doesn't so much physically move through time as rather—" Leonardo spread his hands before him as if to part a fabric curtain "—peer through the veil into another time that is occurring simultaneously as the present."

"So you're saying all time is cyclical?"

"I think more that it is all occurring at once."

The man had lost him, and he wasn't drunk enough to start to figure out any of this nonsense.

"I've used the tritone banned by the church, you see," Leonardo continued. "It exudes magnificent resonance." He closed his eyes and smiled as if savoring a sweet wine. When he opened them and looked about again to see that no one was too close to overhear their conversation, he again pressed across the table. "You seem a man open to the possibility of what's out there, Signore Braden."

Of course he was. He was a soldier, a man of the world, after all. But that didn't imply he could buy into a man traversing into another time. Yet. "You could say that."

"There was once a great man, René d'Anjou, who devoted his life to spreading knowledge. To providing the common man with the ability to learn."

"I knew him," Garin supplied. He'd kept tabs on the man over the decades. Exhausting to consider all he had done in his lifetime.

"Ah! Then we are connected in so many ways. Tell me, did Good King René ever discuss with you the possibility to peer backward through time, to perhaps alter events?"

"Never. I had always thought him a forward-thinking man, actually. What man needs to go back in time? To change history? That doesn't feel right to me. Would not stepping back through time alter your existence now? What if I were to kill the man who was to one day be my very father?"

Leonardo dismissed the comment. "You think on this too much. It's not so complicated as that. I've said you've only the ability to peer into the past. I'm not sure you could actually function within a time frame that is not your own."

And if Garin had the chance to change the one event that had altered his world remarkably, he'd turn it down. It had taken the life of a brave woman, but it had given him an exquisite gift to go on living, somehow.

"Have you heard of the Ordine della Luna Crescente, Signore Braden?"

"I have. The Order of the Crescent is a chivalrous order. Isn't that one of René d'Anjou's projects? They revere the Virgin Mother, yes? Are you recruiting, then?"

"It lapsed after René's death. There is still so much to talk about. Shall we?"

Garin toasted his compatriot with his tankard. "To you, sir! And to the future! And to tending the past with great care, yes?"

"Indeed."

26

Roux leaned on the trunk of Evan Merrick's rental, paging through the notebook as if it were a car-repair manual, and did it really matter if he smudged the ancient pages or even tore them?

Annja's backpack was in the car. Evan had tossed it in there. She drew out the latex gloves and tossed them to Roux. "Please?"

He put them on.

As well, she grabbed the jacket she'd seen in the backseat and laid it across the trunk.

"Have some consideration," she said, directing Roux to lay the precious object on the jacket. It was probably too late to care, but— No, she never stopped caring about the proper handling of artifacts. "I suppose you saw the portrait?"

"What portrait?" Roux asked. He was approximately halfway through the notebook.

Annja decided to wait and see what his reaction would be. He continued to slowly leaf through the pages.

Garin had joined them, peering over Roux's shoulder, ignoring the old man's protests to step back and give him some room.

"Where was this found?" Garin asked Annja.

Evan, who lingered near the driver-side door, popped up to answer, "Picked it up a year ago while visiting some friends at their castle."

Garin's head tilted, as if reassessing the man, and ended with a proud smile. He actually nodded, confirming his approval of Evan's theft.

"Ah," Roux muttered. He must have found the page with his image. Annja noted he was studying it carefully. To have had Leonardo da Vinci capture your likeness must have been an honor. Although, she suspected the vicious label must mar said honor.

"First time you've seen that?" she whispered, aware Evan stood but six or seven feet away from them.

"No. The man gave me a glimpse as he was sketching it," Roux said.

"Apparently he didn't have a very high opinion of you. Care to explain?"

He tapped the word *ladro.* His eyebrows furrowed. "It's ancient history, Annja."

"Right," Garin said. "You've already claimed the sword. Doesn't matter what some slapdash painter once thought of you."

"I'm not following," Annja interjected.

"Sword?" Evan stared at the three of them standing at the car. Annja could almost see the dollar signs flash in his eyes like some children's cartoon. "What kind of sword are we talking about?"

"None of your business," both Garin and Roux said.

"Have you seen the sketch of the *thief?*" Evan asked. "Explain that one, Roux."

"Me, explain something I've just now seen? How do I know you haven't altered this notebook in some way?" Roux spat.

Good one, Annja thought.

"Please." Evan wagged a finger in their direction. "I may be a thief, but I do know how to respect the artifact."

"Pretty funny, if you ask me, isn't it, Roux?" Garin said, tapping the sketch where it said *thief.* "You were so insistent we were not thieves."

"I don't remember the things I did so long ago," Roux muttered and turned the page.

But he had remembered his conversation with Leonardo, and he seemed to have known the neighborhood where the painter's studio had once been. Selective memory, Annja decided. Whatever it was he'd stolen from Leonardo must have been valuable for the painter to so angrily have placed the accusation on paper for the entire world to see.

At least, the world would see it now once she presented the notebook to the proper authorities. They should have some idea from where it had originally been stolen. Possibly. Though if no one had been aware of this notebook, then it wasn't likely to be claimed.

"And what were those things you did so long ago?" Evan moved closer to them.

Ignoring the man's question, Roux tapped his finger on another page. The one that had the diagram of the music box. Garin whistled and leaned in. "I've seen that before."

"You have?" Now Evan was intensely interested and rushed forward. "Where? Why are we searching here for it if you've already seen it elsewhere?"

"Why are you still here, Merrick?" Garin barked. "You're off the job."

"I was done working for you the moment you sent your thugs after me at the bistro. You know, they went after Annja instead."

Garin cast Annja a discerning glance. "She looks no worse for the trouble."

"You going to take that from him, Annja?" Evan asked. "Why don't you team up with me? I've got the cross—"

Annja faced Evan and grabbed him roughly by the collar. Both Roux and Garin gave her their attention.

"How about you hand over the cross and I won't let Garin finish the job he started earlier?" she said to him.

Garin whistled and shook his head. "You should heed that warning, Merrick."

Evan pushed Annja away, but she wasn't done with him. She'd had enough of his underhanded pranks. And while she didn't believe either Roux or Garin knew where the music box was, she'd trusted either of them before she'd trust this opportunistic jerk any day.

"How much are you selling the cross for?" she asked.

"You haven't got the purse for it," he challenged.

"Probably not. But they do."

"I'm not paying that man a dime," Roux said, his attention back on the notebook.

"What? Are you going to steal it and travel through time to hide it away from me?" Evan taunted.

"Let Garin work him over," Roux said. "He'll get the cross out of him one way or another."

And for once, Annja agreed with the suggestion. She shoved Evan toward the towering Garin Braden, who caught Evan by the throat.

"Back inside," Garin muttered. He dragged Evan, struggling and swearing, inside the warehouse.

"Doesn't it bother you at all that you were just giving Merrick fodder for his beliefs that you've traveled through time?"

"Annja, please. Time travel?"

She was about to counter with the fact that he was the one who had begun this bizarre quest, but she was too stymied by this sudden reversal to make a sound.

"They'll think Merrick is unbalanced. And we've got the notebook now, so…no evidence."

"Doesn't matter if we secure the cross," Annja said, joining Roux to preen over the notebook. "If neither of you have a clue where the music box is, then we're at a dead end."

Roux flipped back to the first page that detailed the Lorraine cross. He turned the notebook sideways and ran his fingers along the bottom edge of the sketch, where the lowermost bar of the cross had been done with elaborate scrollwork.

"Tell me what you see there?" he asked.

Annja traced her finger lightly over the arabesques

and quickly realized they were not random curls but letters and… "Numbers?"

"Longitude and latitude. Or so I suspect. You have a GPS on your phone?"

She dug out her cell phone and opened an app that allowed her to enter longitude and latitude to bring up a map location. Roux read off a series of numbers and she typed them in. When the related map came up, she announced the location. "Rouen. France."

They exchanged looks and Annja did not miss the heavy swallow the old man took. Rouen was a particularly memory-laden place for him.

"It can't be," she said. "It most likely links the cross to the city of…" Well, that wasn't right. The city of origin would have been Lorraine, which was east of Rouen.

"Maybe René d'Anjou had the music box?"

"The man was dead when it was already in Leonardo's possession," Roux confirmed. "Where did da Vinci die?"

Annja sorted through her knowledge of the painter. "Clos Lucé, uh…Amboise. In central France. I'm not sure if it was his principal residence. I think…a man named Melzi was the heir and executor of his estate."

Switching from the map app to the browser on her phone, Annja typed in the name. "You knew him?" she decided to ask Roux while waiting for the information to appear on the screen.

"No. Unfortunately not."

"He inherited Leonardo's artistic and scientific works, along with manuscripts and other artifacts."

"I would assume the music box would be another artifact."

"Likely." She scanned the information on Melzi. "His estate is about thirty kilometers northeast of here."

"Then I believe a ride in the countryside is in order."

At that moment Garin strolled out of the warehouse rubbing his knuckles. He rolled his shirtsleeves down and proceeded calmly toward Evan's parked vehicle. "It's in the glove compartment."

"What?"

"What we've been looking for," Braden reiterated. *"The glove compartment."*

Annja ran around the side of the car and opened the passenger door. The glove compartment was locked. "It couldn't have been," she muttered. It couldn't have been right in front of her the whole time she'd been in the car with Evan?

"I need something to pick this lock," she called out.

"Move," Garin said, and he tugged her out of the way.

The former elite soldier was brandishing a crowbar he must have spotted in the warehouse. He pried at the glove compartment and it quickly fell open. He reached in and pulled out the Lorraine cross. Tucking it inside his suit coat, he then strolled toward the SUV he and Roux had arrived in, without a word to either of them.

"You don't know where you're going!" Annja called out to him.

Roux collected the notebook and trailed after her

toward the SUV. Garin was already revving the engine before they both managed to climb inside the vehicle.

"I'd say I'm happy to have you two along," Garin remarked, "but that would be a lie. Where are we going, old man?"

Roux sighed and shook his head.

"Vaprio d'Adda. Northeast," Annja directed.

27

In an hour the Villa Melzi would be closed to the public. The site was on the shoreline of Lake Como's turquoise waters. Annja had joined a guided tour of the grounds and a small museum that offered visitors architectural features and various sculptures.

While she enjoyed the tour, the men had decided to walk through the gardens, which she didn't want to miss, either.

The gardens were an explosion of color, and dozens of tourists lingered, snapping photos. The boardwalk on the shores of Lake Como led to Bellagio, and some tourists headed off in that direction. Annja didn't spy Roux or Garin and suspected she'd find them digging around in some obscure spot far from prying eyes. Or at least, she hoped.

As the tour group was led to the exit, she remained behind a marble column. She'd taken the time to scan along walls and floors and look for hidden doors seamlessly incorporated into walls, but she found no hint or trace of anything out of the ordinary. If she were to find a hiding spot for lost, ancient treasures, it would be somewhere else and not featured on the tour.

"This couldn't possibly be the place," she muttered and went in search of Roux and Garin.

Annja was growing frustrated. What if the music box wasn't anywhere nearby? The da Vinci collection had surely been scattered across the world.

At the end of a path, she spied Roux's white ponytail. He saw her and gestured eagerly, so she picked up the pace. It was past closing time now, but some people were still in the gardens, probably allowed to be there until sunset.

When Annja reached Roux's side, he did not slow down as he said, "We've located the spot where the music box might be."

"How can you be sure?"

"We won't be until we check, Annja. There's property next door that has a château that fits the timeline. Trust me."

"Stranger and stranger," she said and followed Roux, who had just stepped toward a thick hedgerow. Annja thought he was going to walk right through it, but he angled sharply to the right, then went down ten paces and turned left, disappearing into the green shrubbery.

She stared after him, finding that someone other than Roux had pushed their way through the hornbeam hedge. She had to squeeze into the tight space, holding aside the branches to get to the other side of the three-foot-wide block of foliage.

Once she was there, she stood before a small limestone manor home sporting boarded windows and overgrown vines snaking along the walls. The lawn was neatly trimmed, so someone apparently cared for the grounds, yet she guessed the place was unoccupied.

The house was indicative of a fifteenth-century château, a quiet country residence, stately, noble and likely very expensive. Who owned this estate, she wondered?

Roux obliged her with an answer. "Braden thinks this place is mentioned in the notebook."

The urge for discovery never stopped Annja from speculating and trying to put together the pieces of any puzzle and she did so now as they approached the house. The idea of using the front door was out of the question. And this side of the house could possibly be seen from the main road, though she suspected the hedges blocked all but a view of the tiled rooftop.

At the back of the manor was another door, open. The gate that had been screwed into the limestone wall had been forcibly removed and tossed aside with little regard. Garin's work, Annja assumed.

Shaking her head at the man's blatant ways, she stepped into the estate's cool darkness. Inside was a small room she assumed had once been the mudroom or storage area. The walls were bare and the stone floors littered with decades of dust and debris. An old pipe jutted up from the floor, but had been broken off around the eight-inch mark. The place must have been retrofitted with plumbing in the early twentieth century, as many of these old manor homes had done.

Shoeprints led through to another small room, and

still another after that to a vast area that could have been either a ballroom or receiving foyer. Annja brushed her hiking boot over the floor and saw hardwood beneath the dust. Couldn't be the original. On the other hand, it was possible. Not all estates of the time period had marble floors.

Roux entered and his gaze seemed to take in everything from floor to ceiling.

The heavy thud of what sounded like a man jumping up and down drew Annja's attention to another doorway. It was another receiving room, she guessed, and she made for the next room. The light in every room was dim. The sun hugged the horizon outside. They wouldn't have more than another fifteen or twenty minutes before flashlights were necessary.

Garin let out a yelp. A spectacular crash had Annja rushing into an adjoining room. A billow of dust subsided to reveal a new hole in the floor where the boards had broken and fallen into whatever lay beneath.

Annja crept up to the hole, cautious that she might go down, as well. Giving the broken boards a few test pushes with her foot, she then leaned over the gap. She couldn't see anything below, but she could hear a man groaning.

"I'm good!" Garin called up, but the voice sounded less than sure of that.

"Leave it to that bloke to fall into a hole where there isn't even a hole," Roux muttered as he walked up to Annja. "What's down there?" he called into the dark chasm.

After a few seconds, a dim light cast about from

below. Garin must be using a cell-phone light because it was too small and didn't beam far enough to be a flashlight.

"A chest and some rocks."

"A chest?" Annja called back. "Like a storage chest? Old furniture?"

"A traveling chest. Ladders. A broken table. And stacks of limestone. It's roomy down here. It'll fit another couple people."

"Ladies first," Roux offered.

Judging the drop to be about ten feet, Annja sat on the edge of the floorboards and pushed off, landing in a roll that brought her shoulders up against a stack of limestone that wobbled with the impact.

Garin grabbed her hand and drew her away just as the stones tumbled and crashed on top of the chest.

"Good one, Creed," he mocked. "You may have just destroyed the prize."

"Thanks for all your help. Nice catch, buddy."

"Really? Annja, you're a big girl. But if you'd wanted me to catch you, you should have said so."

She grimaced and slapped her cargo pants to get rid of some of the dust. Unbuttoning a pocket on her thigh, she drew out the Maglite and flashed it around.

Roux bent his head down through the hole. "Anything?"

"Yes, I'm fine," Annja said. "Thanks for the concern. You're not coming down?"

"Someone has to pull you up."

"Good thinking."

Garin pulled off a limestone block from the top

of the chest. It landed heavily on the dirty floor. The blocks looked as though they'd be used for a wall or even a walkway. The property seemed extensive and there were likely paths leading to all points.

Garin shrugged off his suit coat and tossed it onto the broken table. "Keep the spotlight on the stones."

She did so, and he shifted a few more away from the chest. The top of the chest had been crushed, and one side, as well. When it was cleared of the stones, Annja kneeled before it and tried the lid. The old bronze lock had been broken in the crash and the chest opened easily.

"Let me," Garin said. Annja made room for Garin to kneel next to her.

What must have once been fabric sifted to dust as Garin held up a candlestick. He set it on the ground carefully.

He lifted a mass of the decayed fabric, and even as it fell apart in his hands, he managed to place the bulk of it next to the candlestick. A wooden box followed, and Garin smiled from ear to ear. He handed it to her to open. Inside were a few silver coins. French deniers. Annja recognized the principal coinage from the medieval ages.

"We'll have to trace who the owners are of the contents of this chest," she remarked.

"Uh-huh." Garin put the box down without further consideration. "But this—" he reached in with both hands and picked up the next item "—is finders, keepers."

The sketch drawn by Leonardo could not have detailed the item more accurately. In Garin's hands was the music box that Annja had initially remarked possessed a certain steampunklike design.

A time-shifting device? She'd curb her skepticism for now. She'd been burned many times before for not believing.

"You got it?" Roux asked from above. As he shifted positions, more dust fell like rain.

"Yes," Annja answered, elated with the find. Finally, the pieces of this puzzle were coming together.

"Pass it up. Then it's your turn."

28

Garin tossed the music box up to Roux. The old man caught it with ease.

"Careful!" Annja exclaimed.

"Yes, yes," Roux muttered.

Annja dug around inside the chest for further treasures. She cleared away the rest of the tattered fabric from a few books, none of them notebooks similar to the one attributed to Leonardo. One was actually a shipping log. It would take patience and better light to decipher the tiny script, though.

A few more loose coins sat at the bottom of the trunk. *They must have fallen out of the box.* If she had a camera along, she'd snap a shot and make a note of the findings to report to the appropriate agency. But circumstances being what they were, she made a mental list of the contents.

"Roux!" Garin called. "I'll toss Annja up and you grab her hand."

"Toss me?" She snorted. "I don't think so."

"You know what I mean. I'll give you a leg up."

Garin clasped his hands together and bent to show her that he'd give her a boost.

"What about one of those ladders?"

"Annja, don't be ridiculous. They're ancient—they'd never hold any weight."

"Fine."

She and Garin waited for Roux to come into view above and show that he was ready for Annja, but no helping hand appeared. Annja probably didn't require a hand up, but it would make things easier.

"Where is that old man?" Garin asked, clearly irritated.

"Roux?" Annja called.

They both listened. Nothing.

"You think he left?" she asked.

"Of course he did. I didn't see that one coming, or rather, I should have anticipated it. The wily coot. He's probably halfway back to the car right now. Come on. Step up onto my hands. We'll get you out of here."

"Then how will you get out?"

"I'll jump."

Annja nodded. Stepping onto Garin's hands, she then straightened her body and arrowed her arms over her head to make as narrow a form as she could. The target above seemed so small now.

"Ready?"

"Go!" she said.

Bending her knees as Garin lowered his hands, she straightened with the lift, and the boost he gave her sent her soaring just high enough to grip the opening and pull herself up and partly onto the floor. Kicking furiously, she launched herself forward to drag herself completely away from the hole. She coughed and sneezed violently from being so close to the dusty ground.

Garin's hands immediately slapped the rough, broken edges of the floorboards. Wood creaked and he cursed, dropping back down into the depths. Annja coughed from the plume of dust and dirt that rose in his crashing wake.

"I'm going to need a wider opening!" he hollered.

"Will do!"

Setting to work, Annja tore away more of the busted floor. It gave easily and she was thankful. She hauled a few boards to the side of the room and could hear a chuckle from below.

"Just be thankful I don't leave you down there," she muttered.

"I'd find a way out and then hunt you down."

"I know! Such a joy having you as a friend."

Garin popped up through the opening in the floor, his arms reaching, and she helped drag him forward until he was able to roll onto his back. "A friend, eh?"

"Well…for today, anyway." She waited for him to get to his feet and catch his breath.

"I know where the old man is headed."

"Where's that?"

"Rouen."

Annja was not surprised. Rouen was the town the coordinates on the drawing had indicated. Rouen was the town in France where the English had burned Joan of Arc at the stake. And now with a time-shifting device in hand, apparently Roux had some history he felt compelled to adjust.

And hadn't Evan mentioned Rouen to her earlier? She felt certain he had. If only she'd paid more attention… "Let's go," she said. "Maybe we'll be able catch up with Roux at the airport."

"If we're lucky," he said. "If we're lucky."

As they headed away from Lake Como, Annja recalled something Roux had said to her a day or two earlier. *I don't want to share it.* Meaning, he didn't want to include anyone else in whatever was found, even Garin.

Should she be worried about Roux? About the music box? She should have thought twice before tossing the artifact into Roux's clutches.

Chastising herself wouldn't change things, though.

"How can we be sure Roux is headed toward Malpensa?" Annja asked as they drove the A8 toward the airport. The road, lined sporadically with tall trees, power lines and businesses, reminded her of a standard Midwestern freeway back in the States. Malpensa was the largest of three airports that served Milan.

"We can't. But does it matter? We've got to take the quickest route to try to catch him. We're just following at the moment."

"You don't strike me as a follower, Garin."

He smiled and flashed her a look, his attention veering briefly from the road.

"So I seem to be on your team now?"

"You're never on anyone's team, Annja. Except maybe that of the tired and poor. The huddled masses—"

"I think you've spent too much time at the Statue of Liberty lately. I just like to do what's right, when I can. And where a possible artifact such as this is concerned?"

"I'll get the box back, Annja. I'm not going to let Roux get away with this one."

A surprising act of selflessness. But Annja wouldn't for one second buy that Garin didn't have his own plans for the device.

"How long have you known about Roux's quest for this artifact? Do you believe in time travel?"

"It's a time shifter, Annja."

"So I've been told. Numerous times. Huge difference from time traveling, I'm sure. Really? Why would you want to go back in time?"

"I don't. And I don't believe the thing works. But on the off chance that it does? It's in the possession of the one man who could change history, Annja. I've known about his search since the day he met Scout Roberts, or Evan Merrick, or whoever he is. I keep tabs, you know."

"You both do. It disturbs me, and then it doesn't."

"Yes, well, keeping tabs has been a lifesaver on more than a few occasions. This time? It could mean preventing a catastrophic change to history as we know it."

"Such dramatics. Cue the ominous movie score."

Garin frowned.

A shrug was the only appropriate response.

"With Roux headed to Rouen," Garin said, "you know what that means."

The landscape rushed by as Annja nodded and tapped the window. Did Roux believe he could stop Joan's execution? Did he not understand the consequences if he actually managed it? He didn't strike her as a man who was overly concerned with the nuances of things. And it must have been a horrid experience for him to have witnessed a person who was so special to him be burned at the stake. But to go back and change the course of everything that had happened afterward was mind-boggling.

Annja dismissed all of it; she knew what she believed. The notion of changing history was absurd. The same was true of time travel. At least the way they were considering it now.

She had to concede to time traveling a lot in the sense that when she was on a dig site, she would sit back and wonder about the origins of a mysterious skeleton or object she'd uncovered. What and who had that person been in his or her lifetime? A peasant? Merchant? King or queen?

"It is possible," she felt the urge to say. "But only through history and science and the knowledge we gain by studying the past."

"Works for me," Garin said. He shifted gears and turned into the Milan Malpensa Airport terminal.

Annja used her phone and went online to check the schedule of outgoing flights.

The only flight to France had left ten minutes before they got to the airport. *Bad timing.* But Garin showed no signs of worry as he drove beyond the main parking lot, toward a smaller terminal where private jets waited. Of course the man would never fly with others, not even first-class.

"Roux didn't take a private jet here?" she wondered.

"I don't know. Not on our team, remember?"

"I'm not really on your team, Garin."

"You don't have to remind me. But just know, I'm the one you should be cheering for this time."

Annja would reserve judgment on that. For the time being, she would stick with Garin because he knew Roux better than she did, and he had the insights to the music box and cross that could be their only advantage.

She thought back to where they had left Evan in the warehouse in Milan. Garin had taken the Lorraine cross and still had it now. Meanwhile, Roux had the notebook. And now Roux also had the music box. Without a piece on the board, would Evan now leave the game?

"Let me see the cross," Annja asked.

Garin reached into his suit coat and then slapped the outside pockets. He swore.

"Don't even tell me," she said. "Sitting at the bottom of a hole on some Sheetrock?"

"I don't think so. That old coot! We argued in the gardens."

"What's new?"

"He shoved me. I shoved back. We had a tussle. I think he stole it from me."

"You'd better hope so. Otherwise we should go back to Lake Como right now."

"He's got it," Garin decided and punctuated his anger with a growl.

29

Roux disembarked from the domestic flight, which he had chosen specifically because Garin Braden would be trying to follow him. He'd only had a ten-minute head start, so he expected Braden to catch up. But by then, Roux wanted to have figured out the time-shifting device.

As he was looking for the exit, a fellow passenger bumped into him, but quickly apologized.

"Désolé," the man offered and straightened Roux's jacket in an attempt to make nice.

Roux walked on, clutching the brown paper bag to his chest. The bag had been the quickest and easiest solution he could find to hold, if not hide, the music box and notebook.

And inside his pocket he had the cross that Garin hadn't been the wiser—

"No!"

Roux spun around, trying to catch sight of the man who had bumped into him. He'd worn dark clothing, but Roux hadn't paid much attention to his face. A good distance away, leading to the parking lot, he saw someone run through the sliding glass doors.

"Stop!" Roux's shout served its purpose. The first face to turn toward him was the man running outside. Blond hair, square jaw and a glint at his ear that must be an earring.

Roux raced down the carpeted aisle, doing his best to dodge other travelers. Had Garin sent someone ahead to trouble him until Garin himself could get here? But why not also take the two artifacts—the music box and notebook? If not Garin, then Evan? He wouldn't have known Roux was in possession of both artifacts....

"Should have ended that man when we had the chance," he muttered, rushing through the open doors leading to the parking lot. He looked left and right.

The blond man hopped into the passenger side of a waiting dark blue sports car and it peeled away from the curb. Roux dashed toward the row of cabs, eyed a limo that was idling and its driver helping a customer with her bag.

No time for explanations.

Roux pulled open the driver's door and slid behind the wheel, tossing the brown paper bag onto the seat next to him. The aggravated driver volleyed French curses at him as he sped away.

Roux shifted into gear and negotiated the labyrinth of vehicles ahead of him. He'd lost sight of the sports car, but it wouldn't be headed out of town, so he veered onto the exit toward town.

The city of Rouen had changed, and it hadn't. A

man could still navigate merely by knowing the location of the Seine, which was to his right.

And ahead, he spied the navy blue sports car.

SEATED IN A COMFY leather chair in the airport's private lounge, outfitted with gourmet food and cocktails—she was surprised there were no sexy women to serve Garin's every need—Annja dug out her laptop. She was pleased to have a Wi-Fi connection.

She'd been in Rouen on a few occasions. One particular time a nasty professor with a Charlemagne complex had been trying to steal her sword for his collection. He'd sought twelve swords to complete his plans to rule the world and had employed some deadly minions who hadn't a care for human life to achieve his goal. Ultimately, though, cancer had beat him to world domination.

As the keep of Joan's sword, she shouldn't be surprised that her adventures would bring her back to the city over and over. Though it was not Joan of Arc's birthplace—that was Domrémy—Rouen was steeped with the martyr's memory, perhaps even her spirit.

"We're headed for the Place du Vieux-Marché?" she asked Garin. It was the site of Joan of Arc's pyre. A monument had been struck in her honor.

He nodded. "The Lorraine cross did have *Rouen* inscribed on it, yes?"

"Yes. And the coordinates are also for Rouen. Did you have an opportunity to look it over, uh, now or a few centuries ago?"

"Leonardo showed it to me, and I remember not

being terribly impressed with it. Simple crosses that people wore around their necks or carried in a pocket were so common."

She glanced around the lounge. It seemed unusually quiet. And Garin seemed to be in an oddly reflective mood. Maybe he was tired. Now that she thought of it, she was tired, too. She should try to catch a few winks before they got to Rouen. But she wanted to check the central square, where they guessed Roux would go, and familiarize herself with all the surrounding streets. Though she'd been there before, the layout may have changed.

At one end of the square stood the Joan of Arc church. It was beautiful. Annja had been inside it a few times. She could spend a lot of time losing herself in the architecture. Of any church, actually.

"Did Roux mention why Leonardo da Vinci had labeled him a thief in the notebook, Annja?"

"No. Will you tell me?"

Garin shrugged.

"Give me a clue, then. Has it anything to do with the Lorraine cross?"

"No. Actually, Leonardo once owned a piece of Joan's sword."

Her gaze met Garin's brown eyes and her heartbeat spiked. Annja knew Roux had traversed the world to track down every piece of Joan's sword, until he'd been drawn to the very last piece—and Annja—by destiny.

"Oh…" She paused, unsure what could be said.

She knew the story after that. Roux had gathered the sword pieces, yet nothing had happened. Until she had looked it over and suddenly she'd held Joan's sword in her hand. And now it was hers, claimed only by her, called from the otherwhere to serve her bidding when she should need it.

Incredible.

"Just thought you'd like to know," Garin said. He tilted his head back against the seat and closed his eyes.

Annja let her fingers fall slack on the keyboard. It was weird how the tidbits of history she gained from Garin or Roux directly correlated with her life. It never ceased to amaze her.

Glancing across the room, she saw Garin snoring. The man had his hands folded on his chest, and his feet up on the chair opposite where he sat. While thoroughly modern in every way, she could easily imagine him outfitted in armor and wielding a sword or halberd while riding siege on an enemy's castle. He had that noble warrior appeal.

Not that he appealed to her, personally. But she could understand why it was easy for him to attract a lot of women. Add to that the private jet and a billionaire's bank account.

"The centuries have been good to you," she muttered.

Powering off the laptop, Annja slid it onto the chair next to hers, then reclined in her seat and closed her eyes. She might not sleep now, for remarkable memories kept her adrenaline racing.

THE BLONDE MAN from the airport had eluded Roux, even though he'd briefly caught up to him while entering the city. He'd lost him in a traffic jam detouring around construction on the Pont Mathilde near the river.

So instead of driving aimlessly in a random search, Roux headed to the one place he expected the Lorraine cross to show up. If Evan Merrick had any clue about how to operate the time-shifting device, he would arrive in the Place du Vieux-Marché.

Forgoing a more predictable watch point in the central square, Roux strode along the rooftop of a building that boasted cafés and clothing shops on the ground floor and apartments from the first to fifth floors. He marked the best angle to view entrance to the square from any street below.

From his position he had a direct view of the statue of Joan of Arc designed by Maxime Real del Sarte. It stood in a corner outside of the Church of Saint Joan of Arc. Put there in 1926, the simple stone statue depicted Joan praying, her eyes cast toward heaven as flames whipped up around her long skirts. Bright red flowers had been planted around the statue, but from this distance they appeared but a blur, almost flamelike.

Roux looked away.

Satisfied with this spot to watch the square, Roux sat and pulled the music box out from the paper bag. Running his thumb over the carved wood and bronze fixings, he closed his eyes and whispered a prayer that he had not uttered since the fifteenth century.

30

Annja answered her cell phone as she strode the short runway toward the waiting limo without plates. The driver nodded to Garin and opened the back door for him. She went to the other side and opened the door herself.

"Creed, I wasn't sure you'd answer my call."

"Evan, where are you?"

"I'm probably in the same city as you right now. And yes, thank you for the concern. The cross is safely with me."

"Really?" Last she'd known, Roux had lifted it from Garin.

"The universe has a way of ensuring things end up where they belong," Annja said. "Ever pause to think that maybe you were not meant to have the Lorraine cross?"

"Bravo! But since it keeps bouncing back into my hands, I'm going to choose to believe the universe actually wants me to have it. So, did you find the box?"

"Box? What box?"

"Yeah, that's not going to work. I know you went

to Villa Melzi. Good call. I wouldn't have tracked it next door."

"You want to make a trade?" Now that they were inside the limo, Garin asked if it was Evan. She nodded.

"Trade? What good is the key without the box? What if I split the profits with you?"

"Fifty-fifty?"

"Seventy-thirty. The sale of the authenticated items will bring in millions, Creed. You'll never have to work on that stupid TV show again."

"I rather enjoy hosting *Chasing History's Monsters*. Only sometimes I end up chasing real-life monsters like you that spoil my day."

"Hey, like I've said, we could have made a great team."

"Where are you, Evan?"

"At the market, in the central square. Bring the music box."

The line went dead, and Annja stuffed the phone into a pocket.

"Where is the rat?" Garin asked.

"The center of town," she said to the driver. The car pulled away from the private terminal. "Evan thinks he's a lot smarter than he is."

"He has managed to hang in the game this long. And find his way here with very little information to go on."

"You forget he had the notebook."

"Yes, but to decipher the clues Leonardo put in there?"

"So you're giving Evan Merrick points now?"

"Never." Garin reached beneath the seat for a slim case and placed it on his lap. He opened it, took out the 9-mm Glock and checked the magazine, then inserted it into the pistol. "Let's go catch us a rat."

THEY STOPPED IN the market square in front of the Church of Saint Joan of Arc. This late at night, there weren't a lot of people around. When Annja had looked at the square on a satellite map, she was startled to find such modern architecture plunked down in the middle of a relatively historic neighborhood. The church and the adjoining parish when viewed from above were positively alien in nature, but gorgeous in their own right.

The park nearby featured a path through areas shaded by massive canopied trees. The nooks offered privacy, even from the cafés directly across the street. Many still had lights on even though they had closed hours earlier.

An eerie solemnity thickened the air. But instead of making her feel calm, the mood prickled the back of her neck.

Walking around the church, she and Garin sought the corner where Joan of Arc's effigy had been preserved in stone behind glass.

Annja had been here before and had seen the beautiful sculpture of the saint—during daylight—so she gasped now when spying it this time. Low spotlights positioned on the ground beamed up through bright red tulips planted around the base of the statue.

Garin sucked in a breath. The image had to be even more dramatic for him.

He turned his back to the statue and scanned about the market square. Chairs and tables were set up before a fountain, which was also lit in the dark hours. A couple sat at one of the tables chatting. But for the most part, the square was quiet, save the occasional taxi rolling by on the Rue de Crosne. Traffic from the nearby river was minimal, but the *schush* of the Seine's waters and the scent lingered even here, blocks away.

Garin strode a few feet away from Annja and spoke into his headset. He'd put the thing on when they'd arrived. He was always working some deal or talking to people in other countries at all hours of the day. He shoved his hands into his front pockets and stared off across the square.

From behind him, Annja followed his gaze. And then she spotted what must have captured Garin's attention. A man on the rooftop directly across from the square. Five stories high, it must be a hotel or perhaps an apartment building. Annja couldn't see any signage because the building front was not well lit. The man had suddenly stood upright as two other men confronted him.

"That's…" Annja squinted to make out the three silhouettes on the building's mansard rooftop. The one defending himself against the other two had a familiar form, and his hair was pulled back in a clasp at the base of his neck. "Roux?"

Garin didn't respond. He squinted and rested his hands on his hips; he was enjoying the show.

"Those are your men?"

"He's got the box and the key, Annja."

"Call them off." She stepped around Garin, but stopped when he held an arm out. It caught her off guard and she wheezed out a breath.

"Give them a minute. They're not going to hurt the old man, and you know it."

"They will if you let them."

This time Garin gripped her by the wrist as she tried to step into the square.

"Annja," he said tightly, "we are not enemies this time."

He winced as her boot crunched into his shin, and he let go of her. "You know as well as I what the old man has in mind to do."

Yes, but it wasn't going to happen. Time travel was a fantasy. No one would ever convince her that a little box with gears and a magical key could perform such a wonder.

"He won't win," he said, staring again at the rooftop. "This time I get to walk away with the prize."

"It doesn't belong to either one of you. It is a historical artifact. That's it," she said, ready to move. "It belongs in a museum."

Garin held his arms out to his sides as if she were making more out of this than was necessary. "I agree."

Annja quirked a brow. Rarely were she and Garin Braden on the same side when it came to such matters. But that didn't mean she had to stand aside and watch Roux get shoved around—

On the other hand… She glanced toward the building just as Roux seemed to knock down one man and then the other. The old Frenchman stood proud, the victor, and looked down over the square. When his gaze landed on the two of them, Roux shook his head and waved them off dismissively.

"Told you." Garin chuckled and glanced at her. "He's on his way."

And she seriously had had enough of these two schemers. Time to seize the artifact and put this whole quest to bed. But there was one piece of the puzzle still missing.

She swept her gaze around the square in search of the arrogant Evan Merrick.

FROM WHERE HE stood inside the dark bistro that edged the market square, Evan had all the players in his sights. Behind him, the shop owner lay on the floor, his hands and mouth bound. Evan wasn't a killer. But he'd needed a quiet place, close to the action, to observe. Fortunately for him, the owner had been working late on his accounts in the back room, and he'd spied the light on as he'd cased the neighborhood.

So Annja Creed was with Garin Braden now? That woman jumped from one side to the other with a dexterity that made him wish he'd been just a bit nicer to her. At the very least, having her with him would have made the poison incident unnecessary. He still felt the burn in his esophagus and wasn't sure he'd ever be able to look at tea the same way again.

Garin was standing next to Annja and looked imposing; more weapons were probably hiding under that expensive jacket. He knew that Garin Braden was a force with whom regular folks should not mess. If he couldn't handle a situation with his guile or those fists, he could easily employ someone to get the job done, and do it in just as imposing a manner as he. Although, given what Evan had just witnessed on the rooftop, he should reassess his opinion of Roux, whom he'd initially pinned as an old man with a bottomless wallet and a penchant for shiny baubles and placing bets. He'd tried to take Roux out with his gambling and keep him distracted that way, but he'd proven more than capable of ditching two or three goons on his own.

As well, Evan suspected Roux knew more about the music box than he was letting on. He'd shifted through time—the notebook with the picture of him labeled a thief was evidence of that.

Evan swallowed. He was by no means a fighter. He was smart, but not so skilled that he thought he stood a chance against either Roux or Garin, let alone both of them.

Annja Creed offered a formidable challenge, as well.

But he did hold the key.

He hoped that would buy him the strength he'd need to win this match.

Roux joined them, and the two men went head-to-head, exchanging harsh words that started in English, then switched to a few French oaths, a splash of German and then a surprising Latin curse.

Annja stood aside, allowing them to get out their frustrations.

Garin didn't make a move on Roux and vice versa, but both maintained an aggressive stance, shoulders back and chests puffed up. They'd been going at each other for centuries. Would their rivalry ever end?

Still, she knew they cared for one another more than they would ever admit.

They eventually settled their ire and stepped back from their posturing when Annja brought up the thought that someone could be observing them.

And when that someone revealed himself, stepping out of a closed shop farther along the street, Annja felt the tension ratchet up again. Garin and Roux were standing beside one another, reluctant allies. Roux had a brown paper bag tucked under his arm. In it, the music box and notebook, she was sure. Garin appeared as if he had no weapon, but of course, the Glock was tucked at the back of his waistband, under his leather jacket.

She stepped in front of them, and Evan crossed the market square, slowing his stride and shoving his hands into his sweatshirt pocket.

"He's got the cross," Roux muttered.

"What?" Garin growled.

"There was an incident when I arrived at the airport. Couldn't be helped."

Garin muttered another curse.

Annja assumed Evan must still think he was in the game; he certainly wouldn't have shown up here unless he still had a piece on the board. The cross could be in a pocket, stuffed down his shirt or even shoved in a sock. Garin and Roux would tear him apart to find it.

She waggled the fingers of her right hand, sensing the sword was close. Her partner in battle, one that never let her down. If she needed to summon the sword, the hilt would find her fingers within milliseconds. Like a thought, it was always there, ever ready. Not a fancy sword, but a solid battle sword that was as much her servant as she was to it.

Not yet, she cautioned herself. But perhaps soon.

31

Milan, 1500

He'd designed it to work only when placed at a specific latitude and longitude. A gift for his friend René d'Anjou, who, sadly, had since passed on. So was it worthless now? A mere fantastical notion he'd managed to construct yet never test? At the very least, it had gone beyond the sketch stage.

Leonardo sat beneath the willow tree in the courtyard near Melzi's estate on Lake Como. In his hands was the music box on which he'd carved the intricate knot details with such care.

He traced over a particular ribbon that wound beneath the bronze gear that turned only when the box had been activated by placing the key within the lock. Why the tritone of musical notes had been banned was beyond him. He did not believe a man could call forth the devil in such a manner.

This device had ceased to hold anything more than sentimental value.

"To shift time?" he said to himself. "Preposterous."

He set the box aside. He was never regretful of the time he spent on his many ventures, successful or not. Always he learned something in the process. And that was what he enjoyed most: learning. Would man ever be able to traverse through time to the past or perhaps even the future? It was a question that was difficult to fathom. And for what purpose was another unknown.

Surely the purpose must always be to advance knowledge. Since by continually sharing knowledge, the vast secrets of life, why, the very universe, could be revealed.

He tilted his head back and closed his eyes. A rare moment of silence on this bright evening beneath the stars. Should man truly master time travel someday, he hoped someone would journey back and introduce themselves to him.

EVAN MERRICK HELD the Lorraine cross out in one hand. Garin stood not ten feet away from him, while Roux flanked him another twenty feet to the left.

Annja stood before their adversary, unsure how to approach this one. Well, she didn't believe in time travel, so why not let the guy insert the key in the device? Everyone would step back in anticipated awe and then—nothing! Ha!

"You brought me a cross instead of flowers," she said. "Aw, now, that's original."

"Anything for you, Creed."

"Hand it over, Merrick," Garin said. He pulled out the Glock and aimed the gun in warning.

"How about a partnership? Just the four of us?" Evan said, wavering too quickly.

Roux shook his head. The brown paper bag crunched in his grasp.

"It's obvious the lot of you know more about this thing and how to use it than I do," Evan continued. "And I'm pretty sure Roux has used it before."

Roux cast Annja a glance that told her he had no idea what the man was talking about.

"You know, Roux," she scoffed jokingly, "when you traveled through time using the device to meet Leonardo da Vinci? That's why he was able to sketch your likeness in the notebook Merrick has all but memorized."

Roux bowed his head, smirked and glanced to Garin.

"Seriously?" Garin said. "You've already used the device, old man?"

"Not you, too," Roux said angrily. "I won't play along with this ridiculous ploy. I have never traveled through time. How absurd!"

"Then how was a Renaissance artist able to sketch your likeness?" Evan persisted.

"A coincidence! Besides, that's not the point," Roux said huffily. "The point is you will hand over that cross now, or the man standing on the other side of Annja will put a bullet in you."

"I like that." Garin nodded and stretched out his arm to better aim at the body in question.

"You're not going to shoot me," Evan spat. "There are tourists over there."

"Only two, and they're casting moon eyes at one another," Garin said. "Another minute or so and they'll be eager to get to their hotel room. As well, it's dark here. And I've a silencer."

"If you shoot me, I'll drop the cross. It'll break and then it'll ruin whatever reason you have for pursuing this. And if you're here, at the site where Joan of Arc was burned, because you think you can somehow save her, I don't think the implications of changing history will go over so well."

"You can't change history," Annja insisted. "It's not possible, no matter if you can travel back in time or not. Whatever has happened, has happened. That's it."

Garin stared at Annja. That brow of his arched either in question or he was impressed with what she'd said.

"As a fan of Joan of Arc—" Garin adressed Evan "—I know something you might have an interest in looking at. That is, if you'd entertain a fair trade."

Annja was curious. What angle was Garin working now?

"And you just happen to have a Joan artifact in your pocket?" Evan smirked. "A desperate man will say anything to serve his needs."

"I've never been desperate in my life." Garin switched the safety off on his gun and renewed his interest in Evan.

"It's Joan's sword," Roux stated matter-of-factly.

Annja craned her neck toward the older man. "Really?"

He winked at Annja. "Go with this one, will you?"

"Take one for the team," Garin added.

The team? she mouthed.

Since when had Garin and Roux ever really been a team? And they only seemed to include her whenever it would serve their interests. And when it didn't? She was left out in the cold, With nothing. Nada.

She should say something about this, bring it to their attention, maybe even redraw the boundaries of their relationship, such as it was.

"Right," she said sharply. "Joan's sword. You want to hold it? You give us the cross."

Against all that felt right, Annja knew the deal had to be done.

She was interested in the music box.

Just a little.

No.

She really wanted to get the Lorraine cross back to the museum in Poland, from where it had been stolen, and then make sure the music box was placed with the proper authorities. As well, the notebook had to be turned in for possible authentication. And as soon as Evan or one of them tested the nonsensical time-travel device and found it worthless, they'd hand it over easily.

"Joan of Arc's sword?" Evan challenged. "The sword she used in battle?"

"That's right." Garin answered.

Annoyed now, Annja couldn't catch Roux's gaze, but she shot him daggers anyway.

"Who's got it?" Evan asked.

"She does," Garin quickly said. "You hand me the cross—"

"Hand *me* the cross," Roux interrupted.

Garin and Roux locked gazes. Two bulls had just clashed horns in the ring. The younger one growled. Yeah, well, it couldn't have gone any other way.

"And I hand you the sword," Annja finished.

"I don't see a sword." Evan gripped the cross more tightly as he looked Annja up and down. She stood ready for action, fingers flexing, feet slightly parted and feeling her weight in the bend of her knees.

"I've got it," she reassured.

"You're lying. Only in movies or on TV shows can they whip out a sword from among the folds of a duster coat. You don't have on anything that would conceal a weapon."

"Yeah, and time travel is real, too."

"Annja, just show him," Garin said.

"You're going to owe me one," she said.

"Yes, yes. In our tally of favors and demerits, I'm sure my side is the most heavily loaded."

On a huge sigh, Annja called the sword from the otherwhere. The sword responded instantly. The hilt fit perfectly into her palm, with a sureness that she had come to admire. A claim that always lifted her, made her thrust up her chin and put her feet at a ready, fighting stance. This was her sword. And she rarely handed it over to another. She could do it. Someone else could hold the sword while she willed it to remain there, only until she wished it to return to the otherwhere. She didn't know how it worked, only that it did.

And that it was breathtaking.

"What?" Evan lowered his hand, the cross suddenly forgotten. "That's a...broadsword!"

"Carried by Joan of Arc into battle," Annja said as she swept the blade before her, noting its shine in the dim light. It wasn't an ornately decorated sword; rather, it had been designed to take a beating and to give as good as it got.

Evan held out his hand with the artifact. Both Roux and Garin stepped forward, but since Roux was closer, he was able to grasp the Lorraine cross. Garin countered the old man, stepping up close to him and staring him down, but Roux would not be so easily intimidated.

"Boys," Annja cautioned. "We'll fight over it later. Yes?"

Again the throaty growl from Garin as he stepped back.

"Give it," Evan said.

Annja presented the sword to him. A jolt of regret buzzed through her nervous system as the exchange was made. She had to focus to ensure it remained in the here and now. And later? She'd show Roux and Garin no mercy. If they thought to use her in their underhanded dealings with a stolen artifact, they'd regret it dearly.

Evan examined the hilt. It was worn smooth from all its many uses through history before it had found its way into Annja's hands. Then his gaze ran along the blade, and he slid his fingertips over the flat of it. Annja thought she felt that touch down her spine. It wasn't comforting. She curled her fingers into fists and fought to hold back a burst of protest.

"This was really Joan's? Have you had it authenticated?"

"It's real," Roux confirmed. He moved into the bright light reflecting the Joan of Arc statue, which enabled him to examine the cross.

Garin remained where he was, guarding Evan. Annja assumed it was in case the man decided to turn and run with the sword.

"Yeah?" Evan suddenly slashed the blade near her, forcing her to jump back a few feet.

She put up her palms in warning. "Watch it. That thing will take somebody's head off."

"And I'm skilled with a broadsword," Evan said, sounding almost giddy. "Took a few reenactment classes in college. So you won't mind if I borrow it a bit? After all, we did just make a fair trade."

He slashed at the air again and again.

Annja winced. She could dissolve the sword from his grip right now. But she did not. They needed time to look at the music box. For Roux to do whatever he needed to with it, before Evan tried to stop them.

She averted her gaze. Roux had placed the cross, like a key, into the mechanism at the side of the music box. He seemed to be trying to figure out how to turn the key, or if it turned at all. Garin had joined him, hands on his hips, the gun tucked away for now. Roux kept his back to the man, making it clear he wanted no interference.

If both Garin and Roux suddenly vanished, she

wasn't sure what she'd do. Run, scream, maybe wish they had taken her with them. But...nothing happened.

Evan was standing at the storefront where he'd been hiding earlier. He was still now, obviously waiting to see if anything would happen, as well. He stabbed the sword, tip first, into the cobbled ground.

Annja had had enough of him. She called the sword back. It disappeared from Evan's grasp. The man yelped. It came to fruition in her hand.

"Where you belong," she muttered, tightening her hold on the hilt.

"I wasn't done yet!" Evan yelled.

Keeping an eye on Evan, Annja approached Garin and Roux.

"Nothing, eh? Well, I'm sorry to be the one to say I told you so, but..."

"I think the key is stuck," Roux said. "There must be a specific pattern to turn it. Give it a go, Garin."

"I don't think so, old man. If it works, I don't want to be cast off into some past land never to return."

Annja switched the sword to her left hand and used her right to trace the carvings on the surface of the cross. "You placed it directly in the box?"

Roux nodded.

"Then pull it straight out."

"That's not how it works, Annja."

"And you know how it does? Because it looks like you're having trouble."

Garin chuckled and walked off to stand beside the statue. He'd resolved that Roux was crazy, and had given up on his quest to wrest the items from him.

At least one of them was thinking smart.

Drawing out his gun, Garin aimed where Evan stood. "Not a single muscle," he warned, "or you'll miss breathing."

32

Annja released the sword to the otherwhere. Roux's hands shook so much she decided he'd bought into the time-travel myth hook, line and sinker. And she found herself agreeing with Garin.

Enough was enough.

"Let me see that."

Frustrated, Roux allowed her to take the music box. It had a good weight, and with the cross inserted in its side, it really did look more like a strange contraption than anything that may have been invented over four hundred years ago to play music.

She pulled on the cross and found it wasn't willing to come free from the slots into which it fitted perfectly. So there must be a means to turn it, or perhaps slide it in order to release the mechanism.

She shifted the key along the side of the box, upward. The topmost portion of the cross slid smoothly about half an inch.

"It moved?" Roux asked over her shoulder.

"Yes. Now. Let's try this."

On a whim, she tried to slide it downward. The

right arm of the cross guided the key gently until it caught. Recalling the sign of the cross the nuns had drilled into her head as she'd grown up in the orphanage, Annja then shifted the cross upward, as if she was making the sign of the cross over her chest. And the final movement was to glide the cross downward, completing the motion.

Something inside the music box clicked. The gears turned. Annja chuckled. From within the box, plinked musical notes could be heard. Annja recognized them as the discordant ones she and Roux had discussed days ago.

"The devil's chord," Roux said in wonder.

Now Garin came forward to watch, intensely interested in what was happening.

So the box could produce music. Shouldn't a music box be required to do as much? That didn't mean it was anything special.

Out of the corner of her eye, Annja saw Evan leave where he'd been standing. She quickly sought to yank the key free of the box to keep the two pieces separate should another fight ensue over the artifacts. But her fingers slid against the Lorraine cross instead and the vibrations emanating from within shuddered through her. The resonance was so strong her teeth chattered. She clamped down her jaw to make it stop, and in doing so, a burst of brilliant light flashed before her.

The air thickened. Smoke curled up around her. Her lungs grew heavy and began to burn. She choked, coughing. Her skin prickled painfully. Finding the ground agonizingly hot, she stepped from foot to foot.

And she realized she stood on flames. Surrounded by a crowd. The eyes of many condemned her. She could not hear the people standing around her, yet she saw their mouths open as if to shout or—could it possibly be—to cheer?

Annja looked about, though her twisting only intensified the searing pain in her lungs. Despite her feet being free, she couldn't move from the center of the flames. She screamed, but she only heard that agonizing sound in her head.

Why wouldn't anyone help her?

Her gaze met a man's eyes through the crowd. It was as if the crush of people parted and an aisle opened directly to the tall soldier who wielded a broadsword. She knew that man. A soldier who had ridden into battle alongside her.

No, that wasn't right. She'd never ridden into battle. Not unless it was on a motorcycle or speedboat. The man she recognized through the smoke and fire was Roux. But he no longer stood beside her holding a music box. Instead he wore a uniform and brandished his weapon. He was fighting to keep the crowd back as they pressed toward the flames, eager to gain a position closer to the horrific spectacle.

Annja sensed she was the spectacle. Where was she? How had she...?

Annja knew she must not let go of what she knew was real for fear of losing it all. She closed her eyes and concentrated on the sword that had been her companion for so long, and tried to reach out her hand for the hilt. It was there. It tingled just out of reach in the otherwhere.

Until that tingling faded and finally receded. Moaning in frustration, she couldn't grasp her most trusted means of defending herself.

Stranded among the whipping flames, they burned and singed her skin. The agony of the heat was crushing her and she dipped her head, breathing in the vicious smoke and feeling tears sizzle at the corners of her eyes.

She heard a shouted epithet. "Heretic!" It was echoed throughout the crowd.

No.

And her thoughts shifted to pray to the one God who had spoken to her all along.…

A confident, steady male voice shivered into her consciousness. It had the trace of a French accent. He called her name. Had Roux managed to push through the crowd to her? Someone seized her hand. Strong and sure, a male hand gripped her by the wrist and tugged her away.

Annja's fingers slid from the Lorraine cross where it had fit neatly into the music box. The attacking crowd shimmered away from the edges of her waking vision.

Her body hit the ground. No flames licking at her now, there was only paved sidewalk beneath her. She rolled over, seeing the sword skitter across the cobblestones, before it disappeared into the safety of the otherwhere.

Feet danced around her. Annja clasped her throat, gasping for clean air.

"What was that?" said a voice she recognized, but it wasn't Roux or Garin. It was that thief, that smirking pest who had attempted to thwart her at every turn. What an adventure.

"Stand back!" Roux instructed. "Give her some room."

"There's smoke coming off her. I think it worked. She traveled through time!" Evan announced.

Annja closed her eyes and passed out.

33

Annja was aware of a scuffle nearby not twenty feet
from where the Joan of Arc statue stood in a recess
outside the church. Two men. One of them was losing
the fight while Garin pummeled him with his fists.

Evan Merrick. She'd recalled his name and now
breathed in deeply, allowing the oxygen to clear her
thoughts.

Where she had been and *when* seemed irrefutable.
Yet how? She may never learn the truth.

Though wobbling, she managed to stand and then
stagger to a bench next to the fountain. Sliding a palm
down her leg and pulling up the hem of her cargo
pants, she thought she would feel angry, burned skin,
but her fingers only glided over the smooth texture of
her intact leg.

Someone paced before her, speaking to her, but she
still couldn't process him. She'd seen him. A knight.
Standing with a broadsword in hand.

She wanted to run. She needed to get away from
here. To sort things out. She didn't care what happened
to Evan Merrick. Nor did she even care about that

cross or the music box. What was going on? Where was she? How would she get home?

Standing abruptly, she began to walk in an attempt to fight the woozy spin that struggled to pull her back down. Footsteps behind her quickened their pace. He followed—the one who had been beside her even then.

She needed to be alone.

"Did you see her?" Roux asked from behind.

A desperation she had never before heard from him made Annja pause. He didn't need to go back in time to change history. Why had he brought her here?

"Annja!"

Breaking into a jog, she called back, "Give me space, old man!"

She wasn't sure where she was going, but it didn't matter. She had to get away from the square and any connection to the brave woman who had died for her beliefs.

TWO HOURS LATER the Rouen police, after receiving an anonymous tip, found Evan Merrick bound to a street pole near the market in the central square. His face was bruised and bloodied. He mumbled nonsense about Joan of Arc's sword. And a Lorraine cross that had been stolen from a Polish museum earlier in the year was found tucked inside his shirt. The caller had also mentioned that Evan Merrick had been arrested on suspicion of stealing the cross, but that no evidence had been found.

The evidence dropped from inside Evan's shirt into a policeman's hand. He was brought in to the station, booked and, after the police contacted Interpol, he was transferred to a Polish jail for holding until a trial date could be determined.

The day following the weirdness in the central square, Annja had left Rouen, got on a train and had returned to Palermo, where Ian Tate waited. He'd shown her the footage he'd edited together during the days she had been in France. It was impressive. And just mysterious enough to make a person wonder. Maybe selkies really did exist.

"How was Rouen?" Ian asked as they strode the stone beach not far from Matteo's cottage.

"It was…" She hadn't given it a moment's thought since leaving the city. She didn't want to think about it because some things should simply be accepted. Like a sword that appeared whenever she needed it.

"Where is the artifact that had been stolen?"

"Uh, I understand that Evan Merrick—the thief—has been arrested. The police found the Lorraine cross on him."

"Awesome."

Ian didn't know about the music box, and in fact, he didn't need that information. As far as Annja was aware, Roux and Garin had battled it out over the treasures, and she didn't care who had gotten them. She could guess who had walked away with the relics. And since they held no personal value to Garin, she suspected he'd sell them to the highest bidder.

A good archaeologist would have stayed to make sure the music box and notebook were sent to a university for study, at least. This was one project she would have to mark down as a failure.

"There's Matteo."

Glad for the distraction, Annja picked up speed and met Matteo, who stood on the shore before his cottage, looking out over the waters. He turned to acknowledge her and Ian, who had the camera on. Matteo noted the camera, but made no comment.

"Figured I'd see you again," he said. He sniffled and tilted his head away from the sun.

Annja did not miss the signs. "Are you all right, Matteo? Where is Sirena?"

"Gone home," he replied and glanced to the ground.

Annja noted where he was looking. A hole about two feet across had been dug in the ground. Or had something recently been unearthed? Sirena's pelt? He'd told her he didn't know where it was.

"I set her free. I thought a lot after you left me lying on the stones."

"You can't keep someone who doesn't want to stay."

"She loved me," he told them. "We loved each other." He faced the camera directly. "I never hurt her, Miss Creed. I can't do a thing like that. I may be a drunk and like to pick fights, but I never laid a hand to Sirena. She loved me. But what the sea gives, the sea takes away. Her first love was always to the sea. She had this deep sadness. I felt it in her every time I looked into her eyes."

Deep sadness was a feeling Annja could relate to. So much had happened to her that she couldn't begin to explain, much less process. And ever since leaving the central square particularly, Annja had been carrying a weight within her that could only be termed sadness.

"So you—" she would be reaching here, but, she reminded herself, it was for the show "—gave her back to the sea?"

Since, after all, some things a person just needed to believe in.

Matteo nodded. "That's all I have to say. Will you turn the camera off now?"

"Ian."

The cameraman lowered his camera and stepped back.

"Story's over," Matteo summed up. "They can't all end happily ever after." He turned and strode off toward his cottage.

France, 1488

THE TAVERN OUTSIDE a small village a day's journey from Lyon was cool and quiet. The evening was quickly chilling as autumn settled across the land, sweeping leaves from the trees and sending animals deep into the forest to prepare for rest.

Roux found a table near the open hearth, ordered the stew—the tavern's only offering—and a mug of hot spiced mead. The sweet drink settled in his belly with a warm splash.

He'd managed to give Braden the slip two days ago while crossing from Italy into France along the Alps. He'd known the man's eyes had fixed on the wench in the Italian inn, and thinking that Roux was going to rest for the night, Garin had taken her upstairs.

Roux hadn't slept. He felt sure he'd gotten a half day's head start on the man. And by veering south instead of north, he hoped he'd given him the slip. For months perhaps. Maybe even years. They two came together through odd, unpredictable ways. Sometimes their union was amicable, and at other times they were opposed to one another. They were destined to play this game for— Who could determine the amount of time they would walk this earth?

Roux tugged out the leather pouch he kept secured beneath his shirt and tied up high so it hugged just under his armpit. He unlaced the opening and tilted the contents into the palm of his hand. Firelight glowed across the small jagged steel pieces. He'd collected many, but there were so many more to be found. It was incredible that they had traveled so far from Rouen, the place where they had originated.

"Forgive me," he muttered, then poured the pieces back inside the pouch and secured it with a tight knot. "I could not save you, Jeanne. But I won't cease my search to bring together your sword."

Who knew what such a quest would lead him to? Might it erase the travesty done against an innocent woman?

He could not begin to guess, but he was confident his quest would not be in vain.

NOT AN HOUR after arriving back at her Brooklyn apartment, Annja signed for a delivery. No return address, but the tracking slip said the package originated from Rouen, France. Something from Roux? She hadn't spoken to him since leaving Rouen. There had been no need.

Peeling away the plastic strip to open the postal box, she had to admit she felt slightly anxious. Inside, snuggly padded in Bubble Wrap, she spied the music box and the notebook. A note scribbled on a plain piece of paper read:

You'll know what to do with these. G.

"Interesting."

She did know what to do with them. Most important? Ensuring the cross, music box and notebook were never again connected to each other. That would be fairly easy. The cross would remain in police custody until it was eventually returned to the museum. The music box she could trace its history and return it also to the castle or wherever Merrick had lifted it from. And the notebook...

The notebook was the key that tied them together.

Annja went to her desk and flipped aside the postal box to reveal what lay beneath. A random ziplock bag. She carefully placed the leather-bound notebook in the bag to keep it from further damage until she could determine the correct place to send it.

She placed her palm over the plastic and entertained the idea of copying the pages before handing it over to the rightful owner.

"At the very least," she said, "the sketch of Roux."

Was the world prepared for what would result should the notebook be preened over and its contents released for all to see? Was Roux prepared? Certainly someone would recognize him and call attention to it.

"Not as if they could convict him of a crime four centuries after the fact." And of what crime could they accuse him? The evidence of his theft was hers to protect now.

She opened the ziplock bag and, grabbing a set of latex gloves stuffed in a drawer, put them on, then pulled out the notebook. Paging to the sketch of Roux, she stopped to consider her options. Did she have options? She could certainly make options. Yet could she live with that choice if she made it?

Annja took the corner of the page in hand and turned it forward, as if to rip it away from the stitched binding. Just testing, she thought as she eyed whether or not the paper would tear easily or instead pulling would result in the removal of more than the single page. The paper was so old it would tear with but a flick of her wrist.

"This is what I can live with," she said and drew in a breath.

She hoped Roux could live with her decision, as well.

* * * * *